ch

Blue Mountain Trouble

Blue Mountain Trouble

MARTIN MORDECAI

ARTHUR A. LEVINE BOOKS
AN IMPRINT OF SCHOLASTIC INC.

Text © 2009 by Martin Mordecai

Mordecai, Martin.
     Blue Mountain Trouble/by Martin Mordecai. — 1st ed.
        p. cm.
     Summary: After being saved from a disastrous landslide by an extraordi-
nary goat that blocks their usual way to school, twins Pollyread and Jackson,
living with their parents high in the mountains of Jamaica, find the strange
goat reappearing at crucial intervals as their day-to-day life is changed by a
series of mysterious events involving the return of a local troublemaker and
secrets from their family's past.
     ISBN-13: 978-0-545-04156-0 (alk. paper)
     ISBN-10: 0-545-04156-2 (alk. paper)
     [1. Twins — Fiction. 2. Brothers and sisters — Fiction. 3. Family life —
Jamaica — Fiction. 4. Mountain life — Jamaica — Fiction. 5. Jamaica —
Fiction.] I. Title.
     PZ7.M78863Bl 2009
     [Fic] — dc22

                                                        2008042648

      10 9 8 7 6 5 4 3 2 1   09 10 11 12 13

                    First edition, April 2009
                Published simultaneously in Canada by
                      Scholastic Canada Ltd.

                    Printed in the U.S.A. 46

                  Book design by Lillie Mear

To Pam,
who believed

Goat

For Pollyread and Jackson, walking down to school around the same time each morning was the same and slightly different. The twins lived in Top Valley, a village high in the Blue Mountains. "On God shoulder," Mama said. Mornings sometimes, when cloud and mist were all around, there you'd be on God's shoulder and you couldn't see his face or his feet. ("Only his belly button," Pollyread said once, looking around for Mama, shocked at her own boldness — and never said it again.)

They looked down the path they were walking, and where a moment ago there was Stedman's Corner and Marcus Garvey Primary, then Cross Point, then Cuthbert Bank and Content Gap, in steps that a drunk giant might take to the hazyblue sea far below — now all of a sudden there was only cloud, thick as Mama's soup, slicking the grass and stones with moisture and making the path where they walked all their life mysterious and new, and sometimes dangerous.

This Tuesday morning the whole world seemed to be moving. The clouds played hide-and-seek with the sun in the steep valleys. You could almost hear them laughing as they twirled around like sails. Pollyread in front, they went carefully down the steep, winding path, walking around the larger boulders, stepping over the gleaming stones. Mama would not forgive them for slipping and getting their uniforms dirty.

Around them, hilltops, stones, sometimes single trees thrust like fists or fingers through the swirling clouds. All of them familiar, all of them, this morning, new, different.

And this morning, out of that green-and-white mystery of stones and floating trees, out of it this perfectly normal Tuesday morning came the goat.

One moment there was just the clouds and the rocks and the bush, the next moment it was there. Huge, its dark head with grandpa beard unfurling a pair of horns like Jericho trumpets.

There, floating in the path, in a pool of brightness from an unseen sun. The twins could only see a huge head, with a billowing beard and horns like they had never before seen, on a goat or any other creature. It was like a mask, of a size that would've had a body as big as a minibus carrying it. Unsupported, it floated next to a big round rock — just where they would walk.

2

The twins stopped dead. There was no way around it. The goat's eyes pinned them, flashing dark fire. The eyes seemed sightless but seeing everything too, down into the very darkest corners of their terror.

For a second or two, all was still: the goat-mask, the twins, even the clouds. They saw something like teeth. The goat tossed its head.

Then the cloud shifted and it wasn't there anymore. As effortlessly as it had appeared, made of cloud but very real, it was gone.

The rock behind it reappeared, humpbacked, familiar. Cloud rolled away on silent wheels, unfurling the valley and hillsides like a banner. The twins were surrounded by things well-known and intimate, comforting as Mama's arms. But they were shivering.

Jackson's hand touched Pollyread from behind. "Go on nuh?" She didn't, couldn't move.

Then the ground vibrated beneath them. As if Jackson's touch had tilted it. The hump of rock that the goat-head had hung in front of trembled. The guango tree behind it shook with a sound like rattling teeth. And as they watched, the hillside in front of them slipped away and crashed into Bamboo River below. They looked down: A meter ahead of their feet was — nothing. What was left of the hillside looked torn and bleeding, earth dribbling away like blood.

Birdsong and the soft rattle of leaves filled the pool of silence that settled around them.

Pollyread and Jackson looked into each other's wide bottomless terror. First, the goat. Then . . . it hadn't rained for weeks, the earth hard as cement. There seemed no reason for the landslide.

"Maybe Mass Cleveland get a new goat," said Jackson tentatively. "I hear him talking to Poppa one day, say he looking about some high-class ram from a man in Saint Ann that bring them from foreign. No ordinary ram goat."

"Well, that certainly wasn't no ordinary goat," said Pollyread.

All day they'd waited, expecting some other extraordinary thing to happen. They had no idea what they were expecting, but they'd know it when it happened. Like the goat. But nothing happened. No one said anything unusual. No one did anything unusual. They went through the day feeling as if an X was marked on their foreheads. But no one looked at or spoke to them in any way strangely. And they had hardly spoken to anyone, even each other, all day.

Now they were lying in bed on either side of the curtain that divided the room they shared. They'd said

4

their prayers rather more quickly than normal, though Jackson had remembered to give thanks for being saved from serious injury and possibly worse. They hadn't mentioned the goat directly. On the other hand — they knew. But they weren't sure of what the goat *was*. Or of how to talk about it.

Jackson turned on his back and cupped his hands behind his head. He sighed as he gazed up into the black roof.

"I hear Mass Cleveland tell Poppa he going to crossbreed" — his tongue relished the word — "the foreign ram with them scrawny-looking goat him have running up and down hillside eating out people vegetable garden."

"So the new goat not going to eat vegetable and flowers? Is that you saying?" He heard the change in Pollyread's tone, like she was turning over the page to a new story.

"Don't be stupid! Goat born to eat everything, even condense milk can. One goat can't be different just 'cause it have a different father. I meant," he went on, shaping his words carefully, "that the goat that Mass Cleveland crossbreeded, if he get the foreign goat from the man in Saint Ann, would be a different kind of goat from what we custom to see in these-here parts. You understand now?"

That tone infuriated Pollyread, but sometimes Jackson couldn't help himself, she deserved it. She would tell him he wasn't her teacher so please not to speak to her like she was no dunce up in front of the class. When Mama heard him speaking like that, she would tease and call him "Politician."

"Different in what way, Mr. Know-it-all?" asked Pollyread, her voice sweet as custard, but with lime on the edge.

Pollyread felt her brother stiffen on the other side of the curtain, and was pleased.

"It will look different," he began irritably. "It will be taller and have more meat on it and —"

"From all those cabbages and flowers and cucumbers, I suppose," his sister said in her driest voice. "The same ones Mass Cleveland goat dem eat now, and still skinny like puss."

"Cho man, Polly," Jackson cried out, hitting his mattress. "You too stupid!"

She could not let that pass. "I wish to do no more than remind you," she said in *her* teacher's voice, "of our respective placements according to last term's reports, and indeed for some time now."

There was a long sigh from the other side of the curtain, which Pollyread's little grin swallowed like a sponge.

"Anyway," she said after a while, and quietly, "I don't think is Mass Cleveland foreign goat, even if he get it already."

"So what you think it is?"

"I think," she began, and then turned and put her head right up close to the curtain where she knew her twin's was and, wondering if God was still listening to them, said in a whispered rush, "Ithinkisaduppy."

"Duppy?" Jackson's voice came right back, loud.

"Sh-h-h!"

They listened for a sign of the parents in the next room.

Generally, singly or together, they discussed anything unusual with Mama when they got home from school. But they hadn't been sure how to mention the goat, or of what sort of discussion might follow: Mama frowned on talk of duppies and obeah and other "manifestations of darkness," as she termed such matters.

Besides, Mama had been in bed when they reached home, an unusual development in itself. A strong woman who often worked beside Poppa in the ground they planted, she seldom felt poorly. But this morning she'd complained of dizziness and a funny feeling in her stomach. And after supper, though she was feeling better, Poppa had shepherded her to bed at the same time as the twins.

"Duppy?" Jackson's voice caught between disbelief and agreement.

"Is something," said Pollyread, soft but firm. "Something not from this place." Jackson knew she didn't mean just Top Valley. "A spirit thing."

"Like . . . rolling calf?"

"I suppose so," said Pollyread, trying now to sound casual about the fantastical shape-shifting creature that gave every child nightmares.

"Rolling goat maybe."

Pollyread had to giggle, but her brother's attempt at a joke evaporated immediately into the darkness, leaving their thoughts to settle like slow running water into the crevices of this dark idea that had been gathering shape all day.

Silence, like rope let down into a well.

Out of that well of silence, rising like the mist that was almost surely rising somewhere in the sleeping valley, came Jackson's voice:

"Our Father. Who art in Heaven. Hallowed be thy name . . ."

"Thy kingdom come," Pollyread joined in.

"Thy will be done . . ."

"On earth . . ."

Ground

Every morning after that, they watched out for the goat, peering intently into whatever mist and cloud they encountered on their way to school. Someone had erected a makeshift fence around the place where the ground had fallen away, and a new path to Stedman's Corner was already forming. Mama seemed recovered and was back at ground with Poppa. The world was as it had been, was supposed to be. "The goat like it gone on holiday," Pollyread said, disappointed and a little irritated, on Friday.

Very early Saturday morning, before daybreak, Jackson found himself stumbling after Poppa, whom he could hear more than see, on the path that led up one side of Top Valley, and then disappeared over into another valley that everyone called Morgan's Mount, after the name of the peak on the far side.

Jackson wanted to cry out to Poppa to hold down and wait for him, but he knew better. Poppa was a hurrier. When the twins were babies, he would try to walk with them at their speed, but even then he was usually a step ahead, and the distance lengthened as they found their feet and learned their way around. He would lead, they must follow, and if they couldn't keep up, they knew the way home. He wasn't out for no Sunday stroll, he'd say. Mama it was who had taken them for walks, and kept their toddling pace.

So Jackson, still not fully awake, was quiet, his eyes on the path that slipped in and out of focus ahead of him. He relied for direction on the thump on the ground of Poppa's lignum vitae stick that he seldom left home without, and the uneven smack of the thick leather sheath that held Poppa's cutlass against his leg as he walked. Jackson's own little cutlass, an old one of his father's worn down over the years of use and sharpening to the size of a large kitchen knife, was stuck in his waist in a protective scabbard of banana leaf.

Something flashed past Jackson from behind and vanished into the darkness ahead. Cho-cho. Jackson cried out as though something had hit him. That set off the little mongrel, who came dancing back like a spirit in the gray half-light, barking to wake the dead.

"Cho-cho. Hush!" Jackson said, fierce as a flame. Which only made Cho-cho bark more. "Cho-cho!" More barking.

"Blasted dawg," Poppa grumbled up ahead. Quite close by, which made Jackson feel better.

"Not me bring him, Poppa," Jackson said quickly. "I did think we pop him when he sleeping."

"Sleeping? That dawg don't sleep!"

"Must take Cho-cho back, Poppa?"

"Him will only follow you again."

Jackson heard the rustle of leaves as his father resumed walking up the path, his boots and stick stamping in an uneven, angry rhythm. After a while Jackson released Cho-cho, who had the good sense not to run forward again. Gradually, Poppa's tread settled, and Jackson relaxed. Cho-cho ran between them, sniffing the ground and putting little marks of pee on randomly chosen bushes and trees.

They were going to what Poppa sometimes called "Jackso's ground." The Gilmores, like almost every family in Valley that grew things, had a piece of land, or "ground," that was generally separate from whatever small pocket surrounded the house they lived in. That Gilmore ground was some distance from the house, but on the same side of Bamboo River. It sloped gently down to the river and several Valley families had their ground there; some, like the Gilmores, for three or more generations. Original ownership of the land, if there was such a thing, was lost in the government records in Town. Individual boundaries had been established over the years by a tree, a large rock, a line of yam hills. Everyone knew their ground.

The Gilmores were unusual in Top Valley for having two grounds. Even before the twins were born, Poppa had leased the other one — the owner known this time, a Mr. McIntyre who lived abroad — over in Morgan's Mount. He had leased it, Poppa said, so as to avoid the *palampam* that often broke apart families upon the death of the father, with the already small inheritance having to be divided up, usually among several children. Whatever happened with the Bamboo River ground, for which there was no paper, Morgan's Mount would be a Gilmore ground as long as a Gilmore wanted, with paperwork to back it up locked in a lawyer's office in Town.

Morgan's Mount was too far away to go to every day. Every few months Poppa and a friend would go up there with a day's supply of water and cooked food to clear the place. To establish possession, Poppa would say. So that people would know the land belonged to some-one nearby and wouldn't think they could just capture it for themselves. The last few times he had taken Jackson with him. "Because is *his* dead-lef," he'd explain to Mama when she complained that Jackson was too young for such hard work, or he had homework to do, or some other reason. "He must learn to look after his own things." Jackson didn't mind hard work. To keep poverty and shame in their proper place, life was a struggle to the grave. Valley children learned that lesson with their growing, the way they learned the landscape of the district and the faces of the people around them. Besides, he loved being in the bush with Poppa and his friends.

But he didn't like to think of the Morgan's Mount ground, or even Bamboo River, as being his own. Deadlef meant an inheritance after Poppa died, and he didn't want to think about *that*. To do so would be to open the door to a world without Poppa, and the twins had daymares enough when he was away in Town for even a week, as he had to be sometimes.

And there would only be Pollyread to share any ground with — up to now anyway. Land could come to girl children, but Pollyread had no interest in owning land or planting things, only in selling them. God made things grow or not, according to his mysterious will. It wasn't in her place, certainly, to interfere with the divine process. Or to get sweaty and dirty doing it.

With Jackson, it was a different story.

"Jackso born with him hand inna dutty," Mama would

say, her tone conveying different things, depending on whether she was rowing with him for dirtying his clothes, or showing off the various flowering shrubs and plants he helped her with around the yard. There were times when not even the best game of cricket or football, or the best mark in class, could provide the satisfaction when he saw the pink shell of the ginger lily he'd planted under their window aflame in the soft light of morning. It was a blessing, and the breaths that he took while looking at things growing, whether he had planted them or not, could make him feel as light as the air around him.

And now, as the sun woke up and stretched, releasing its breath of light into the air, Jackson had the impression that they were climbing into the sky. No longer afraid of losing sight of Poppa, he stopped at one point and looked back down Top Valley. He spotted their house, tiny and fragile in the blue air and, farther down, a piece of Stedman's Corner and the main building of Marcus Garvey Primary.

At the top of the hill dividing the two valleys they ran into a wall of blazing sunlight and stumbled down the slope, half blinded, to the refuge of a guango tree. Cho-cho squatted between them, tongue hanging.

Shading their eyes while catching their breath, they looked down.

Morgan's Mount was, in fact, a valley much like Top Valley, even to the ribbon of river at the bottom like a zip holding the two mountainsides together. But this valley was not as populated or as well planted as Top Valley. The patches of haphazard cultivation amid the larger splotches of bush and trees were threaded with tentative pathways like pieces of twine. Perhaps half a dozen shacks were visible, widely scattered like tiny dark boxes thrown down on the slopes. One such, on the far side of the valley, flew a pennant of smoke.

Poppa's arm swung up from his side suddenly, the cutlass pointing. The sun glancing off the blade startled Jackson. At first he thought Poppa was pointing to the river, which caught the first sunlight and threw it back at them. But the blade, as Poppa stood straight now against his lignum vitae stick, was pointing to the far slope. Jackson vaguely remembered that the Gilmore ground would be somewhere in that direction. Following Poppa's arm, Jackson saw two dark figures like large insects in a field that was tidily planted in rows. Above them was the hut with the smoke. Lights seemed to flash from the men-insects as they moved. Jackson heard a growl, which he thought was Cho-cho, or distant early-morning thunder. But it came from Poppa's throat.

Then Poppa set off. And at a pace! His big stick plunged at the ground like a piston, driving him down toward the river. Jackson tried to keep up with him, feeling like a toddler again. Except that if he had been three or four he would have called out to Poppa to wait. Now he knew not to say a word. He could hear Poppa's breath pumping in and out of his lungs, and Cho-cho's yapping, which Poppa ignored, concentrating on the dark brown path his feet must follow, studded with little rocks and tree roots that could trip him up. Poppa's hands were swinging vigorously, the stick flying out before and behind like a warning to Jackson not to get too close, the other hand with the cutlass chopping at upstart bush.

In no time they were down at the river, by a line of small rocks that zigzagged across the stream. Jackson remembered them from the last time, and the intricate dance he and Poppa had woven across the river. This time, dry season, the river was low, and without any hesitation Poppa, ignoring the stones, splashed straight into the water, balancing with his staff. Cho-cho leapt after him unthinkingly, and as quickly retreated to dry land, where Jackson scooped him up.

"Poppa," Jackson called out, not loud, more an automatic reaction to uncertainty. As if to back him up, Cho-cho yelped twice. But Poppa paid no attention, perhaps didn't even hear them. He was now on the other side of the little stream, his trousers wet below the knees and clinging darkly to his legs. Jackson called again, louder.

His father spun around as if yanked by an invisible rope. He was framed between two of the stringy trees that shadowed the stream, silhouetted against the sunlit slope behind him stitched with rows of small plants. In one corner of the frame, a man was squatting on his haunches, pulling weeds.

"Whaddapen?" asked his father impatiently.

Jackson wasn't sure what to say next. He hadn't seen Poppa this agitated in a long time.

"Use the stones and come cross," Poppa said sharply, turning away again. "And hold the dawg."

Lifting Cho-cho, Jackson did as his father instructed. The stones were dry and stood well out of the water, so his running shoes had no problem finding a grip, but with the wriggling dog to contend with, every stone was a challenge. On the far side Cho-cho expected to be put down, and wriggled even more when he realized that he was still a captive. To calm him, Jackson knelt and rested the dog on the ground between his legs, stroking him softly while holding his collar.

By now Poppa was thirty or forty meters ahead, marching up the slope. As Jackson was wondering whether to try and catch up, his father turned and held his stick high: *Stay!* Poppa resumed his striding across the ground, the steepening slope affecting his pace but not his determination. He was not stepping over the foot-high seedlings planted neatly in the rows he crossed. He was crushing any that fell under his angry feet, slashing at others with stick and cutlass.

"Oi!" shouted a man from the bottom corner of the ground, trying to catch Poppa's attention. Poppa, marching away from the man, didn't even pause. He continued straight toward the upper part of the ground where there was a little shed perched on a ledge of level ground under a spreading shade tree. There, a man crouched over the fire that sent a bright thread of smoke into the air, the one Jackson had seen from the hillside. As Jackson watched, another man emerged from inside the hut, rubbing his hands over his face as though he had just woken up. He saw Poppa and stopped, still as a statue.

From Jackson's vantage point the man seemed tall and well built, an impression heightened by a big crown of locks: Rasta. He was shirtless, and the sunlight danced on the bunched shoulders and muscular arms crossed on his chest. Something dangled from one hand. A stick, Jackson thought. Then it glinted: a cutlass.

Poppa was now no more than ten meters from the Rasta above him. He stopped and balanced himself on the sloping ground. His right arm lifted and Jackson caught his breath. But it was Poppa putting his cutlass into its leather sheath. Jackson sighed. The two men watched each other. The man crouching over the big pot on the terrace beside the Rasta continued his tending of the fire, but watched Poppa also.

Cho-cho whimpered. Jackson relaxed his grip a little. There was something familiar about the big man. Jackson had seen him before. He found himself moving forward without thinking, crablike on his heels, with Cho-cho between his legs. Who was this man? He thought and thought, but could not remember. But the sense of the man's familiarity persisted, and it wasn't comforting.

Poppa took a few paces forward and stepped up onto the little terrace. They were on the same level now, and about the same height. But Poppa's wiry body was like a yam hill against the man's tree.

Jackson, too far away to hear the words, saw their mouths moving. They maintained their distance, Poppa standing almost at attention like a soldier. The Rasta appeared the more relaxed of the two. But there was a coiled stillness about him.

The Rasta smiled, and even from his distance Jackson could see that it wasn't friendly and knew that his father wasn't returning the smile. The Rasta's teeth against his dark shadowed face scattered the sunlight, and Jackson, as though catching the pieces of light in his mind's eye and making a pattern of them, realized suddenly why he knew the man, and who he was.

Jammy!

James Parchment — but no one except his mother and the police used either name — was a legend and a tonic in Top Valley. Parents warned their boy children they'd turn out like Jammy if they didn't listen to their elders. The children, before they were old enough to reason the finer points of right and wrong, knew that Jammy led an exciting life, a lot of it "out there," beyond Top Valley. As they grew older, details of Jammy's adventures fell like potato peelings from adult conversations: Jammy was in Tower Street in Town, which they only slowly learned was the address of the General Penitentiary. Jammy was in "foreign," abroad; and they gathered enough from other scraps of gossip to know that he couldn't be there legally because no one in their right mind would give Jammy a visa, which was something necessary for travel to said foreign.

Lately, Jammy had been *somewhere*. No one had seen him in Valley for the past couple years, and now here he was. *Large as life and twice as ugly,* as Poppa said about people he didn't like.

Jammy was still standing with his arms folded, grinning, his teeth bright like stars. Poppa threw his arm into the air, one hand carrying the lignum vitae stick aloft. Poppa looked like he was threatening Jammy, but Jackson knew that wasn't the case. Poppa didn't threaten, he acted. A peal of mocking laughter reached Jackson like garbage thrown down the hillside. Cho-cho yelped as Jackson's hands impulsively squeezed him.

Poppa spun away from Jammy's laughing face and started back down the hill.

"I-man will be right here, Mass Gillie," Jammy called to Poppa's back, loud enough for Jackson to hear. "We not going anywhere."

"You going back to prison, Jammy. I promise you that," Poppa shouted, half turning his head. "Where you belong! All o' you!" He swept the air with his stick. The sun behind threw Poppa's shadow ahead of him like a puppet as he tramped down the diagonal of the hillside toward Jackson. He pulled out his cutlass and slashed viciously at the little plants that his path crossed.

"Mind I-man sue you for damages, Mass Gillie," Jammy shouted, but he was laughing.

Poppa stopped and half turned. For a moment he seemed about to go back up the hill, this time with cutlass and stick. Jackson squeezed Cho-cho. But Poppa raised his staff, not the machete, at the mocking man above him. "Sue me, Jammy," he said. "I *want* you to sue me." And he resumed his walk, without waiting for a response from Jammy, slashing at more plants as he came toward his waiting son and the watchful, quivering dog.

Amazingly to Jackson, when he reached them he was smiling, as though he had told himself a joke. Almost tenderly, he slipped his cutlass back into its leather sheath.

"Come, son," he said. His voice was gentle, as it was when Jackson or Pollyread hurt themselves. He touched Jackson's shoulder and helped him to stand up. "Let's go home."

Standpipe

Jammy!" exclaimed Bollo, hitting the side of his head with his hand. "You mean Jammy is here?!"

"Jammy?" echoed Trucky.

Jackson couldn't help himself: A laugh popped out of his mouth. Just a little bark, like one of Cho-cho's.

"Jammy same one," Jackson said, as serious as he could be.

They were at Standpipe, as they generally had been around this time of day most days, in dry season at least, from when they were still in the arms of their mothers. There were mothers and babies there today, as well as Keneisha, Trucky's sister, who would soon be a mother herself.

Jackson's announcement of the return of Jammy had had the effect he'd hoped for. Bollo — known as Calvin Tomlinson to the teachers at Marcus Garvey Primary, but to no one else in Valley — worshipped his cousin, and would hear no word said against him. If he had known that Jammy was back in the district, everybody else in Top Valley would've known.

"Jammy come back," he said, speaking to himself. "And he don't even come to say howdy." Anyone else in the valley would have been surprised if Jammy *had* announced his presence. But Bollo was crushed at his cousin's bad manners.

"And he turn Rasta," Trucky added in wonderment. Robert Gordon had been, from babyhood, built like a small truck. He and Bollo lived close to each other and were seldom apart.

"Jammy not no Rasta," said Pollyread sharply. "He hiding behind the locks so police can't find him."

"Who say police looking for him?" asked Bollo defensively.

"If they not looking for him now, they will soon be," said Pollyread.

"So what Jammy had to say for himself?" Trucky asked quickly, to head off an argument.

Bollo and Trucky were looking expectantly at Jackson now, waiting for more information. He wanted to tell them what he *had* heard, but somehow knew that Poppa, who had made no mention of the encounter with Jammy all the way down to home, or since, would have regarded that as a betrayal.

"I couldn't hear what they say," Jackson said. "But they never smile with each other."

"Mass Gillie never like Jammy from time," Bollo muttered.

"*Nobody* like Jammy from time," Pollyread shot back.

"Nobody don't *understand* Jammy, that's why," said Bollo, a little less aggressively. "Everybody think Jammy is a bad bwoy, but he have plenty things he want to do with his life."

"And do them with things that don't belong to him" was out of Pollyread's mouth like a whip. Jackson saw Bollo flinch and felt sorry for him.

But as the four of them busied themselves with their plastic water containers, which they had been taking turns to fill from the standpipe while they talked, Jackson felt anger begin to puddle in his stomach. He remembered a time a few years back, right here at the standpipe, when Jammy had shown (yet again!) his true colors.

There had been a line of children waiting turns for the trickle of water. Jammy had been part of the line. Which was moving far too slowly for his liking. So eventually he'd done a Jammy thing: simply walked to the front of the line, lifted the bucket that was filling out of the way and put his own container there. There was a flurry of protest and then silence: Jammy had a temper, and he was bigger than anyone there.

Bigger even than Miss Icilda, whose grandson Jonathan had been waiting just ahead of the twins. Miss Icilda emerged from under one of the shade trees nearby, walked over to the standpipe and, without a word, kicked over Jammy's bucket. Jammy made to grab her, but she pushed him off.

"You must wait you turn like everybody," she said angrily. "Learn discipline."

Jammy took a step forward, raising his hand. "I soon discipline *you*," he shouted.

Miss Icilda stepped forward also. "Lick me, then," she said quietly, looking up into his face. "You is bad man and I am a little old woman. Lick me. Show these pickney how big man is to behave — lick me!"

Jackson was certain Jammy *was* going to hit Miss Icilda. But, after a moment when his hand wavered above the old woman like something that didn't belong to him, he spun away from her and stamped off, scattering children like chickens. Later, he'd caught a ride down to Town and wasn't seen in Valley for several weeks.

"So, Bollo," Pollyread called out now, as they were helping each other hoist the full, heavy water buckets onto their shoulders, "why Jammy must pick Poppa's land to do him business on? What him have against Poppa?"

Pollyread, not for the first time, had plucked Jackson's thoughts and put them into words. He was not particularly surprised that Jammy had captured land, for whatever reason, and Morgan's Mount was an isolated spot, so perhaps no one would notice, for a while anyway. But why their land? (*My land*, he thought.)

Bollo started to shrug and then remembered the teetering bucket of water atop his bullet head. "You would have to ask Jammy," he said carefully.

But the little ripple of Bollo's shoulder, and his noncommittal words, only irritated Pollyread, her bucket perfectly poised. "I don't have no question asking Jammy," she snapped. "My father will deal with him."

"Maybe," Trucky ventured, shifting feet and shoulders to find a balance for his own bucket, "maybe is Mass Gillie do Jammy something." Jackson hadn't missed Trucky's pause, nor the tone of his voice, suggesting his classmate, and therefore Bollo also, knew something about Jammy and Poppa that he, Jackson, and Pollyread, didn't know. Jackson felt uncomfortable all of a sudden.

"Something like what?" he asked, bristling.

"How I to know?" asked Trucky, withdrawing a little from Jackson's sharpness.

"Ask Mass Gillie," said Bollo.

The air around the four friends crackled with unease.

Again

Mama was at Stedman's Corner when they got there on the way home from Standpipe.

It isn't a corner at all, really just a large, level, open space with a shop and a rum bar on one side, owned by Mr. and Mrs. Shim; Miss Clarice's cook shed where she sold soup, cooked food, and sweets on the other; and a large, barren guinep tree that people wait under, out of the sun or rain, for the minibuses that intermittently grace Valley with their bone-rattling service. All paths meet there: It is the crossroads of social and economic life in Valley. Almost everyone who is not a babe-in-arms or an invalid crosses the little scrap of concrete-hard dirt and pitchy-patchy grass at least once every day.

Mama called to them from Shim's, though it was Keneisha, Trucky's sister, who heard her. She had walked with them — more like waddled, she was due any day — to Stedman's Corner, sent by her mother for a few groceries. Really for the exercise, she told Pollyread, as the three of them fell into a laborious progress up the hill from Standpipe while Trucky and Bollo went home another way. The buckets of water on the twins' heads were as heavy as Keneisha's belly. Pollyread, who had little interest in dolls, was galvanized by real babies and anything to do with them. Jackson plodded ahead, the girls' chirpy voices blending with the cries and coos of birds coming home for the night as evening soaked up the light from the sky.

Jackson didn't hear Mama's call because he was deep in thought. About Jammy. Squatting on Gilmore land. Growing plants that he'd never seen before — nor Poppa, who knew a lot about plants. It was the one question Jackson had ventured on the way down from Morgan's Mount. "Nothing like that grow around here," Poppa answered, and said nothing further on the matter. Jackson had wished then, and wished now, that he had thought to pick up a piece of the unknown plant. Maybe Miss Bovell, his science teacher, would know what it was. But what Jammy and his ruffians might be growing was not as important as *where* they were growing it. On *his* ground. And Jackson was also curious about the why — especially after Bollo and Trucky's mystifying remarks.

"What a way you favor star apple," Mama said to Keneisha, smiling as she came out of Shim's to greet them, holding a plastic bag of groceries to take home. Jackson knew Mama's views on Keneisha's pregnancy: much too young, not churched or even living with the father (whose identity was the source of endless speculation around Valley). Another girl pickney "drop," her future blighted. A reason for lamentation. But a baby was always welcomed with delight. Even Jackson could agree: Keneisha, the prettiest girl in Valley anyway, had bloomed around her baby belly into a glowing . . . star apple.

"When the baby due?" Mama asked. "Should be soon, not so?"

Pollyread knew the answer before Keneisha gave it: "Soon-soon." She'd told Pollyread the same thing on the way up from Standpipe. Babies were born all the time in Valley, but each one was a wonder and mystery to Pollyread.

Now, though, another mystery was occupying space in her brain. Jammy. And Poppa. And the possibility that there was something about the family that others knew and she — they — didn't. Pollyread liked to know. That was her *thing*. Knowing.

Bollo and Trucky had said to ask Poppa. But Mama

must know. And here she was, all by herself. With a long walk home.

She waited. Not an easy thing for Pollyread at the best of times, and this wasn't. The pail of water on her head made her neck ache. But if she put it down now, it would be worse when she took it up again, as she would have to. Waiting a few yards away as Mama chatted with Keneisha, who just glowed all over from her baby and being the center of attention, Pollyread stood as still as she possibly could, until she felt the water bucket drilling her into the ground of Stedman's Corner.

Then she noticed the smell. Sharp, burning her nostrils and eyes. And it got darker, like a cloud had covered the sun. But it hadn't. The sky everywhere, though sliding toward evening, was clear. The duskiness was only here, over the part, the little part, of Stedman's Corner where Mama and Keneisha stood talking and Pollyread and Jackson waited a few yards away.

Curiouser and curiouser, Pollyread thought, remembering Alice. But this wasn't Wonderland. Everything here that she was looking at was exactly as she'd known it from before she knew herself.

Then the murky air around them moved. Congealed into little wisps of cloud that danced. And the pungent smell grew stronger.

Pollyread, statue-still, trying to keep the pail of water from tumbling and wasting a whole afternoon, knew. Like it had been waiting for them.

Jackson noticed too.

It quivered to one side of the little group, a mass of grayish cloud as big as Mama, forming, so to speak, the third point of a triangle between the twins, and Mama and Keneisha, who were still chatting. If either of them had turned they would have looked straight into the eyes of the goat, because it wasn't noticing the twins at all. Which for some reason made Pollyread vex.

"What you want now, Mr. Goat?" Her tone was as sharp as it had been with Bollo at Standpipe.

That got the goat's attention. The cloud turned slowly and the pebble eyes bore into her. And they laughed. Shone with humor like moisture, and the air shimmered without losing the shape of itself, beard and horns and all.

Pollyread's face opened up in amazement at herself, and at the goat's reaction. Without the heavy pail of water to anchor her, she'd have started to tremble.

Sensing something, Mama turned. "What happen to you, Pol?" she asked.

"She catching fly," Keneisha joked at Pollyread's open mouth. The jibe shut Pollyread's mouth, snap. But she still couldn't say anything.

The goat was looking from the twins to the women to the twins. It was having a fine time, shimmying like a dancer.

It was trying to attract Mama's attention! And Keneisha's. And they couldn't see it. Him. Whatever. Only the twins could.

That realization broke the lock on Pollyread's frozen self.

"Please, Mr. Goat," she said, polite now, as she would talk to a grown-up, "why you come?" *And where you come from?* formed in her mind, but she couldn't find that much voice.

The twirling mist stilled a moment, as if listening to her. The goat's eyes brightened, burning into Pollyread's. She couldn't look away. The face wavered, going in and out of focus. The head tossed, perhaps in the direction of Bamboo River — or beyond. Like he had *heard* her unspoken question.

But then his attention turned to Mama again and the rotating resumed. *Like when I was a child,* Pollyread thought. Performing for attention.

Mama looked right through him at the twins. "What you just say, Pol? You was talking to me?"

"No, Mama," she mumbled. "Not you."

"Stop. What is this smell?" Mama looked around —

again, right through the goat. "And what this cloud doing here?" As though a child had strayed. "Is it smell so? Something burning round here?" Mama took a breath and scrunched up her face. Keneisha beside her took a step back and spat on the ground.

Goat was not pleased. Pollyread could tell from the sudden stillness of the air. She thought it funny and was about to laugh when — again as though reading her mind — he looked at her. Hurt. His feelings. That's what she thought, and frightened herself with the thought. A cloud, a puff of something like smoke — with feelings! A duppy goat that could read her mind. Crazy.

Mama turned back to Keneisha. "Better go on home now. Miss G will be worrying about you."

"Okay, Aunt Maisie," Keneisha said, also looking through Goat at Pollyread. "Walk good, Polly." And turned to waddle over to Shim's.

"Let me help you with that pail of water," Mama said to Pollyread, putting down the plastic bag of groceries on the ground.

But as she watched Mama's face coming closer to her, hands reaching out for the pail, Pollyread saw the face crumple as if grabbed from within. In slow motion, she saw Mama toppling toward her.

*   *   *

Mama didn't fall, because Pollyread was right there. And Pollyread only staggered as Mama held on to her. But the pail, after wobbling around on Pollyread's frantic head for what seemed like minutes — *that* fell, splashing water over everyone's legs and setting Jackson to wobbling. Matters weren't helped by Goat, whose swirls of cloud and sulfurous smell only added to the confusion. And the noise: Mama's moans as she tried to stand upright, Pollyread shouting to Mama as if she was over at Shim's instead of holding on to her shoulder, Keneisha crying out, "Whathappen, whathappen" as she ran back toward them. And the pail of water teeter-tottering on Jackson's head, trying its hardest to join Pollyread's.

Through it all, Jackson was held tight by the thought that Mama had not tripped or been pushed. She had collapsed. Something from within had thrown her down.

Finally getting himself balanced and stable, he carefully removed the pail from his head and rested it on the ground. It was getting darker by the minute. But that wasn't the reason Mama's face looked gray. And when he reached beside Pollyread and held on to Mama her skin was cold.

He saw the same worry in his sister's eyes.

Mama's breathing was mixed with little moans, as though something inside was sticking her sporadically.

Goat was still, like a slow-burning flame, a few yards away now. He was looking steadfastly at Mama. Anxious, Jackson thought. Like the twins.

"You okay, Mama?" It was all he could think to say.

She tried to smile but grimaced instead as the thing inside stuck her.

"Come," Pollyread said sternly. "Come sit down." And they led Mama between them to the only place in Stedman's Corner outside of Shim's where there was a seat, an ancient tree trunk that had fallen years ago and been worn smooth by generations of Valley bottoms. It was just where the path from the Gilmores' house met level ground. People who lived up that way often rested there before attempting the trek up.

"I sorry 'bout the water, Pen," Mama said, when her breathing returned closer to normal.

"Is not your fault, Mama. Is the goat."

"Goat? What goat?" Mama looked around, including in the direction of Goat.

"No goat, Mama," Jackson jumped in. "Water seep into her brain."

"I am not crazy," Pollyread announced loudly. She

appealed to Keneisha, who was still hovering around Mama. "I look crazy to you?" Then, without waiting for an answer, she pointed. "See him there!"

Jackson, his breath like a big dumpling in his mouth, looked. And Goat was there. Looking at the little group from few meters away, still and serious as a judge, as Mama herself would have said. Had she seen him.

"You see any goat?" Keneisha was appealed to again, this time by Mama.

"No, Miss Maisie," the girl said.

Mama giggled, the sound music to Jackson's ears. "Pen? Maybe this time you brother have it right." Her tender tone did not appease Pollyread, who, Jackson noted, was staring at Goat with fire in her eyes.

"Come, pickney," Mama said, bustling to her feet. "Time to go home. I never expect to be out this late, I never even bring the flashlight, and is almost dark already. Keneisha, next time I see you, you might be a mama by then, eh? What a thing." She gave the girl a broad grin. "Happy landing, and give Miss G a big howdy. Walk good. Mind Pen goat don't trip you." She giggled again.

Jackson saw Pollyread thinking to say something but, thankfully and unusually, she thought better of it. He collected his bucket from where he'd put it down and asked his sister to help him settle it on his head.

"I don't finish with that goat," she said fiercely, her voice low so only he could hear.

Jackson looked up the path leading to their house. A little way up, there was a glow like a candle flame, illuminating the route they had to walk.

"I don't think he finish with us either," he said.

A Long Day

Mama and Goat were fighting. Or playing. They were shouting at each other. Or laughing. It was hard to tell in the tangle of smoky cloud and limbs. Pollyread's feet were planted on Stedman's Corner concrete ground like a tree that could not be moved. She couldn't even scream. To add insult to injury, Jammy was sitting on the tree trunk, legs crossed like he was in his own living room (if he had one), laughing his head off at all of them. Jackson — of course — was nowhere in sight. Nor Poppa.

But Pollyread woke, head ringing with the violent dream, to the sound of bees. Bees were among those small creatures — including ants, forty legs, and cockroaches — which Pollyread hated: Invariably, if one were in her vicinity, it stung her. The sound they made, like old men whispering together, was not soothing, as she'd read in a book: It alarmed her. This morning it brought her to wakefulness abruptly. And alert enough to realize that the sound couldn't be bees — unless there was a frighteningly huge swarm of them out by the gate. So, she thought, perhaps it was (this being Sunday) a group of real old men on the path, saying their prayers. In the gray half-light that surrounded her, that crazy thought really woke her up.

She began again, touching base with herself. The murmuring sound was coming from out in the yard. It was not a swarm of bees. The sounds *were* human. People talking. One of the voices was familiar.

"James —" she heard Mama say, and a rumble, the sound she had awakened to, followed.

As she was running through the short list of Jameses that she knew, Pollyread heard a voice that, though she had not heard it in a long time, she recognized immediately.

"Touch not the Lord's anointed!"

At that, like a match struck in darkness, Mama's voice flared. "Your frowsy head anoint with weed. And it dutty like a drain!"

Pollyread knew the expression well, and Jammy was right to be offended. He was highly offended. His outrage was expressed in a string of words not usually heard on a Sunday morning, and certainly not in the Gilmore yard. They banged like stones against the windows of Pollyread's ears and demolished the last shadows of sleepiness.

41

But as she stamped out of her room, anger boiling with words to throw back at Jammy, she bumped into Poppa stumbling out of his room, rubbing his eyes. "Wha-appen?" All arms and legs, he looked like an oversized doll. "I hear —"

"Jammy outside!" was all Pollyread had to say to wake him up fully and send him through the front door, grabbing his lignum vitae stick as he went. She was right behind.

An extraordinary scene greeted them, stopping them cold for a moment: Jammy's clenched fist raised high as Mama doubled over and spat explosively onto the ground between them. In the gray light, the sun still many mountaintops away from Valley, they looked to Pollyread like dream figures. Nightmare figures.

A wordless roar erupted from Poppa as if tearing him open. He rushed toward the two figures, stick held high in one hand. Jammy, looking down at Mama, saw Poppa late but had the sense to jump to one side as the stick slashed through the space where he'd been. Pollyread ran to Mama, still bent over but trying to stand. She put her mother's heavy arm round her shoulders for what support she could offer.

"Going kill you here today," Poppa said in a cold fury Pollyread had never heard in his voice before — and which she shared. She hardly felt her mother's weight on her, so intent was she on willing her father to get at Jammy.

Poppa, crouched, legs apart, his stick trailing half behind him on the ground like a broken wing, was stalking his prey. Jammy, eyes wild with weed but also from fear, had taken refuge behind the ackee tree, the nearest shield. His Rasta head peering around the trunk at Poppa's advance looked like an outgrowth of the tree itself.

"I never . . . touch . . . her . . . Mass Gillie," he stammered, edging around the tree as Poppa began to circle it. "Never touch . . . her, sah."

"But I going touch you," Poppa said, his voice low and urgent. "Touch you good."

"Miss Maisie," Jammy called out. "I . . . I touch you?" Appealing to Mama but not taking his eyes from Poppa.

Pollyread felt Mama's body double over, as though Jammy's words had hit her in the belly. She convulsed and vomited. Pollyread's eyes, as if somehow separate from herself, identified a piece of Lucea yam from last night's supper on the ground. Bent over, waving her arms while trying to stand straight, Mama was struggling with words.

"Miss Maisie —"

"Shut up!" Poppa barked. "And take you lick like a man."

Mama squawked, "Gil . . . bert."

"What?" He didn't turn or lose his sight of Jammy.

"Don't . . . lick him." The words were dressed in spittle.

"Why?" Poppa, looking like a black land crab, moved a half step closer to the ackee tree. "Him lick you. Is *you* should lick him."

Lick him! Pollyread heard herself scream silently.

"Him never . . . lick. Me." Mama's voice was a hoarse whisper.

As though he hadn't heard her, Poppa raised his right hand, the stick quivering.

"No!" Mama's scream was an explosion of pain. Her body sagged against Pollyread's shoulder.

"What happen, Maisie?" Poppa's voice was tinged with fear.

"Mama say him never lick her," Pollyread shouted at Poppa, who had taken another step toward the terrified Jammy.

Poppa stopped, but kept his hand with the stick raised. "Say what?" Pollyread couldn't see his face but puzzlement was clear in his voice. She could see Jammy's eyes, which were as big as the ackee seeds in the tree above him. "I see him!"

44

"Gilbert," Mama said firmly, pushing herself away from Pollyread's supporting shoulder. "No. You *think* . . . you see him . . . hit me." *I see!* Pollyread yelled inside her own head but kept her mouth shut. "But same time he look like he was going to hit me, the sickness take me and I double over." Mama was breathing hard but holding herself straight and stern.

Poppa stopped and straightened. "You sure?" He didn't sound convinced, and turned to face Mama and Pollyread, as if searching for proof.

That was a signal to Jammy. He seemed to fly from behind the ackee tree and through the gate, flashing past Pollyread and Mama in a smelly swoosh of ganja fumes and pursued by a livid Cho-cho, who had been stalking him right behind Poppa. As Jammy went through the gate, the little dog lunged and just missed the man's bare ankle. His custodian's duty accomplished, Cho-cho fetched up and marked the gatepost with pee as Jammy disappeared up the path back toward Morgan's Mount.

Pollyread looked quickly at Poppa to see what he would do. She was surprised at the little smile on his face, which softened his eyes. He glanced at Mama and she smiled too.

Pollyread saw nothing funny about anything.

As she was helping Mama back to the house, Jammy's

voice, cursing Poppa, floated down into the yard like pieces of dirty paper.

"How you feeling now?" Poppa asked. His voice was gentle, and a little anxious.

They were sitting at the table, the four of them — Jackson having stumbled out of bed as they entered from the yard — letting Sunday's silence settle around them.

"Not too bad," Mama said, patting her husband's hand resting on the table. "But I don't think Reverend Forsythe will be seeing me today."

"Me neither," Poppa said, sounding tired himself.

Pollyread didn't like the sound of this. *Something wrong*, particularly in Mama's gray face, which looked as though it was evening at the end of a long day, rather than barely dawn.

Pollyread and Jackson exchanged questions. Many questions. Jackson's was a simple one: *What did I miss?* Which Pollyread couldn't answer at the moment. Her own were like heavy black flies buzzing around inside her head. Jammy hardly figured in her thoughts. Or Goat, despite the dream. They were distractions. Mama was at the center. Yesterday evening's collapse. This morning's vomiting. And now, too sick to go to church.

Poppa staying home with her. *Definitely a story there,* she thought. Not a good story either, her gut told her.

The twins generally liked going places by themselves, together or separately. Shim's grocery, carrying messages around Valley and as far, now they were big, as Cross Point, even to Miss Brimley at the library in Cuthbert Bank (though that was farther, so they had to go together). But AME Church on their own was a different matter, nothing to do with distance. You had to be well behaved from the moment you stepped through your gate because any adult had the natural right to correct the bad-behave of any child — and, if the adult so chose, to report such behavior to a parent. (Which brought a double dose of censure: for the bad-behave and for the worse sin of "shame-me-in-the-street.") In church itself, once service began you couldn't fidget or whisper to other children. And there were no comforting props (in their case, Poppa; Mama sang in the choir) to lean against and catch a little doze or at least a daydream during Reverend Forsythe's convoluted (a word she'd learned for Common Entrance) and interminable (learned on her own) sermons. Not a good scene.

"What you was fixing to make for breakfast, Mama?" Pollyread asked, her voice bright and helpful. She tapped Jackson lightly on the head as she moved into the kitchen: *Come on.*

47

They took, as Mama would have said if she'd noticed, their own sweet time fixing breakfast. Never had onions and tomatoes been so finely diced, never a regular-sized cabbage yielded such a mountain of finely shredded leaves. Her brother's surgery on a fairly small chunk of saltfish made Pollyread wonder whether this was the real story behind the feeding of the five thousand. Her own fingers ached for hours after from kneading the flour, baking powder, and water for the johnnycakes. The plantain from the tree in the yard was lovingly (and slowly) sliced and carefully (and slowly) sprinkled with cinnamon for frying. All that effort yielded a meal no larger than Mama would have put together, and certainly no tastier. But what would take their mother half an hour at most occupied her painstaking children twice as long.

Which was exactly the point. And the parents didn't notice. Mama had been taken by Poppa to lie down and had dozed off. Poppa wandered out into the backyard and became preoccupied, as he generally did, with watering and weeding around the plants growing there. Meanwhile, as they were working, Pollyread filled Jackson in on what had happened before Cho-cho's furious barking woke him. Their whispers danced around the question of Mama's health. That was a dark pool of memory, which they didn't want to put even a toe into.

The twins were complimented on the flavorsome meal, which, after prayers of thanksgiving for the food and that Mama wasn't harmed, proceeded almost silently. Pollyread said nothing that would draw attention to time passing. Jackson, she noticed, chewed every mouthful with unusual thoughtfulness. (*A ruminant*, she thought, remembering a word she had recently learned: her brother the cow. Or the goat.) She was lost in such thoughts, mingled with her wild dream and flashes of the drama with Jammy, when Mama spoke.

"Is you him come to," Mama said. Her voice, weak but sounding more like her own, told Pollyread that she was teasing Poppa, a good sign.

"Me?" Poppa's voice was a deep growl.

"He say he want to see you about something."

"At this time of morning?" Valley people were early risers, but a visit at this hour was unseemly. "The only thing I want to see Jammy about at any time, I will see him about in courthouse in Town."

"He must be don't have nowhere to sleep," Mama said. Pollyread was surprised at the note of sympathy in her voice, considering what had happened less than a couple hours before.

49

Poppa snorted, put down his knife and fork, and ticked off his fingers. "Him have him mother yard. Him have other family here in Valley and in the district. I hear say him have a girl in Town carrying baby for him — *she* must live somewhere. And him have my ground at Morgan's Mount that him capture — him all build shelter on it. The bwoy have more place to sleep than you and me, Maisie."

"He never sleep nowhere inside last night, that's for sure," Mama said. "Dry grass and leaf tie up in his locks."

"All kinds of grass tie him up," Poppa said, surprising Pollyread with a little laugh.

"Him was high, yes," Mama agreed. "When he come inside and I go to pick something out of his head, the bwoy step back and rail up and tell me not to touch the Lord's anointed." Pollyread heard that voice again in her head, thunderous and dark.

"Is not the Lord anoint him with weed," Poppa said.

Mama cackled. "Is that I tell him, make him let out a string of badword I never hear the likes of before. Only from them madmen in Town."

"Jammy mad, yes." Poppa said it quietly, as if summing up Jammy. There was, Pollyread thought, a sort of sadness in his voice.

"Is why Jammy take a set on us like that?" Jackson

asked before biting into his third johnnycake. "Is like he think we have something for him."

Poppa grumped before sipping and swallowing his coffee. "I nearly give it to him this morning." He chuckled at his own bad joke.

"But I don't hear him troubling anybody else since he come back," Jackson argued. Bollo didn't even know his own cousin was in the district.

Pollyread, with a shiver of anxiety, wondered if Jackson was going on to talk about their exchange with Bollo and Trucky at Standpipe the day before.

Mama sighed a big sigh. All eyes turned to her. A wisp of a smile lifted her face. "Him was such a mannersable boy."

"Mannersable?" asked Jackson.

"Who?" Pollyread asked.

"James," Mama said softly. She wasn't looking at either of them, but into the past somewhere.

Jackson's body shifted as though he was getting up from the chair. "Jammy?" His eyes scanned Mama's face like flashlights for something he didn't find. He looked at his father. He was fussing with his food.

Pollyread spoke his question: "In this house?"

"Yes." The word dropped from Mama's mouth like a feather.

The twins, speechless, locked eyes for support.

Poppa stepped into the silence. "Maisie, you hardly touch you food."

Mama's mouth corners turned down as her smile faded away. "I not tasting it." Pollyread felt a pang of embarrassment. Which Mama sensed. "Is not the cooking, Pen," she went on quickly, but sounding tired. "Is me. My tongue feel like cardboard." Carefully, she took the empty plate that had held the johnnycakes and covered her own plate. "Put it on the stovetop to keep. I will eat it later." She eased herself up from her chair and shuffled toward her bedroom.

Then she paused in the doorway. "But wait . . . you pickney going be late for service at AME."

The twins suddenly showed an interest in what was left of their breakfast.

Mama sucked her teeth and wandered inside. The twins, dutifully and quietly chewing their food, listened for the creaking of springs as Mama lay down, and the sigh as she relaxed. Then they knew they were out of danger.

Guessing

Mama sick."

"Oh, so you is doctor."

"I not a doctor. But I have eyes in my head. And ears."

"Big ears."

"Maybe so. They hear Mama throwing up the breakfast we fix."

"The saltfish spoil."

"Saltfish don't spoil, that is why they salt it."

"So you is a expert on food as well as doctor."

"I not expert, Pel. But you know Mama sick too."

"How I know?"

"You was in and out with her whole day today."

"Because she . . ."

"Because she sick, just like I just say."

"She say is gas."

"Is not gas."

"How you know? You is doctor?"

"No, but I have sense. And sense tell me is not gas Mama have."

"How?"

"When Mama have gas, she make so much noise Aunt Zilla stay next door and know."

"I bet you I tell her what you just say."

"Tell her. I hear Mama say so herself. So."

"So what?"

"What is really wrong with her?"

"I supposed to know?"

"You was inside with her the whole time when I was out and about with Poppa at ground. You never talk?"

"Of course."

"So?"

"   ."

"So?"

"She say I not to tell anybody."

"Me is not *any*body."

"Not a living soul. That's what she say. And you not dead."

"She in the way."

"What!"

"Shhh."

"What?"

"I think Mama is pregnant."

"She never tell me that."

"Then what she tell you?"

"   ."

"Tell me I wrong."

"You wrong."

"That is what I think. And I think you think so too."

"You will have to go ask her yourself."

"You ask her?"

"No."

"Then how you know that I wrong?"

"How you know that you right?"

"You could ask the goat."

"Ask the goat what?"

"If Mama pregnant."

"Goat would know?"

"Maybe."

"Then you ask him, then."

"How you mean?"

"Don't you and him is big friend? Having conversation and everything."

"When?"

"Last night. Down at Stedman's Corner. It wasn't the goat you was talking to?"

"So what if it was?"

"Is a duppy."

"Sh-h-h."

"Quiet in there. School tomorrow."

"Yes, Poppa."

"But you see him too, not so?"

"I didn't talk to him."

"But you see him."

"'Course."

"Why you think that is *we* see the goat?"

"You mean — if is we it come to?"

"Yes."

"You think is so?"

"Maybe."

"Maybe it come *for* us."

"Poppa!"

"What going on in there? Don't I tell —"

"Jackso trying to frighten me."

"Jackson?"

"Yes, Poppa."

"You frightening you sister?"

"No, Poppa!"

"He telling duppy story, Poppa."

"Jackson?"

"Yes, Poppa."

"You telling you sister a duppy story?"

"Not really, Poppa."

"Well, really stop that and really go to sleep. Both of you. Or I going to really come in there to you."

"Yes, Poppa."

"Yes, Poppa."

"Jackso."

"What?"

"Why you want Mama to be pregnant?"

"How you mean?"

"You don't remember the last time?"

"   ."

"You remember?"

"Yes. I remember clear as day."

"Me too."

"So why you want her to be pregnant?"

"I remember the blood."

"Me too."

"And Poppa —"

"Crying like a baby."

"And darkness, like it say in Genesis. Forty days and forty nights."

"Yes."

"So, Jackso."

"What?"

"Why you want her to be pregnant again?"

Common Entrance

For the next few days, though they didn't discuss it, the twins watched their mother closely. There was no more early-morning vomiting, and she was up and doing as usual when they came home in the afternoons. She didn't complain about being dizzy or tired. Or gas. She seemed to sit down a lot, but that may have been her back, which gave her trouble from time to time.

On Wednesday morning when the twins reached Stedman's Corner, Trucky was waiting for them, bouncing up and down.

"What happen, Trucky?" asked Pollyread. Something was always happening with Trucky.

"You don't know what day it is?" he asked, excitement bubbling in his words.

"Wednesday," said Jackson impatiently. Trucky never came straight to the point.

"You never see Miss Phillipson go down to Town yesterday morning and come back in the afternoon with a big envelope in her hand as she get out the car." It wasn't a question.

"I never notice," said Pollyread dismissively: She always had more important things to do than watch the comings and goings of others — though somehow, Jackson thought, she usually knew about them.

"Me neither," said Jackson, who had, in fact, been kicking ball with Trucky and some other boys yesterday afternoon on the piece of level ground in front of the school. He'd been aware of Miss Phillipson's return from wherever she'd gone, but hadn't taken any interest in what the principal had in her hand.

"Well," said Trucky, dancing beside them as they continued toward Marcus Garvey, "*I* notice her."

"You is a real newspaper, Trucky," said Pollyread, in a hurry to hear the real news, whatever it was.

Trucky beamed. "Well, when she leave, she only have her car key in her hand and her big hamper basket handbag over her shoulder."

"And when she come back?" prompted Pollyread, an avid reader of mysteries.

"She leave the handbag in the car," said Trucky, who relished the smallest details of everyday life.

"So what was in the big envelope?" asked Jackson sharply.

"Who say anything about any envelope?" Trucky stepped in front of them with mock astonishment on his face.

"Nuh you," said Jackson, irritated now. "You see what was inside the envelope?"

"No," said Trucky. "How I was to see?"

"You mean she never come over and show you?" Pollyread's tone was sarcastic enough for even Trucky to understand.

"Is one of those big yellow envelopes from the Ministry," he said, a little defensive as he stepped aside and they resumed walking toward school.

"Cho," said Jackson, not letting up. "She get those envelopes from the Ministry all the time."

"Maybe it have salary money in it," said Pollyread casually.

"It too thin to have salary money in it. Besides, is the middle of the month."

The twins knew that there wasn't anything else to do at this point but to wait until Trucky was good and ready to tell them what he knew, if he really knew anything.

"Then," Trucky exclaimed dramatically, "this

morning . . ." He paused. Now he had their attention again. "Auntie Mavis CB her sister."

It was a point of pride for the Gordon family that they had a citizens band radio in their little house, one of only two or three in the whole district, which didn't have telephone service and had no hope of getting it anytime soon. It had been installed over the protests of Trucky's father, who preferred to go on with his life as much as possible at arm's length from the rest of the world, particularly of Town. But Mrs. Gordon came from a large family scattered across the island, and happily accepted the gift of her baby brother, who had a small electronics and computer shop in Town. He had come up and installed it one weekday when he knew Trucky's father would be down in Town. Mr. Gordon was not well pleased with his wife on his return, but had more sense than to throw the paraphernalia down into the gully behind the house, which was his first instinct. Now the crackles and screeches and rasping voices were part of the soundscape in that little corner of Top Valley. Trucky's Auntie Mavis in Town, who had never visited Valley, nevertheless was known to dozens of his friends as the source of stories behind the stories on the radio, and some that were not on the radio.

"Auntie Mavis CB her sister," Trucky repeated, his tone and the reference to his mother in the third person a sure promise of soap opera melodrama.

"Somebody dead?" asked Pollyread briskly. They were approaching the school gate by now; her attention was beginning to wander to the other children arriving with them.

"Nobody don't dead, at least not for us," said Trucky. "That's not why she call."

"So why?" asked Jackson, sighting Tafiri Smith, who was bringing marbles to trade with him today.

"She CB to say," announced Trucky, pausing for effect, rising on tiptoe, "that Common Entrance results coming out in the papers tomorrow. They will announce in school today!" He waved a hand at the world and ran off into another group of children, no doubt to replay his little drama of superior knowledge.

"Just weekend gone . . ." Jackson started saying, and then heard his voice, as if it were somebody else's, die away.

The Common Entrance exam stood like the Gates of Heaven and Hell for eleven-year-olds and their families all over the island. The common part of it was that everyone took the same exam at the same time everywhere. After that, the entrance was what mattered: Heaven was admission to the secondary school you wanted, hell was that the school didn't want you. As Miss Galbraith, the Sunday school teacher at AME, would say from time to time to summon backsliders to contrition: *Many are called but few are chosen.*

And now, if Trucky's news was to be believed, the day to be chosen — or not — had arrived.

Jackson and Pollyread walked in silence through the gate of Marcus Garvey Primary, caught up in the same thoughts, not needing even to share them. They didn't remember anything about the exam itself, but the lead-up to it had been a difficult time for all the Gilmores: months of dread and drilling for the twins, extra lessons paid for by extra hours in the field and at Redemption Ground market, at the carpentry table in the shed, or down in Town trying to make business. And studying until they felt their bottoms glued to the chairs around the dining table, with Mama and Poppa taking them up on endless study sheets, everybody weary and worried.

"What is for you cannot be un-for you," Mama had said when they came home from the exam-taking, to calm them.

"When you do your best, the angels can't do better," was Poppa's contribution.

Today, Jackson thought, they would find out what was for who, and who would need angels. Miss Watkins,

Marcus Garvey's grade-six teacher and extra-lesson tutor, confidently expected the twins, in the school-yard lingo derived from American sports television, to nail the exam and get their first choice of school, St. Giles, Mama's old school. Unless disaster struck like a biblical plague.

Given Pollyread's marks through their whole time at Marcus Garvey, that was as unlikely as snow in Top Valley. Jackson knew that his case was, as Mama liked to joke, a horse of a different story. Not that she joked about Jackson's marks. "Bwoy, you brain have sieve?" she would ask sometimes, tapping his head gently but firmly. "Everything just run through it like banana water." Pretty much everything, Jackson had to admit, except numbers. They stuck. He was always top of whatever class he was in for mathematics, regularly beating even Pollyread. Words were a different matter. Jackson couldn't see the point of studying about words. He never had a problem getting people to understand what he wanted to say, and he could read any book from the library in Content Gap. But he wasn't very good at answering the kinds of questions that Miss Watkins and the people at the Ministry in Town asked on the test papers. They didn't seem to make sense in the way that sums made sense to him. Sums were real, and useful. And if you understood numbers, they could be as fanciful as the big words that Pollyread liked to throw at him.

But there had been nothing fanciful about the words or the figures in the Common Entrance exam.

As he walked through the half-broken-down gate-posts of Marcus Garvey Primary beside his sister, who was all but skipping with anticipation, Jackson felt his belly-bottom tighten into a fist.

Assembly

Assembly took place in the open yard between the two blocks of classrooms, which ran parallel to each other. The children stood in ranks there, according to grade. The sixers, also generally the tallest, were at the back. The teachers sat on chairs on a raised covered passageway that ran between the two classroom blocks; it served as a kind of stage for morning assembly.

The teachers sat very still, barely noticing one another . . . or the children. Miss Watkins looked steadfastly down at the second graders, whom she had nothing to do with. She had hardly a glance for her grade-six charges at the back of the serried ranks, shuffling their feet and trying hard to appear casual. Miss Sharpton, who had taught the twins reading and writing in grade two and encouraged their love of books thereafter, looked down into her lap, perhaps already saying prayers.

Tension hung in the air like a fine dust that you breathed.

When Miss Phillipson appeared in the doorway of the old school building, all chatter and movement subsided into the yellow stillness. She was about the smallest member of the staff, but seemed taller to the children because of her position as principal, and because her back was as straight as a post. When Jackson looked at Miss Phillipson he thought of the people he used to draw in second- and third-grade art class, all straight lines. She wore pale, simple blouses tucked into dark, straight-cut skirts ending just below the knee, and neat black shoes with little heels. The outfit was so consistent — as was the hairstyle, which was not really a style, just pulled back in a bun — that the slightest variation was noted immediately. Today, above the usual dark skirt, there was a burgundy blouse with long sleeves, and, as though that wasn't enough, a large yellow rosebud in the lapel. As well as the battered old Bible she always brought to assembly, she carried in her left hand a large brown envelope.

Jackson, without looking, could feel Trucky's smile of satisfaction from five spaces farther down the grade-six line. The twins seldom stood together at assembly, but this morning, without thinking about it, they found themselves side by side, touching shoulders from time to time.

Miss Phillipson came to rest at the lectern placed in

the middle of the row of teachers' chairs, putting the Bible on the lectern but continuing to hold the envelope. She looked out at the gathering.

"Good morning, Marcus Garvey Primary," she said. She didn't speak loudly but her voice carried easily to the grade sixers at the back of the assembly.

"Good morning, Miss Phillipson," everyone replied, including the teachers. She gave them all a brief, thin smile.

"Well, brothers and sisters," Miss Phillipson began as usual — though her tone always made it clear that any relationship with her good self was a remote possibility — "we all know what day today is."

The grade-six line rustled. Knowing smiles were exchanged but quickly turned inward.

"But first," Miss Phillipson said, "let us pray."

Normally, there was a reading from the Bible, one of the Psalms perhaps, or from something uplifting that the principal happened to be reading. Kahlil Gibran was a favorite, as was Maya Angelou and, on days of national importance, Marcus Garvey. Prayers were generally read from prayer books that lived in a space below the canted top of the lectern.

But Miss Phillipson made no move toward the Bible she had put on the lectern, nor the prayer books underneath. Instead, she lowered her head slightly. As though theirs were all connected to hers, all the other heads went down too. "Perhaps the Good Lord will find it in his mercy," she said in her flat voice that carried beyond the children to the row of coolie plum trees marking off the quadrangle from the rest of the school yard, "to work a few miracles on the papers I got from the Ministry yesterday, and bring joy where I saw only sorrow."

There were whispers and shifting feet, a few giggles. The twins didn't dare look at each other but touched shoulders briefly.

"Dear Lord," Miss Phillipson began her prayer, "you who turned water into wine, we beseech you in your loving-kindness . . ." Her singsong stream of words coiled around the supplicatory thoughts of her students like smoke from a wood fire, carrying all up to heaven. Jackson heard Pollyread, a more attentive Sunday schooler than her brother, whispering to herself: *The Lord works in mysterious ways his wonders to perform.* Jackson's own plea was defensive and kept to himself: *Remember me, Lord, when you come into your kingdom.*

"Ah-*men!*" Miss Phillipson's conclusion was, as always, emphatic, cutting off any further dialogue with the deity. Heads restored themselves to their normal angles. To Jackson, the small familiar figure before them suddenly seemed strange and powerful: She had

70

assumed absolute control of the grade sixers' lives, simply because of what she knew about them inside that envelope.

Miss Phillipson, in the brisk manner that she did things, flipped open the big envelope and drew out a thick sheaf of paper. She wore glasses for reading, small oval lenses in a delicate gold frame. They rested on the flares of her nostrils, which were oddly broad for her small face. She touched the glasses tenderly, a habit of hers.

"Well, school," she began, "this has been a momentous year. For some of us, this will be our last year at Marcus Garvey." Her eyes, light dancing off the gold-framed spectacles, swept the line of grade sixers at the back. "I have here in my hand the results that we've all been waiting for, I know. For the Common Entrance examination," she added, as if anyone were in any doubt. The principal paused. "Some of you have probably done better than you yourself expected, and certainly exceeded the expectations of myself and Miss Watkins." Jackson felt a lifting of his spirit, but it didn't last: He thought he knew how badly he had done. "But others," Miss Phillipson continued, "others have not done as well as expected." She paused again, searching the line of sixers. Jackson felt a paintbrush dipped in cold water touch his heart. "As I call out your name, you will come forward and stand in front of the school here beside me." One finger pointed imperiously to a spot slightly in front and to the left of herself.

"Albert, Aidrene."

"AA," as she liked to refer to herself — "Miss Fancy" to some of her classmates — who was always first in everything arranged alphabetically, pulled herself away from the line and marched up to the front of the assembly to stand right beside Miss Phillipson, grinning with self-satisfaction, as though she belonged naturally at the focus of attention and acclaim. A few hands clapped, but Miss Phillipson silenced them with a swift glance and a curt "Later, please."

"Darby, Jeremiah." The class clown, who wore the biggest and thickest pair of glasses anyone had ever seen on a small mongoose face, zoomed out of the lineup with his arms flailing like those of a minibus driver swerving in and out of traffic in Town, changing gears as he navigated the stretch of school yard up to the principal and coming to an abrupt stop, with bobbing head and air-brake sighs, beside Miss Fancy, whose smile had faded. Jeremiah had been driving everywhere, in and out of school, from the time he was able to walk. The teachers had long ago given up trying to curb him, except in the classroom itself. Besides, in class he was attentive — and got very good marks.

Miss Phillipson, a rare smile on her face, waited for the bus driver to completely settle beside Aidrene Albert.

"Newton, Kerry-Ann."

Jackson's body had been stiffening, as if anticipating a blow. When the blow came, he didn't even feel it — Pollyread did. Jackson felt his sister go wood-stiff beside him. Miss Phillipson had skipped over G for Gilmore! Whatever the names being called out meant, they belonged to the children who had habitually come at the top of grade six. But Pollyread, who had come first overall more often than all the others — she had been completely ignored.

She was staring straight ahead. Jackson knew she wasn't seeing anything. Nor was he, just the blur of movement as Miss Phillipson called out another name, which Jackson didn't even register.

"These," he heard Miss Phillipson say from far away, "are our star students, whom we are sending off into the great noisy city down below to their first choice of schools. You have to be very good to get into your first choice, because all across the land, other children are trying to do the same. Let us *now* give them a big hand of applause."

Jackson didn't hear the sounds made by the fluttering hands around him. Their pale palms were like butterflies, silent in his ears. He didn't feel his right hand slapping against his left. He was feeling Pollyread beside him, the shoulder touching his thawing like a piece of meat from Mama's fridge, but no other sign of life from her. And he was thinking: *The world has turned upside down! The angels were asleep.*

The flickering hands settled. Miss Phillipson had raised an arm, which all knew was a command for quiet. The hand clapping and cheers died away like windows closing.

"This is the best set of results Marcus Garvey Primary has *ever* had," Miss Phillipson said, raising her small self on tiptoe and making her audience the gift of a smile. "And there are several students who have been given their second choice of schools, which is a worthy achievement also. Miss Watkins will have the list and will take it to her classroom after assembly." The principal turned and handed over the papers from the Ministry to the grade-six teacher.

"But —" She paused and seemed to rock back and forth slightly. "Splendid as these young people have performed, there is even better to come." The principal's face seemed to swell a little before their eyes, as though she were trying to swallow something. "I've saved the best for last."

A ripple of murmurs and foot shuffling. *She's going to*

give us a holiday, Jackson said to himself, though the thought didn't give him any kind of pleasure.

"You all know that each year the Ministry awards a few scholarships." A pause. "To the very brightest children." Another pause. "The *very* brightest. And," she continued after another dramatic pause and an eye sweep of her audience, "we've never had one of those brilliant students in our school, with their name and their school's name in the papers and everybody biggin' them up." Miss Phillipson paused to allow her audience time to appreciate and savor her knowledge and use of school-yard slang — no one about to point out to her that it was already out of style. "Well," she continued, pleased with herself and her news, "we have one of those *very* people *right here* with us at our *very own* Marcus Garvey Primary School." She glowed like a ripe mango.

Jackson didn't allow himself to think. He noticed, however, in the pin-drop silence, a quivering beside him. Pollyread seemed to become a couple inches shorter, and he realized she'd been standing on tiptoe all this time. Then she grew again, bright eyes fixed on the principal. *Holding on for dear life,* Jackson thought.

"Students and staff of Marcus Garvey Primary." Miss Phillipson's voice rose a notch. "I present to you our very own government scholar for this year, one of only seventeen across the land and the very first government scholar from this august institution. . . ." She paused and flung her arm out, finger pointing toward the middle of the anxious line of grade sixers. "Penelope Gilmore!"

In the split-second silence between the calling of her name and the beginning of the clapping, Jackson heard, clear as a pane of glass, "Ohmigodsaveme" whispered beside him. And then Pollyread — Penelope on her birth paper, Pel to her twin, his first word, Pen to Mama and Poppa except when they needed to make a point, Polly to other family and longtime friends because she started talking before walking and hadn't stopped since, and Pollyread to just about everyone because when she wasn't talking she was reading — dropped down in a crouch.

Had she fainted? That had happened a couple times that Jackson could remember, and he bent over to aid his sister.

"YES!" Pollyread screamed, bouncing Jackson out of the way as she shot up into the air, fisted left arm straight, television-sports style. "Yes!" Again, softer, pulling her arm down to her side to complete the ritual.

Then, with the big cat grin that Jackson knew so well, she pranced along the line of grade sixers and up to the front of the gathered school, floating on the applause.

Afterward, even years afterward, Pollyread could have told you, in minute detail, about the announcement and the explosion in her head, the green and blue stars silently bursting, the walk through the applause like she was a knife in an avocado pear; and of the feeling she had, walking toward Miss Phillipson and the place of honor that Aidrene Albert made by shuffling away from the principal, that she was walking away from herself, her life until now.

And she could have told you, afterward, of the coolness of the principal's congratulatory hand, soft as baby powder, and of her smile, not much warmer — Miss Phillipson, who'd been overheard to say, *That Gilmore girl is too bright for her own good.* She could have told you, as she told a multitude of people, of the little dance by Jeremiah Darby in front of her, stamping his feet to the tight rhythmic clapping of the rest of the school.

And she could have told you about the beginning of her speech, responding to the cadence of hands, feet, and shouts of: "Speech! Speech!" She had to recall it afterward, because she didn't have any idea at the time of what she was doing or saying. She just remembered, laughing at herself as she told it later, sounding like one of those stars on the television (though the Gilmores didn't have TV, the children were allowed to watch occasionally at one or other of their few neighbors who did) winning an Academy Award or something like that. She remembered having the good sense to begin by thanking Miss Phillipson and Miss Watkins before even Mama and Poppa. And she remembered saying something about how wonderful her fellow grade sixers had been — and thinking: *Why am I saying this? I don't even like some of them.*

Clearest in her memory was of turning to the line of teachers behind her to find Miss Watkins. And of running and throwing herself into Miss Watkins's arms and bursting, finally, into tears and wanting to disappear from happiness into that large cushiony woman, whose arms felt as cool as sleep.

Facing
the Music

The lone johncrow floating on the hot morning saw children running all over Valley at a time when none but the smallest should have been visible. But Miss Phillipson had declared a holiday for the thirty-seven grade sixers, even those who had not covered themselves in glory. Some of these, as the observant johncrow would have noticed, were not rushing in the direction of home, where the principal had sent them, or indeed rushing at all. Bad news weighs a lot.

Those who had something to celebrate, however, tumbled through the school doors and scattered in the direction of their homes — or elsewhere. At Stedman's Corner there was further division, onto the paths leading up and down the valley sides like veins.

As often happened, the twins found themselves in a loose group with classmates who lived along the same path. They came to Christine Aiken's gate first. A sweet-natured girl who dreamed of being a beautician and had more interest than Pollyread in the dolls that Pollyread used to get for Christmas and birthdays, Christine had nothing special to report to her mother, who had four other children younger than Christine to worry about, with no resident father. Christine's departure to Town, had she won a place, would have thrown her mother into a panic: Where would the money come from and who would help her mind the smaller children? But there had never been much chance of that. Christine would go on to Cross Point All-Age, which her mother had attended, continuing to look after her younger brothers and sisters and style the hair of her classmates, until time came when Christine would begin having children of her own. Her mother had had her at sixteen.

As she stepped inside the gate to her little yard, Melody, born early last year, came toddling toward her on rubber legs. Christine, with the ease born of practice, scooped her sister onto one hip, balanced the schoolbag on the other side, and gave the dirty, glowing face a kiss.

"See you later," she called out brightly to the twins as she closed her gate. "I glad for you."

"Thank you," said Pollyread, as two more children tumbled out of the little house on hearing their sister's voice.

The twins looked at each other, two impulses balancing in a momentary seesaw. Sometimes when walking back from school they raced each other home from some point that was determined in a flash by one or the other. Now Pollyread crouched, one hand fiddling with the hem of her uniform skirt. But Jackson turned away, looking back down the path to where Jonathan Purdy, the other member of their little group, walked slowly up toward them, head down. Pollyread sighed and straightened.

Jonathan was not a very popular member of the Marcus Garvey school community, though no one could have told you exactly why. He wasn't clever or slow, good at games or clumsy, mean or generous, good-looking or ugly, fat or skinny. Had he lived elsewhere in Valley, he would have been almost unknown to Pollyread and Jackson outside of class. As it was, they knew more than they really wanted to know about him. Jonathan — and that was another thing about him: He didn't have a nickname or pet name — was minded by his grandmother, left there by his father when he got a prized place on a crew to go to Florida to cut sugarcane. Jonathan was less than two years old at the time, and no one had seen or heard of the father since. His mother was unknown to everyone except, presumably, the father. That in itself was not unusual: A lot of Jonathan's

81

schoolmates were minded by grandmas, aunts, or even unrelated "aunties." But none of the others had Miss Icilda raising them. A foundation member of Zion Pentecostal Tabernacle, Miss Icilda was a firm believer in the biblical injunction: Spare the rod and spoil the child. Jonathan was not spared, though no one else would have called him a wayward or disobedient child. The Gilmores, though living more than a hundred meters up the path, were aware of every occasion on which the rod — actually a leather belt — was applied by Miss Icilda, a wiry woman in her sixties who smoked a pipe and still dug her own ground. The worst thing was that as he got older, Jonathan had stopped crying out, which made the thwacking sound of the belt, tearing the air like paper, all the more startling.

The twins stood side by side now just above Christine's gate, waiting for Jonathan to catch up. He approached with head still down, and perhaps would have gone right past them if they hadn't, between them, been blocking the pathway.

"You want to come up by us?" Jackson asked. They all knew what awaited Jonathan a few meters up the road. His Common Entrance marks had put him in the middle of the class. With someone to argue for him, a place could probably be found for Jonathan in a high school in Town. But there was no one to make the case. So he would go to Cross Point All-Age and return every afternoon to Miss Icilda.

Jonathan shook his head without looking up.

"Maybe your granny not there," said Pollyread hopefully. "Come stay by us until she come back."

He looked at her. A smile like the shadow of a bird wing crossed his lips. "Is okay," he said softly, and seemed suddenly a little old man, not eleven years old.

The three of them walked in silence to Jonathan's gateway, which was an opening between two big tree ferns that formed an untidy but beautiful arch of mottled green sunlight into the yard behind. Into the trunk of one of the ferns had been hammered the lid of a tin of Milo for visitors to knock on with the bolt from a latch, which hung at the end of a string. Miss Icilda had lived in Valley most of her life, but only Jonathan came into her yard unannounced; if there was no answer to your knocking, you went away.

"Okay, then," Jonathan said, pushing the gate. "See you."

"You sure —?" Pollyread began.

He spun back around as he walked away from them and waved a hand, forefinger pointed in the air.

"Congrats, yow," he called out with a smile. Then he turned and went, head down again, toward the shut door of his home, framed by the lovely arch of ferns.

The twins didn't wait for him to reach the door. They wanted to get away as quickly as possible.

A few steps up the path from Jonathan's gate there was a big breadfruit tree. As they passed it, Jackson a step ahead, and without a word being spoken, the race for home was on, Pollyread breaking first and bouncing Jackson's shoulder. Generally, it was a game; it conferred bragging rights for the first fifteen minutes or so after they got there. But today it was a race in earnest: to be the one to tell Mama the news, good and not so good.

The topography of the path, dotted with trees and stones, step-ups and sideways leaps, decreed a complex strategy of speed, agility, and balance, with the ever-present risk of injury to pride and person. The clamor of their cries and grunts and the clattering of shoes on the hard-packed dirt filled the air that surged around them. They left drops of sweat behind like clues. More than once they were tempted to shrug off the backpacks they carried to lighten their load and increase speed. But the consequences of throwing away a bag of books would be longer-lasting than the pride in winning the race. So they groaned and whinnied and yelped their way up the winding path, first one, then the other leading past strategic markers. They raced around the goat rock without a thought, their lungs filled with pain and excitement.

Cho-cho decided the winner. The little mongrel picked up their cries when they were still a distance from home and came prancing and barking down the path, further complicating the progress and tactics of the race. His rush carried him past them, and they managed to get ahead of him for a few meters. But when the pathway that had been twisting like a piece of twine suddenly straightened at the blackie mango tree marking the boundary of Gilmore land, Cho-cho caught up with them. He flew past Jackson, a few meters behind his sister at that particular point, and leapt up at Pollyread, aiming perhaps for the flashing white kerchief in her hand. Or perhaps it was that Pollyread's foot fell on one of the several overripe blackies lying on the path, squishy as oil. Either way, she pitched forward in what Miss Phillipson would have called an unseemly manner, the deliriously happy dog tangling her up just long enough for Jackson to leap over the writhing duo and bolt through their gate with a shout of triumph.

Even after they had all achieved the sanctuary of the yard and the twins were catching their breath on the gray granite boulder just inside the gate, Cho-cho wouldn't stop barking. He ran up the path toward the house and barked at it, as though summoning Mama inside. No one appeared. Then he trotted back to them, still barking, looking from Pollyread, who was furious with him, to Jackson, pleased with himself and ignoring the dog. Then he pranced back to the house, spinning round every meter or two to see if they were following. They continued to sit on the rock, drawing longer and longer breaths, smelling each other's sweat.

"Okay, Cho-cho," said Jackson finally, standing up and making a couple steps toward the house. "Cease and settle, man."

"Damn dawg," Pollyread muttered angrily.

Getting some response at last, the dog ran to the house again, tail wagging. Mama came into view from around the side of the house, carrying a bunch of carrots in one hand and some fresh-cut gerberas in the other.

"But stop!" she said, stopping herself. "What you pickney doing home this time of morning?"

Until she remembered what in fact they were doing home, Pollyread felt guilty for a moment.

"Common Entrance, Mama," she announced, recovering herself and grinning at her mother.

Mama didn't smile in return. "What you mean, Common Entrance? Don't is long time you take Common Entrance?" She looked suspiciously at them.

"Results, Mama," said Pollyread, aware of Jackson shifting nervously beside her.

"A-oh," Mama sighed, relaxing.

"Pel get scholarship!" Jackson blurted out.

Mama froze. "A-true? Scholarship? Pen?" Her face opened up like the ortaniques the twins found on the table some mornings, golden with her joy. "What you saying?" She dropped the things she was carrying in her hand and didn't even notice. Pollyread, inching forward, giggled, and Mama looked embarrassed. Then Mama half squatted and held out her arms, and Pollyread waddled like a duck and fell into them. Mama tumbled over and they rolled on the ground, over and over — something that, under other circumstances, would have brought the wrath of Jehovah down on Pollyread's head. Jackson couldn't help but smile, even as he felt tears prick his eyeballs. His news wasn't going to make Mama so happy.

The thought also flitted through his mind that Mama hadn't been well, so should not be rolling on the ground like pickney. They were cackling like yard fowls, Jackson thought, beginning to get irritated. He wanted to get his part of this over and done with quickly.

As though she read his mind, Mama brought the rolling to a halt and untangled herself. "So what about you, Mister Man?" she panted, standing up and brushing off her clothes. Pollyread, leaning against Mama as though unwilling to break the contact, was silent, looking at the ground.

He shrugged.

Mama looked at him and repeated his movement. "That's all?" She did it again, to underline her question.

"Second choice," Jackson mumbled.

"What that you say?" She cupped a hand behind one ear, a habit of hers when she wanted you to speak louder.

"King's, Mama." A little louder.

Mama's face began to open in the direction of a smile, and then her lips tilted in puzzlement. "King's?" She looked down at Pollyread. "Is that him say? King's?"

"Yes, Mama," Jackson cut in before his sister could answer. "King's College."

"What about King's College?" Mama was truly perplexed, and Jackson's heart sank: There was going to be no easy way.

He took a deep breath and let the words out. "I got into King's College in Town."

"King's College?" Pollyread had detached herself

from her mother's shoulder and was walking back toward Jackson and the schoolbags. She was still not looking at Jackson. Mama meanwhile was looking from one child to the other. "Don't is Saint Giles we wrote on the Common Entrance paper from the Ministry?"

Jackson could only nod.

"For both of you?"

Nods from both of them this time.

"*You* going to Saint Giles, Pen?"

"Yes, Mama," Pollyread said, hitching her schoolbag over her shoulder and standing beside but a little apart from Jackson.

"So, Mister Man," she said, looking fixedly at Jackson, "how come you saying you going to King's College?"

King's College was one of the most acclaimed high schools in the island, and any parent would be delighted to know that their child had been selected for it. Jackson watched Mama's face intently, hoping — against everything he knew about his mother — to see a window into something like congratulation. But she had not reached that far yet.

"You mean to say," Mama spoke quietly, but clearly, "that you didn't get into Saint Giles."

It wasn't a question. "No, Mama."

The slightly bewildered look didn't change. "How that happen, son?"

Jackson's shoulders shrugged before he thought, and he realized immediately that that was not any kind of answer to give to his mother. But what was the answer? What words to use? And to express what, exactly?

"I don't know, Mama," he said, mostly for something to say.

"You must know, Jackso," she said. She was using her pet name for him, and her voice was gentle. Jackson squirmed. If she had been angry with him, or upset in some way . . . But she was trying to understand what had happened. And Jackson wasn't helping her. He just stood there, hunting frantically for words which were suddenly missing in action when he really needed them, looking at Mama, holding tight to a curtain at the back of his eyes, right behind which was a river of tears bigger and stronger than Bamboo River. If he could just find the words, he told himself, then the river could be held back.

Mama beckoned him to her. "Come. Let we go inside and talk."

Jackson watched himself walk toward Mama like a robot in a movie, barely lifting his feet. He was aware of Pollyread slightly behind him, and of Cho-cho a little in front, like the two of them were guarding him in some way. And then he was aware only of Mama's right arm, dusty from rolling on the ground with Pollyread, heavy as a tree limb as it closed around his shoulder and also light as warm air. The curtain gave way.

"Lordy lord," Jackson heard Pollyread say behind him.

Holding Court

That night, as they were settling down to sleep, Jackson described the afternoon as "Princess Polly holding court." Tart words sprang immediately to Pollyread's mind but, unusually, she bit her tongue. Jackson's tone was teasing rather than malicious, and besides, he wasn't entirely wrong.

Pollyread couldn't remember another time when so many people found their way to the Gilmore house in one afternoon. They didn't come all at once, in fact never more than two or three at a time, but there was always somebody there, until dark drove the last ones home. By then, Pollyread's head was swollen tight with praise and flattery, and Mama's very skin seemed to shine with pride. Because everyone — neighbors, Mama's church sisters, Poppa's drinking partners from down at Shim's, and some who were, in Mama's words, just out "ketching breeze" — was drawn by news of Pollyread's scholarship. In Valley, news seemed to be carried by the birds and butterflies, up and down hillsides and through doorways and windows to the next yard, and the next. News as big as this — the first scholarship anyone could remember — went on the breeze itself.

By evening, though, Pollyread's fingers were swollen from squeezing limes and Seville oranges to make wash for their guests, and there was no sugar for next morning's breakfast. Poppa, who liked his coffee syrupy sweet, would have to be content with just condensed milk. Mama was a little tired by the end of it but had borne up well, Pollyread thought. No sign of dizziness or upset stomach.

Lunch had been eaten almost without words, Jackson's head down in the food that he was picking at, Mama and Pollyread teasing him silently with rolling eyes and winks at each other. Pollyread figured that Mama, who usually didn't waste time when she had something to discuss with one or both of them, was waiting for Poppa before she reopened the matter of Jackson's results. She probably didn't want to risk another river of tears.

As Pollyread picked up plates to begin clearing the table, Cho-cho exploded under the table, where he'd been dozing on Jackson's sad feet, and flew to the doorway, quivering with furious barking. An equally loud screech from outside almost caused Pollyread to drop the plates.

"Hold dawg! Hold this bad dawg before it eat poor little me!"

Mama and Pollyread looked at each other, Pollyread frowning in irritation, Mama smiling indulgently as Pollyread went to calm Cho-cho.

"Afternoon, Miss Singh," she said politely to the woman standing at the bottom of the steps into the house. "Hush up, Cho-cho!"

"Hold that bad dawg," Mrs. Anita Jayarasingh said sharply, scowling at Cho-cho, who stood to attention on the top step, tail trembling, doing his best to appear fierce. The woman's eyes locked with the dog's. They were at the same level, not because the steps were that high but because Miss Singh was very small, probably the smallest adult in Valley. All her several children, except the youngest, Laxshmi, who was in grade six at Marcus Garvey Primary, were taller than her. They took after their father in that.

Pollyread bent down and scooped up Cho-cho. "He not going to trouble you, Miss Singh," she said, patting the dog's head. "He just barking to make noise."

"One day," said Miss Singh, coming up the steps while shaking a disapproving finger at Cho-cho, "one day that bad dawg going to eat up somebody and you father going to be in courthouse!"

Pollyread managed to keep a straight face at the image of Cho-cho, who now rested placidly in her arms, "eating up" anybody, especially Miss Singh, who was not just small but bony. "Yes, Miss Singh" was all she said. Miss Singh said the same about the dogs in every house in Valley that she visited or passed, though she had never been bitten, as far as Pollyread knew. But all the dogs barked at her.

"Howdy, Anita," Mama called out from the table. "Don't mind the stupid dawg."

"He stupid, yes," Miss Singh snapped, darting a ferocious look at Cho-cho as she reached the top of the steps and could look down at the dog. As abruptly, she looked at Pollyread, and her stern face cracked with a ravishing smile.

"Scholarship girl." She beamed, as delighted as if her child had won the prize. And, ignoring the dog that a moment before had been a ravening beast, she enveloped Pollyread and Cho-cho in a cocoon of sweat spiced with turmeric and rose water. "You could take the dawg with you to Town," she laughed when she let them go. "They have plenty terrorist in that place, it will be right at home."

Pollyread couldn't help but laugh too. She put Cho-cho down. Ignoring Miss Singh, the dog went back to his place by Jackson's feet under the table.

"You must be proud of you pickney, Miss Maisie," Miss Singh said, slipping off her worn sandals at the door and advancing into the house. "Both of them. You do good too, young man." She patted Jackson's head as she passed around him to sit down in the empty chair next to Mama. The myriad bangles, gold and silver, that covered almost the whole of Miss Singh's left forearm tinkerbelled in a blessing.

Jackson looked up at Miss Singh with a grin like a death mask, as if she had caught him doing something wrong. Pollyread felt herself squirming in sympathy with him.

"Any wash leave, Pen?" Mama asked. "Bring Miss Singh some, please."

"But, Maisie, how you can have the big scholarship girl pouring lemonade like ordinary pickney, eh?" Miss Singh and Mama cackled with each other. Pollyread couldn't be upset at Miss Singh's teasing. With her bony hands and scaly long-toed feet that could easily be imagined gripping a branch, Miss Singh had always reminded Pollyread of one of those parrots that flew high overhead some days, a dozen of them together, squawking and laughing with one another. And Miss

Singh's style of dressing — almost never skirt and blouse, though she put her daughters in them, but saris, reds like hibiscus flowers, yellows and pinks like poui blossoms — could pass for plumage. Pollyread went into the kitchen and poured out the last of the lemonade that Mama had made for their lunch.

By the time Miss Singh had thanked her and taken the first sip, Cho-cho was up on his feet and barking again. It was Aunt Zilla, their nearest neighbor and some sort of cousin to Poppa. Without waiting to be asked, Pollyread went back into the kitchen to make more lemonade: She sensed how the afternoon would unfold.

Each new visitor would wrap her possessively in a fleshy or thin, dry or sweaty, fragrant or not-so-fragrant embrace, for the moment claiming Pollyread's achievement for him- or herself, and rain down congratulatory kisses and words on her increasingly muddled head. She began to understand how a doll would have felt in the hands of several girls playing together. From time to time she took a suck of one of the sour oranges, just to remind herself of her self.

But she was also pleased and sweetened like the lemonade she was continually mixing. This was the moment she had worked and hoped and prayed for for a long, long time. She felt light-headed, a little drunk on all the words swirling around and in and out of her head. Like Christmas with a particularly nice present, and then the Christmas lunch when Poppa allowed them a small glass of sherry wine that made them giggle. From time to time now, despite her aching fingers, Pollyread giggled to herself.

But she was brought back to herself when she looked out the kitchen window into the backyard and saw Jackson. He had changed into his yard clothes and slipped through the noise and confusion to where Pollyread knew he was happiest, tending the plants.

She was angry with him. Not for being outside enjoying himself while she was in the kitchen grinding her fingers. This wasn't fun but it was better than digging and weeding. She was angry because he wasn't in here soaking up the words and the congratulations (though every now and then a visitor flung some words at him, which he waved at like he was catching them in his hand). He should have been a scholarship winner too, and it was pure don't-care on his part why he wasn't. It was bad enough that he didn't do as well as everybody expected him to — though, she had to admit, better than probably eighty percent of the children in the island. What really was making Pollyread angry with her brother was that now they would be going to different schools in Town. He would be at King's College.

While she would be alone at St. Giles. She didn't like that idea at all. Only rarely had they ever spent more than a day apart. Now they were looking at — Pollyread knew she was exaggerating, but it was Jackson's fault — the rest of their lives, hardly seeing each other, having different teachers, different homework, nothing to talk about anymore. . . . She was *so* angry.

Pollyread had known, from about grade three, as the twins worked their way to the top group of their class and stayed there, that this moment would arrive. They didn't talk about it in the family, though, because everyone knew what it meant. And now it was here! Wonderfully, a Christmas present in the middle of the year. A source of joy. But also — Pollyread felt it in her belly — like one of Jackson's seeds: Who knew how it would grow? (God, perhaps, but he wasn't saying anything.)

Praise and flattery, at Marcus Garvey this morning and from this afternoon's visitors, were very welcome. And she felt a deep pleasure for Mama, glowing like a lantern among her friends. But she also felt excluded by Jackson's dogged, tender ministering to his plants. She felt the silence from outside begin to worm its way into her thoughts, undermining her anger. She didn't have a clue what he was thinking. He was out there with his plants, talking to *them*. Not a thought for his sister, his *twin*, and the situation he had placed her in. He was probably telling the plants about tra-la-lah-ing off to Town and all the fun he was going to have at King's College. Without her. Well, there'd be no plants for him to talk to in *that* concrete jungle. Nothing grew there except weeds — and "weed" (ganja). Who was he going to talk to then? (Though even as she thought that she remembered the large back yard of Aunt Shiels, Mama's sister, and Uncle Josie, with whom they'd be living in Town. That would suit Jackson just fine. And not many books for her in that house, mostly Aunt Shiels' about nursing.) Apart from a few relatives, Pollyread knew not a soul in Town.

Her mood for the rest of the afternoon wavered like the afternoon light outside, between brightness and shadows.

Different Horse

You is not Pen, and Pen is not you," Poppa was telling Jackson that evening, not for the first time. "Same horse race, different horse." There weren't any horses in Valley, only a few donkeys, but Jackson understood what his father was trying to tell him.

They were outside under the shed where Poppa kept his tools for planting and for carpentry and masonwork. He had come home from Town to encounter Mr. Grandison, the last of the congratulatory visitors, on his way out. Fortified by a drink of rum Mama had poured him, Mr. Grandison was in a lighthearted mood.

"Aha, neighbor," he greeted Poppa. "The proud father of the bride." With a flourish of his hand, he removed an imaginary hat atop his glistening head and bowed to Poppa. A bewildered Poppa, not knowing whether or not to smile, or even to come into his own yard. "Congratulations, Gillie," Mr. Grandison cried out as he disappeared down the path, no doubt on his way to Shim's.

Poppa, hurrying off the bus and straight home, didn't know what day it was. "What sweet Mr. Grandy?" he asked Pollyread, who stood grinning at the top of the steps into the house. She gave an elaborate, theatrical shrug as she stepped aside to let Poppa in.

Jackson, hearing Mr. Grandison taking his leave of Mama and Pollyread, packed up his tools and was putting them next to his father's in the shed when Poppa arrived. The moment he had dreaded all afternoon had come. Why hadn't Poppa been home earlier? To hear the bad news and get it over with.

At the same time, he didn't want to *not* be there when Poppa got the news. That would be worse, so he scampered up the steps and into the house behind his father.

"You all were having party in here?" he asked, looking at the dining table, which was still cluttered with several empty glasses, mugs, and plates with crumbs.

Mama, busy in the kitchen, pretended to ignore him. "Ask the pickney dem." There was a tinkle in her voice and it made Jackson even more anxious. The liveliness of the afternoon from which Jackson had excused himself persisted in his mother and sister, and in a moment would infect Poppa, when he heard Pollyread's news. And then he would have to hear Jackson's . . .

"Somebody birthday that I forget?" Poppa asked, a half-smiling question crinkling his eyes.

"Nobody birthday," Pollyread laughed, dancing around her father with eyes as brilliant as her feet. "You don't know what day it is?"

Poppa put down his old leather bag that he always took to Town and swiveled around to look at Jackson. Caught in his father's half-serious glare, Jackson felt naked. His mouth was dry. He managed a shrug. Poppa turned back to Pollyread.

"Wednesday?"

"Common ENTRANCE!" Pollyread shouted, throwing her hands in the air and preening on tiptoe.

"Common Entrance?" Poppa said, puzzled. "I thought that was Febru . . ." His voice died away, and then he grinned. "Today? The results?" He looked from Pollyread to Jackson and back again, his grin widening.

"You have a scholarship pickney," Mama said from the kitchen doorway, drying her hands in a towel.

Poppa dropped into a crouch so that his eyes were level with theirs, put his hands on his hips, cocked his head, looked from one to the other several times, and made a sound of a rooster crowing in the back of his throat. His face flooded with pride and delight, like Valley at sunrise.

"Say what?! My babies? HA!" And he gathered them

into his arms and squeezed them close for a long moment. Pollyread and Jackson felt something trickling through their hair like crawly insects, but they didn't move. Pollyread thought of Mama's favorite Psalm, the twenty-third: . . . *thou anointest my head with oil; my cup runneth over.*

Jackson, feeling like a cheat, thought to himself: *Let this cup pass from me.*

"So . . ." Poppa released them. His eyes were bright with water, his cheeks wet. Jackson couldn't remember ever having seen his father cry, and felt that Poppa somehow knew his son, from whom he and everyone else had expected great results, had let him and the family down. Jackson was close to tears himself. Beside him, though, he felt Pollyread, Miss Perfect, bubbling.

"So," Poppa said again, " tell me. . . ." He looked again from Jackson to Pollyread and back. "Both of you?"

Jackson's finger was quick: He pointed to his sister.

Poppa straightened and held out his hand. "Congratulations, Miss Gilmore," he said. He and his daughter shook hands formally. Then hugged again and spun around.

Letting go of Pollyread, he turned his full attention to his son. "And what about you, Little Man?"

Jackson looked at his father's chest, at the little crescent-shaped scar that was sometimes visible just above the top button of certain shirts. "Second choice," he mumbled.

He felt Poppa's finger under his chin, lifting his face so he couldn't avoid his father's eyes. "What that you say?"

The room around him was still, Mama and Pollyread like the furniture.

"Second choice, Poppa," Jackson said, forcing himself to be clear. Poppa hated mumbling.

Poppa's expression didn't change. "What that mean?"

"I get into King's."

"King's?" Poppa turned to Pollyread. "And you going to —"

"Saint Giles," she said, her voice muted.

"I see," Poppa said, finding Mama's eyes.

"Them mix up Jackso's paper, Poppa," Pollyread cried out.

"What you mean, mix up his paper? Who mix up his paper?" Mama's voice was sharp. Jackson wished his sister to shut up.

"Miss Watkins say it happen all the time at the Ministry," Pollyread babbled on, looking sternly at Jackson as though he were the cause of all this.

"How Miss Watkins know about Jackson's exam paper?" Poppa asked.

"Hush up, Pen," Jackson said fiercely, before Pollyread could say anything else. "I get second choice. That's all."

"That's all?" Pollyread's eyes flashed angrily at Jackson. "All? What I am supposed to do at Saint Giles, me one and God? Eh? Tell me that!"

Jackson was tongue-tied by his sister's explosive attack.

"Calm down, Pen," Poppa intervened. "That is not important right now."

Jackson watched as Pollyread gathered the thoughts that would set her father right as to exactly what was and was not important — and then thought better of it.

"Come, Jackso," Poppa said. "Let we go wash up for supper. How you get so dirty?"

"Outside," said Jackson with relief. "Weeding."

"Thank you," said Poppa, and led the way outside.

There, while they washed their hands side by side, he waited for his father to speak. Poppa scrubbed his hands and forearms as vigorously when he came from Town as when he came in from the backyard or ground. He washed his face as well, with the same carbolic soap,

106

though Mama made sure there was face soap out there also. Jackson worked at his fingernails with a worn bristle brush: They would be inspected, slyly, at the table.

"You is not Pen, and Pen is not you," Poppa said quietly. He was drying his hands on a towel. "Same horse race, different horse."

Jackson, knowing what his father was referring to, continued washing his fingernails.

"You do well to get second choice. First choice would be better, of course, but second choice is still good. Don't let anybody tell you otherwise. Plenty family up and down this island tonight celebrating second choice, and plenty more sucking on piece of cloth."

Then Poppa chuckled. Jackson glanced up to find his father looking straight at him.

"It don't exactly surprise me, you know," Poppa said lightly, as though he was about to tell a joke.

"What don't surprise you?" Jackson asked, trying to sound casual, though he knew instantly what Poppa meant.

"Second choice."

"What you mean?"

"You don't even break a sweat with the books, talk the truth."

Jackson looked into his father's eyes, which were

smiling but still steady on his. He looked away at his soapy hands and then came back to his father, as he knew he had to.

He shrugged. One shoulder. Poppa understood. He smiled briefly, a breeze blowing across his face and then gone.

"All well and good," Poppa said quietly, keeping his voice below the clinking of cutlery and plates coming from inside, "but your mother is not sure what to think right now, and your sister is *too* sure what *she* think." He smiled to himself. "You sister get scholarship, so the government will pay some of the cost. Them say that is free education, but nothing not free in this life, and certainly not education. But we will find the money for you."

Jackson took a deep breath. "I don't want to go," he said, forcing himself to stay in Poppa's eyes.

Poppa's eye corners crinkled. "Don't want to go where?"

"Town. King's." He couldn't find the words to make whole sentences, or the strength to look for them.

Poppa put his head to one side, as if trying to see his son more clearly in the dim light of the little bulb above them. "What you mean?"

"I could just stay up here," Jackson said.

"And do what?"

"Dig ground. Plant things. With you. And Mama. Here."

To Jackson's dismay, Poppa put back his head and laughed. He kept the sound down, but he laughed for a long time. *Like a donkey braying,* Jackson thought, puzzled. He hadn't said anything that he meant to be funny.

"And what," Poppa said, bending slightly toward him, "you think you sister would be saying about *that?*"

Jackson couldn't help smiling at the thought.

"But you can't stay up here," Poppa continued, serious again. "Not now anyway. Farming is good. Nothing wrong with it. Is work with dignity, and if you farming your own land, it free you from the oppression of other people. I feel proud when I see the things come up out of the ground the way God mean them to. But is a hard life, Jackso. You know that. Look how hard you work. You want to be doing that all you life?"

"Yes," Jackson said simply.

Again his father surprised him by smiling. "That's what you say for now. And you can come back up here if that is what you really want to do. But the world is a big place. Go see some of it before you make up you mind what to do. And you need skills to do that." He handed Jackson the towel he had been using. "You have to go to high school to get those skills. And then university."

"You didn't go to university," Jackson said.

"That is why you have to go." He crouched down so that he was looking up at Jackson a little. "When I was your age, same way I treat the books. I like to read like you, but I like to dream too. Just like you. When I look like I was studying, I f-a-r away." He stretched out the word and laughed to himself, not taking his eyes from Jackson's. "Just like you — chip don't fall far from block, eh." Jackson smiled with him. "But dreaming don't get you anywhere. Remember that, son. Book learning —"

"Jackso! Gillie." Mama, calling them inside to supper.

"Soon come," Poppa called back.

"Come now."

Poppa's eyebrows danced. "Book learning, Jackso. And you can't get it up here."

"But what about ground?" he asked Poppa, revealing what he'd been thinking about all afternoon. "Morgan's Mount."

Poppa laughed softly. "I still have some life left. I will keep it for you."

"What about Jammy?"

Poppa's eyes clouded over and his mouth tightened. "Jammy going to be gone long before you might be ready for Morgan's Mount. In fact —"

"Gilbert!"

"— before school give holiday. Come."

As he straightened up, Poppa paused and bent over. Jackson felt his lips rest for a moment on his head top.

Pollyread, after they joined hands around the supper table, said grace. From the first few words, Jackson knew that this would be a long one. More than once, he had upbraided her that God didn't have the time to listen to no long grace, when he had poor people to feed and gunmen in Town to smite with justice, but it made no difference. Mama always took her side: "He is God, he can do anything he like. He have time to listen to your sister. You should talk to him more often."

Tonight, Jackson didn't bother to fuss. His head was full of Poppa's words, and with the smell of Mama's supper — salt pork, with cabbage, tomatoes, and seasoning from the backyard, and cornmeal dumplings.

". . . make the person at the Ministry find Jackson's right and proper paper, and . . ."

After he kicked her shin under the table, he didn't hear anything else until "amen."

At the end of the meal, Poppa got up and went to the glass-fronted cabinet in the corner, next to the chair where Mama sat most nights, sewing and listening to the radio, and brought out a bottle of dark sweet sherry. Rum was kept in the kitchen, easily available for anyone visiting. The "good wine" only appeared on birthdays and at Christmas. From the same cabinet, Mama brought out four small, delicately fashioned pink glasses that had belonged to her grandmother. Poppa poured full measures for himself and Mama, and half glasses, "a tups" as she insisted, for the twins.

"Give thanks and praises," Mama said, raising her glass.

"For clever pickney," said Poppa, lifting his.

Pollyread beamed as she clinked her glass against everyone's.

Jackson, bouncing his on theirs, didn't know what to think. He wondered whether the baby in Mama's belly — if it *was* there — would be clever like Pollyread or dreamy like him.

Thief in the Night

That weekend, Saturday night, the long spell of dry weather broke. The first clap of thunder woke the twins.

Rain at night when it wakes you in your bed under a zinc roof (as long as the roof doesn't leak) is the sweetest thought you can think, the warmest memory you can own. When you sleep your whole life under open windows in a place so quiet you can feel the night sky move, then rain when it wakes you is like God telling you stories. While you're listening to the crackling laughter of lightning and the thunder clearing the sky's throat, your feet search the bottom of the bed for the sheet Mama always leaves there, even in the hot months, and your toes wriggle into it so it becomes a second skin.

And through the boisterous rain-telling, and the rumbling thunder, beneath the thumping of your own excited heart, you listen for the sound you know will come: whining that is like a jagged knife tearing through the hullabaloo. This is Cho-cho. Who, by strict parental edict, is not allowed inside the house once the door has been closed for the night until first light next morning. "Lightning not going kill him," Poppa said more than once when the twins pleaded for the little mongrel. "He can stay under the house bottom like all the rest of the dawg them."

Cho-cho does — right under the twins' window. It is there that he begins his campaign, with a pitiful whine that comes through the heavy shroud of rain as easily as a needle going through cloth. Then, sensing some movement or interest above, no matter how faint, he scurries around to the door and starts scratching, scratching. The door is nearer to the parents' bedroom than to the twins', and Mama is a light sleeper. Like a strangely shaped creature joined by the darkness, the twins tiptoe to the door, slide the bolt, lift the latch, and swing it open to pull in the shivering dog, lock the door and carry the dog back to their rooms and get back into their beds — all in a few seconds and without a single word being exchanged. Cho-cho plays his part too, unaccustomedly silent in gratitude.

His coat being soaking wet most times, there is no question of the dog being allowed further concession.

To take his richly smelly body into either bed would be tantamount to signing a confession. So Cho-cho is bundled under one or other bed, covered with whatever can be found to keep him warm, and is shushed to sleep amid the stories that the night leans over the windowsill and tells, spitting raindrops onto your face.

Sometimes the rainstories become your dreams, and your dreams are a bridge back to the morning, and the whispering of Mama's ancient house slippers across the creaking and sighing floorboards as she moves around her small bedroom before coming out into the dining room and opening the front door on the world. Her wakening rituals lift you briefly to the surface: the clearing of her throat, the splashing of water on her face, a little fart, an exchange of words grunted between the parents that sounds like the rumble of distant thunder.

But this morning it was an explosive fit of coughing from Poppa that popped the dreams of Pollyread, who stuck out her foot and toe-poked Jackson, who leaned over and grabbed Cho-cho by his tail just as the dog was getting ready to go into the living area. He unceremoniously dangled him over the windowsill and let him drop the couple feet to the wet ground as he heard Mama open the front door and say to herself, "Where's that dawg?" Then, "Oh, there you is. You sleep late this morning," with a chuckle.

Jackson and Pollyread relaxed back into their beds with a shared sigh and listened to Mama walking around the far side of the house for what she called her morning "breeze-out."

They didn't have more than a few moments to savor their escape from disaster.

"Oh, my Savior!" they heard Mama exclaim. "Gillie! Come! Come, Gillie! Come quick!"

"What happen, Mama?" Jackson shouted in answer, scrambling out of bed and colliding with Pollyread.

"Wha', Maisie . . . you call me?" grumbled Poppa, lurching through his bedroom door into the living area. He was still in his sleep clothes, a singlet and baggy underpants, and rubbing his eyes. He and the twins tumbled through the door and raced round the side of the house to Mama, Cho-cho greeting them with yelps.

The sun was some way from clearing Catherine's Peak, but it was light enough for everyone to see clearly.

Mama stood frozen, legs apart, staring out at their

116

little provision ground sloping gently away from the back of the house.

"What the matter, Maisie?" asked Poppa, grabbing his wife's shoulder. "You feel sick? Why you get up . . ."

"Look," Mama said, her arm pointing straight out at the back of the yard.

Their eyes followed her arm.

It was obvious from everyone's first glance that more than the rain had moved through their backyard last night. For a moment Pollyread wondered if the wind had been stronger out here than it had seemed to them inside. Plants and bushes and small trees were lying on the ground like smudges on what had been an orderly pattern of planting. Pepper and tomato bushes had been thrown down, cho-cho vines and yam hills pushed over and torn from their posts. Carrots had been uprooted. Large heads of cabbage had been wrenched from their beds and tossed about as in a frenzied game. In the soft, clear morning light, the colorful vegetables gleamed in their ground as they always did, but with skins bruised and innards scattered across a space that looked like a finger painting by a furious child.

"Oh, Gawd, Gilbert," Mama moaned. "Is who would do something like this?" Pollyread could see just the side of her face, squeezed tight like a fist. For a moment Pollyread remembered last Sunday morning and her confrontation with Jammy. Was she going to vomit again?

Poppa's hand fell from Mama's shoulder and, like a man still asleep, he walked away from them into the ruined planting.

The twins remained frozen beside Mama. They didn't want to even look at each other.

From time to time someone's animal would get loose and wander from its base into a neighbor's ground, trampling, uprooting, and eating precious plants, fruits, and vegetables. This was the cause of much kas-kas and botheration, testing friendships and widening enmities. It was one of the reasons that Poppa didn't keep animals.

But this wasn't the work of an animal — not a four-footed one anyway. Even from where they stood the twins could see the sliced yam heads looking like amputated limbs, some of the tomato and pepper bushes rendered cleanly topless.

Poppa stepped carefully between and over the broken rows. Every little while he picked up a broken bush, a shattered vegetable, examining it carefully before putting it down, as tenderly as he would an egg.

Suddenly, with a wrenching roar, Poppa picked up a cabbage and threw it. The green ball, its loose leaves like wings, arced over their ground and their fence into the government bush that ran down to Bamboo River. Then he picked up one of the stakes that had supported a tomato plant and started beating the world around him, the plants and the ground and the air, as if fighting a duppy, attacking the plants that he himself had put into the ground, and nurtured and coaxed to bloom with care and tenderness. He wasn't shouting now, but furiously cursing, using words that he would have been shocked to know that his children understood.

"No, Gilbert, no," Mama moaned, walking like a dream figure toward her husband. "No, Gil. Darling. It don't make no sense. It not doing any good."

"It doing good, yes!" Poppa spoke fiercely, in rhythm with his savage swings. "I practicing. What I going do. To the brute. Who do this. When I ketch him."

With a vicious swoosh, he decapitated a perfectly healthy bush, scattering leaves and peppers like butterflies, and then fell into Mama's arms. She patted him and cooed into his ear like she did to the twins when they had hurt themselves; she seemed to be holding him up. Pollyread felt anger rising as if out of the very ground where she stood beside Jackson, moving up her body in a warm flow.

Stealing crops was a fact of farming everywhere, even in remote communities like Top Valley, and the Gilmores were not exempt. Nothing caused more bad feeling than "tiefing." Animals, when they got loose, didn't know better. But human scavenging was deliberate. And the worst part of it, thought Pollyread, now so angry she was beginning to tremble, worse than having the produce destroyed or stolen, even things that you desperately needed for selling, was that your little private postage stamp of a world, the envelope of your life, had been violently torn open while you slept.

Looking at the crumpled figures of her parents, holding each other up like invalids, Pollyread felt that their lives had been invaded by an evil that was in the very air around them. She wanted to lash out violently. But at who?

Mama turned toward the house, pulling Poppa.

"Come, Gillie," she said gently. "Come have you bickle."

He stood still, feet planted, reluctant to abandon his ruined ground. Mama tugged him.

"Come," she said firmly, sounding almost angry,

though she wasn't. "You can't do anything else out here now. Come eat something."

Trailing behind her, Poppa let himself be led back toward the house, both of them stumbling over plants and roots and sticks as though they were going through an obstacle course. Mama's face was carved in a fixed glare that excluded everything, even her children, as she passed them by. But her eyes glistened with tears. In contrast, Poppa's face struggled with itself as though little creatures were fighting under his skin.

Pollyread felt her own eyes suddenly prickle, like something was sticking her pupils from behind. But, mixed in with her fury and her desire to find the person responsible for this desecration and tear him into pieces as small as the shredded leaves of the cabbages they'd left behind, Pollyread felt something else tickling her mind. And as she turned to follow her distraught parents back into the house, her eyes touched Jackson's, and she understood what was troubling her.

If Cho-cho had been left to sleep outside last night, Jackson thought, *none of this would have happened.*

The invader would have been routed before such awful damage could have been done, or at least those inside the house would have been alerted to his presence by the dog's insistent barking.

Jackson felt so upset that he didn't know whether even confessing their crime would make him feel better. Confession usually did. But all his former wrongs suddenly seemed like childish pranks compared to this one.

"We have to tell him," said Pollyread, scanning Jackson's thoughts through his eyes.

"You mad?" was his immediate reaction. But he wasn't sure if that was how he really felt.

Truth is the lightest basket to carry, Poppa had told them more than once, when they'd been caught out in an evasion. But the consequence for confessing to so large a transgression was beyond estimation. Bright in Jackson's mind's eye was Poppa with the stick a few minutes ago, slashing all around him like he was fighting devils only he could see. He had never beaten the twins — an occasional single clap on the bottom when they were smaller was usually enough to make the point. Now that they were older, his cold voice or a big-eyed glare was sufficient. They had never seen him so distorted by anger as he had been just now. He had become a stranger before their eyes, transformed by an explosion inside himself, his whirling stick and chanted obscenities chilling the morning air around them. Nor had they ever seen him so broken afterward. That was even more frightening.

"*You* really want to tell him?" asked Jackson quietly, challenging her.

Pollyread studied her big toe drawing lines in the dirt as if it didn't really belong to her, and didn't answer.

Fresh air blow away shame was a favorite saying of Mama's, and it rang in her daughter's head right now.

The silence between herself and Jackson filled with the chattering of birds waking. Cho-cho, ignored, followed his nose out into the devastated ground and through the broken plants, quivering at the unfamiliar tang of the intruder. From inside they heard the murmur of their parents' voices, Poppa's still flickering with bitterness, Mama's pouring balm on his resentment as she moved around getting breakfast ready. Pollyread smelled the hot oil from the kitchen, heard it sizzle as the first little balls of johnnycake dough were put to rest in the frying pan. The belly-scratching of hunger was not enough to distract her from the dilemma they faced.

Jackson liked to call her Miss Goody-goody and Miss Galbraith *Junior* (after the prim old lady who'd taught Sunday school at the African Methodist Episcopalian Church in Top Valley for longer than anyone could recall). She chafed at this. She was no goody-goody, as Jackson well knew. He just didn't appreciate it when she pointed out to him the ethical shortcomings of some project or mission dreamed up by himself or his friends, such as raiding Mass Charley's mango trees, whose fruit didn't *quite* hang over his boundary fence by the river, which would have made them fair game. (At the same time she was not herself immune, once the mangoes were picked, to the succulence of those little blackies that just popped into the mouth and dribbled sweetness into the back of your throat. Being good, try as you might — and Pollyread really tried — was not a straight-forward road from A to B to C.)

Like now. Last night. That was evil, no two ways about it. Who would do a thing like that? In the middle of the night and in a thunderstorm — to a neighbor! Because it had to be someone from Valley. Who would leave their home in that weather and come all the way from Cross Point or farther down to destroy someone's livelihood? Pollyread looked across the pathway that ran outside their fence and saw Mass Charley's rows of pepper and tomato like little Christmas lights in the new sunlight — untouched. So why the Gilmores'? Pure bad mind. Pure — evil.

This was like Town — Babylon, as everyone routinely called the place — where evil flared like a knife-edged flower. When she was a child growing up in Top Valley, and thrilled at every opportunity to go down to Redemption Ground, where all the vendors greeted her by name, Pollyread hadn't fully believed the stories she heard adults telling about Town: of people robbed and raped and murdered, acid thrown, knife fights on the buses. Even in schools, she'd heard. Few Valley people knew anyone to whom these things had happened, but everyone would swear to the truth of the stories in the grand scheme of wickedness that was the city of twinkling lights and traffic. Something like last night would have made a weird kind of sense in Town. But last night hadn't happened in Town, and Pollyread knew in her bones that no one from Town was responsible.

Despite the sun rising over Catherine's Peak, she hugged herself from the chill she felt inside herself.

"Breakfast," Mama called.

*   *   *

The children filed up the steps with heads down. Inside the house was shadowy, the only light coming from the window looking out onto the backyard. Fortunately, the yard sloped away from the house and could not be seen from the dining table, just mountains in the distance, and sky.

Mama offered grace. Normally, Poppa pronounced the blessing, or they joined hands in silent thanks. This morning he sat hunched over, with tight lips, staring at the round empty plate in front of him.

"Bless this food to our use," Mama said softly, "and us to they service, O Lord, our strength and our redeemer." As they all murmured amen, she cried: "And strike the wicked person who —"

"Maisie," said Poppa firmly. Mama pulled herself up short, and the twins exchanged a glance: Poppa didn't often "correct" Mama like that. "Today is Sunday. Let us give thanks that none of us come to any harm," Poppa continued, softly, sounding more like himself again.

"Amen," they said again, Mama also.

They ate the meal in virtual silence, speaking only when they needed something on the table that they couldn't reach.

As Poppa was dipping his last piece of johnnycake into his cup of coffee, Jackson said, quietly, as if he was asking for a favor, "What we going to do, Poppa?"

For a moment Pollyread wondered if Jackson was asking Poppa for guidance as to whether they should tell him about their role in the debacle they had awakened to this morning. She looked at Jackson sharply, in a panic that he was having one of his crazy minutes when he would completely surprise her with something he said or did. Her brother was paying no attention to her at all, which worried her even more. His eyes were resting on Poppa's face as though the whole world balanced on the blunt tip of their father's nose.

"I don't know, Jackso," Poppa said wearily. "I still thinking 'pon it."

Jackson seemed disappointed at his father's answer, but Pollyread sighed audibly with relief.

"So we not going do nothing?" asked Jackson. "You not going to call police?"

For a moment there was complete silence: No one, not even Jackson until he said it, had thought of the police.

"What they going to do?" asked Poppa. "The brute well gone from this place by now." His voice had that sad edge of earlier.

Mama sighed. "Philbert will be at service," she said, referring to Corporal Philbert Letchworth, more widely, and respectfully, known as Corpie, who was second in command at the Cross Point police station and lived in Valley.

"I will talk to him." Poppa pushed back his chair. "Remember to feed that dog," he said to Jackson. The twins listened for any sign in Poppa's voice that he knew the source of his troubles, but there was none.

Give Thanks

If I didn't know better," Corporal Letchworth said to Poppa as they surveyed the wreckage side by side, "I would say is Jammy. Or someone like Jammy." They were still dressed for church, from which Corporal Letchworth, who lived on the other side of Valley, had sent his own family on without him and come home with the Gilmores.

Jackson, changing swiftly into his yard clothes, had sauntered around the back, far enough behind Poppa and Corpie that he wouldn't be noticed but close enough to hear what they were saying.

"Could be Jammy, yes," Poppa said.

"But nobody don't see Jammy this long while."

"I see him."

"What!" Corpie's voice was almost a screech. "Where?"

And Poppa told him about Morgan's Mount.

The corporal prided himself on knowing everything

that went on in the district. And Jammy was a particular interest of his. Their paths had crossed continuously from when Jammy was a boy going under fences to pick fruits that, had he asked for them, would probably have been given out of respect for Miss Mildred, his mother. Angry farmers had enlisted Corpie to "speak" to the boy. No amount of "speaking," even of the most forceful kind, had helped. It merely made the growing Jammy more cunning.

Jammy's activities had crossed the line from pranks to crime on his fourteenth birthday, when he and his friends decided on a curry goat feed for the auspicious occasion. It went without saying that nothing had been bought. As the party went on it got more raucous, and despite its remote location in the upper reaches of Bamboo River, it inevitably attracted the attention of someone who summoned the law. Jammy was escorted personally by Corporal Letchworth from Juvenile Court in Town to Rocky Hill Approved School for Young Offenders.

Two years in Rocky Hill had not rehabilitated Jammy at all, merely widened his sphere of operations beyond Top Valley and enlarged the list of possible accomplices. But these new accomplices were no brighter than his first set. They kept making stupid mistakes that led Corporal Letchworth back to the tidy little front yard full of flowerpots that Mildred Trout presented to the world, as if to wipe the shame of Jammy from her eyes. As he grew older, Jammy had taken his activities away from Valley. Somehow, though, he always came back. And now here he was again, the perennial thorn in Corpie's side, back, and foot bottom.

The corporal looked to Jackson as though there might indeed be stones in his shiny Sunday shoes. He wriggled his feet as he listened and edged around until he was facing Poppa.

"When you find him in Morgan's Mount?" he asked sharply when Poppa was finished.

"Saturday."

"Yesterday?" He sounded like he was interrogating Poppa.

"No. Last weekend."

"And is only now you telling me?"

"I will deal with it," Poppa said, looking out at the ruined backyard. Jackson saw his back straighten slightly.

"Squatting is against the law."

"Only if I lodge a complaint. Is my ground."

"Breaking and entering and malicious destruction of property is against the law also, Gillie."

"Is my property."

There was a warning in both voices. Jackson could only see the policeman's eyes, but they were staring hard at Poppa, whose shoulders were rigid. Neither of them noticed him. He kept as still as possible, Cho-cho sitting at his feet.

"You is the only person," Corpie said grumpily, "who take up for that bwoy, apart from him mother. And not always at that."

And Bollo, thought Jackson.

"I not taking up for him. I going to deal with Jammy." Poppa sounded like he was explaining a homework problem.

"You better," said Corporal Letchworth heavily. "Or I will deal with him, *my* way. I tired of that bwoy."

"He not a bwoy anymore, Philbert," Poppa said, still in his homework voice. "He is twenty years old."

"Then he old enough to know better."

"Yes," said Poppa, so quietly Jackson barely heard him, "that is true."

"I'm sure Miss Mildred teach him better. She is a decent woman."

"That she is," Poppa agreed.

"And the other pickney turn out okay."

"Yes," Poppa agreed again.

"So —?" Corpie raised one eyebrow. He wasn't

looking so hard at Poppa now, but he wasn't looking anywhere else either.

Poppa gave a small chuckle. "A long story, Philbert," he said.

"Not a laughing matter, though."

"No, no laughing matter. Jammy is not a laughing matter at all."

Corporal Letchworth heaved his shoulders and sighed deeply. "Okay, Mass Gillie. I leave it to you. For now."

"If is Jammy," said Poppa, waving his hand across the yard.

"Who else it would be?" Corpie was in no doubt as to who was responsible.

It was Poppa's turn to shrug.

Corpie looked at Poppa and rested a hand on his shoulder. "You can be a Christian, Gillie," he said. "I-man have to be a policeman."

"Seen," said Poppa.

"Tell Maisie I will see her at choir practice later."

"Okay."

Poppa turned to watch Corporal Letchworth leave and noticed Jackson for the first time. He frowned slightly, but only said, "Time for lunch," as he walked past Jackson back to the house.

Jackson meanwhile was thinking about what Jammy was growing up at Morgan's Mount. *It's something funny,* he said to himself. *Jammy is not a natural planter.* Somehow he had to find out what it was.

Mama said grace again and then moved quickly, once they'd started eating, to question Poppa about his conversation with Corporal Letchworth in the backyard. She asked the same question: "Who else it could be?"

"But it don't have to be Jammy," Poppa said, sounding a little defensive now. "Plenty bad boys in the district."

"None of them would do this," she said roughly. "This is evil."

"You just come from church and calling somebody evil?" Poppa tried to make a joke of it.

"Evil is as evil does."

There was only the clatter of knives and forks scraping on plates for a while.

"So what is Philbert doing about . . . ?" Mama's voice, sounding a little less angry now, drifted off, but everyone knew what she meant.

"Philbert don't have to do anything," Poppa said calmly. "I dealing with it." He sliced a piece of yam and put it into his mouth.

They all waited for him to finish chewing, to tell them how he was going to deal with — whoever. He scooped up some rice and peas and a small piece of chicken, saying nothing further.

"What you going to do to Jammy, Poppa?" Pollyread piped.

Poppa's voice lashed her. "*You* know is Jammy?"

Pollyread flinched and put down her fork, staring down at her plate.

"Gilbert." Mama dropped Poppa's name on the table like a stone.

Jackson felt the piece of chicken in his mouth turn to ashes. When Mama and Poppa quarreled — and this could be the beginning of one — it was like a cold fierce wind caught inside their little house.

Poppa put a forkful into his mouth. No one else was paying any attention to food. Jackson saw, as Poppa chewed, that his father's jaw muscles started to relax.

He swallowed, took a sip of water, put his knife and fork down on the side of his plate. He looked at Pollyread with sad eyes. "I'm sorry," he said. "There was no cause."

Slowly they began eating again, carefully, as though they were waking up.

"I will talk to him," Poppa said eventually.

"You think is him, Poppa?" Jackson asked.

"I don't know," Poppa said. "That is why I will talk to him."

"You think he going to just tell you?" Mama's words were like pebbles bouncing off the dining table. "You don't tired to talk to that bwoy?"

"I tired, yes," Poppa said, chewing slowly. "But he not a bwoy any longer, Maisie. Hear say woman have pickney for him in Town."

"That don't make him man," Mama said scornfully.

"Maybe not. But him have pickney, and him is twenty him last birthday."

The twins' eyes rested on each other's again: How did Poppa know Jammy's birth date? Where was the anger of this morning?

"Miss Mildred raise him bad."

"The other children she raise don't turn out bad," said Poppa. "Besides, Mildred not the only one who raise Jammy."

"You on that again?" Mama's voice rose a notch.

"Maisie . . ."

Jackson knew well the tone in Poppa's voice; sometimes it was in Mama's voice, directed at Poppa. It was like a policeman's hand directing traffic: *Stop right there.* They were trying to ensure that nothing further was said about a particular matter at that particular time.

Because that matter had "story" behind it, and that story was "big-people business," not to be discussed in front of children. But this one was a contention *between* them. Jackson watched Mama's eyes flare at Poppa before looking down at her plate. Her mouth tightened to a slit, as if locking in the words she wanted to say. He felt the hot breeze of irritation around the table.

Pollyread's eyes on his were serious and unblinking. This story, they both understood, the one they had been denied all but a glimpse of, was to do with Jammy — and also with Mama and Poppa.

Curiouser and curiouser, Jackson thought, the phrase from *Alice in Wonderland* rising like a smoke signal.

Lunch was completed in silence.

Out of the Rain

You think God love Jammy?"

The words were out of Pollyread's mouth before the thought had even begun to form.

"How I to know what God think?" Jackson grumbled.

Pollyread had not expected any other answer anyway. Jackson didn't think like she did. Not about things like this.

She didn't really wonder whether God loved Jammy or not — that was God's business. It was more that when she had something difficult to work out, she tried to look at it from above, to see everything at the same time, like a hovering bird would. Like, she imagined, God did. The question about Jammy didn't really require a sensible answer.

But Jammy was becoming difficult. Even when he was doing his badness up and down Valley, it was easy to ignore him most of the time. But he was getting closer and closer to the family now. Last night's invasion — and Pollyread, despite Poppa's apparent unwillingness, was herself certain that it was Jammy — was bad enough. But worse were the thoughts that had begun creeping around in her head like slimy things.

"It sound to me," she said, "like they know Jammy."

"Who?"

Pollyread tossed her head in the direction of the house. "Them," she said.

They were sitting on the front steps, looking out into the yard. Pollyread's bottom was on the floor of the house and her feet on the top step, where Jackson sat, his feet on the cool earth floor of the shed, really an extension of the roof propped up by two posts. It was where Poppa stored his tools for the field, and the bags and baskets that needed to be kept dry on days like today.

The rain on the zinc roof sounded like gravel being poured by an unsteady hand. It had returned right after lunch, a balm on the valley — and on the little weeds of tension that had grown up during lunch. Mama and Poppa were inside their room, the door closed. The twins had quickly become bored with lying in their beds reading, though Pollyread still cradled a book, a finger marking the page.

Nothing seemed to be happening outside either. No one was about on the path that ran past their house. Not surprising, with the rain.

"Of course them know him," Jackson said.

"I mean —"

"I know." Jackson sounded grumpy, as though he wanted to sleep or had just been awakened.

"You think so?"

Jackson nodded.

"How?"

He shrugged.

Pollyread heard Bollo's voice in her head: *Ask Mass Gillie. Ask Jammy.* It was as though Bollo, and Trucky — and who knew who else? — knew something about her family, her father, that she and Jackson didn't know. Lots of stories were always circulating in Valley, about almost everybody. Pollyread herself would carry story sometimes. It hadn't occurred to her before now that people were saying things around Valley about Poppa, and possibly Mama. And about them and Jammy! How could there possibly be *anything* between her parents and Jammy? And Poppa sounding as though he was *defending* Jammy. After everything Jammy had done to them (Pollyread was sure it was Jammy!) . . . What did that mean?

God, perhaps, loved Jammy; he probably had to, being God and all. But she didn't have to, and she didn't.

"I going to ask Poppa," said Pollyread. "When he get

up." She felt anger twitching her bare toes. Some of it anger at Poppa, for keeping secrets.

Staring out into the curtain of rain, Jackson didn't say anything.

It seemed to Pollyread that it might well be raining not just in Valley or the island but over the whole world. It certainly felt like the world was draped in wet clothes.

Then a sudden breeze, like a hand sweeping away a cobweb, created a space in which she saw a flash of white. Just a flash. Then the shroud of rain descended again. Pollyread focused on what she thought was the spot, and in a few moments, in another sudden shift of breeze, there was a second flash of white, this time more like a glowing.

"Pel." She heard Jackson whisper and felt his elbow jab into her shin. At the same moment there came, from beneath them under the house, a warning growl from Cho-cho.

The glowing acquired a shape. A now-familiar shape, hovering in the rain.

"Yes," she whispered.

Her knee bounced his shoulder and stayed there. Jackson's hair, from the length of which he had skill-fully deflected Mama's attention for weeks, was suddenly held from behind in powerful fingers. Pollyread's book landed in a clatter beside him on the step and then slipped onto the dirt floor. They didn't even notice.

It was hard to tell exactly where it was at first. It seemed to be dancing with the wind. Then, in an instant, the goat was right at their gate, twenty meters away, throwing its large head and those trumpet horns from side to side, looking at them. Yearningly.

The great white head, with its untidy billy goat beard, brushed the air. Its eyes, bright like the large black buttons on Mama's Sunday dress, seemed to be speaking. As though it was calling them to the fence, or asking for permission to come closer.

Pollyread, bottom fused to the steps, felt her toes wriggle under Jackson's bottom like they were hiding. Cho-cho had inched on his belly out to the edge of the dry space beneath the shed. The hairs on the dog's spine stood up in a ridge, his whole body quivering in the direction of the goat.

As if someone else were lifting his hand, Jackson waved.

And the goat nodded.

"Who you waving at?" Mama's voice from behind startled them both. "Somebody out in this rain?"

Pollyread heard Jackson struggle to answer,

words tangling up in his throat. Her own mouth wouldn't open.

The goat's eyes brightened and it nodded again, as though acknowledging Mama's presence.

"Plenty cloud out there. But I don't see anybody."

Everything trembled: the smiling goat — yes, Pollyread decided, it was smiling now — the shifting uncertain light, the twins' ragged breathing.

Then a gust of rain threw a curtain across the yard. When it cleared moments later, the goat was gone.

"No, Mama," Pollyread finally said. "Nobody out there."

Pollyread felt let down and angry. Angry at Mama for chasing away the goat. Disappointed that the goat had gone. She could not show her anger to Mama, who in any case had gone into the kitchen. And her disappointment with the goat was beyond expressing in words. All she could think to do was jam her feet farther under Jackson on the step below her, deriving a small satisfaction from forcing him to shift to one side.

For fully a minute after the goat's disappearance the twins said nothing, listening to each other breathe.

Cho-cho had retreated back under the house, and was silent. It occurred to Pollyread that, just by breathing, they were inhaling Goat as part of the air; he was now a part of them, like food, or water. Her chest tightened.

"Why you wave at it?"

"'Cause it was nodding at us." Jackson sounded as though waving at an apparition was simply the polite thing to do. "Besides" — he turned to look at his sister, a twinkle in his eye — "you was asking it question the other day."

Pollyread couldn't answer. Everything Jackson said was true. She wasn't frightened of the goat. The first time, yes, when it had reared out of the cloud on a perfectly normal morning walking to school. But it had also saved her from falling off the edge of the path. Then the second time, it had, in a manner of speaking, saved Mama by providing a glowing light for them to find their way home from Stedman's Corner in the near-dark. And it had not tried to frighten them. Not then or just now. It had kept its distance every time. Just now, it seemed to her, it had been asking *them* to come closer to *it,* when it could so easily, she realized, have simply zoomed right up to where they were sitting. *That* would have been terrifying.

But where did it come from? And, most of all, why? Why was it here? Why now? Did it have anything to do with Jammy, who had reappeared in Valley around the same time? And around the time that Mama started feeling sick — did it have anything to do with that? It had looked heartbroken at Stedman's Corner when she'd collapsed. But why just the twins? No one else seemed to see Goat. Not even Mama. Though maybe Cho-cho . . . Some old people believed that dogs could see duppies.

The rain was lighter now, coming straight down, and the wind had died. More of their familiar world was visible, though still no other people. The wisps of cloud left had no particular shape.

From inside the house behind them, like the rumble of faint thunder, came the soft muffled voices of their parents talking to each other. Usually this was a reassuring sound, but it made hardly a difference to Pollyread's unease.

And then a sunbeam burst through the clouds and rain, splashing into the yard in front of them. It was abrupt and brilliant, startling Pollyread, and as she watched in wonder, the rain was burnt up in its blaze and ceased falling. As the light spread, it seemed to absorb all sound.

The goat, it occurred to Pollyread, had appeared in the darkest moment of the afternoon. Had the creature been driven away by the approaching light, or had it ushered it in?

Later, as the twins were under the shed washing up for supper, Nurse Blackwell — Valley's midwife, and the nearest thing in the district to a medical person — passed on her way home with the news that Keneisha had just birthed a healthy baby girl.

Pollyread, who had gone to the gate to take the message, asked Nurse, "What time Keneisha's baby born?"

"'Bout four o'clock. Was pouring rain," said Nurse. She gave a broad smile that lit up the darkening afternoon. "Then, just as she born, the sun come out."

Jackson had followed Pollyread to the gate. Pollyread turned and they looked silently at each other.

Decisions

Miss Know-it-all.

Pollyread knew that was her nickname among the Marcus Garveyites who didn't like her — teachers too. She also had a reputation for sharpness of tongue, however, so she didn't often hear the gibe made openly. But Sharon Wilson's voice was quite clear in the yard as grade sixers tumbled out for lunch break, everybody heading for Shim's grocery or Miss Clarice's cookpot.

"Watch them nuh? Miss Know-it-all and Miss Fancy. Nose in the air a-catch fly."

Pollyread's first impulse was to ignore the taunt. But Sharon Wilson was Jammy's half sister. And Aidrene Albert — whom Pollyread hadn't noticed until that moment was right next to her — bristled and stopped. They didn't say a word to each other but turned on their heels together to see Sharon Wilson and Idris Morgan a few meters away, Sharon's face bug-eyed and vacant as usual, Idris's lips tweaked in a mocking smile. One that disappeared swiftly, with its owner, when she saw Miss

Know-it-all and Miss Fancy advancing in tandem, definitely not smiling. Sharon's eyes widened with awareness of her sudden solo condition.

"What you say, Miss Know-nothing?" Aidrene's voice rasped like sandpaper. The insult bounced off Sharon's hard head, but her eyes, Pollyread noted, registered the lowering of Aidrene's head. That head, crammed with intelligence and information, was also a weapon feared in the school yard and passageways of Marcus Garvey and beyond, the subject of many stories. (Pollyread had always thought that Aidrene used her head in a fight so that she would not risk damage to her manicured fingernails — an opinion she kept to herself.) At the last moment Sharon stepped out of the way of the advancing Aidrene — directly into the path of Pollyread. Who merely stretched her arms out. Momentum alone sent Jammy's sister stumbling backward, her broad backside abruptly meeting the ground to a tinkling of laughter from the children who'd seen. Without even glancing at each other, Aidrene and Pollyread turned and went their separate ways.

But the incident brought Jammy back full rush into Pollyread's consciousness. His face, so close in look and expression to Sharon Wilson's a few desks away, hovered in her thoughts in the after-lunch session of school.

By the end of the school day, without talking to Jackson about it, Pollyread had decided that Mama had to be told about their role in the depredation of the backyard during the rainstorm of the night before last. She loved the word *depredation*, which had come to her freshly minted in a passage Miss Watkins had read in class that morning. After class she had fished out the dictionary she always carried in her schoolbag. "An attack involving plunder and pillage," the dictionary said. Pollyread knew what plunder and pillage meant — they had a ring to them too. Turning them over in her mind like those hard paradise plums that Miss Clarice sometimes sold, she tasted their sweet sounds, but also the bitter images of the Gilmore backyard after the depredation. Guilt about bringing Cho-cho inside, against specific and clear instructions, prickled her thoughts.

Clear conscience sleep through thunder, Mama would say when she was trying to coax the truth from one or both of them. It usually worked. This time, Pollyread was determined she wouldn't have to coax or wheedle: Pollyread and Jackson would bring their wrongdoing to her and take the consequences.

Pollyread was already feeling better for having made the decision, even though she hadn't actually told Mama anything yet, and really didn't want to think about that part of it anyway — that was for later. But she did feel . . . lighter.

Except that, at the end of school, when she was ready to go lightly home, she couldn't find Jackson. They didn't sit near each other in class, so she hadn't even noticed him leaving the classroom at the end of Miss Grange's health science session. Out in the school yard he was nowhere to be seen. Her eyes found first Trucky, then Bollo, then Janja Forbes. They were all together, and she noticed a cricket bat and some stumps — but no Jackso with them. She looked toward the market garden plot, where Marcus Garvey Primary students competed for prizes for the best vegetables and fruits, and where, if he wasn't playing soccer or cricket, Jackson was generally to be found. Not a sign of her twin. She searched her memory like she did the school yard: No, he hadn't said anything to her about his after-school plans. Where the devil was that bwoy?

"Pollyread!"

The sound of her name from behind spun her around. Aidrene Albert was running toward her, followed by Christine Aiken. The voice had been Christine's, always a little husky, as though she had a cold. "You coming?" Christine called as they came up to Pollyread.

"Coming where?"

"We going to see Keneisha baby."

"No you're not," said another voice right beside them. The three girls spun and looked up into the stern face of Miss Watkins.

"Why not, Miss?" asked Pollyread, who hadn't even made up her mind if she was going.

"The baby just born yesterday."

"We know, Miss," Aidrene said, puzzled by her teacher's attitude. "We going to be the first to see her." She grinned with anticipation.

"Her grandparents and her uncle and auntie see her already," Miss Watkins pointed out in her teacherly way.

"We know that, Miss," said Christine, her face alight. "But we going to be next."

"No you're not," Miss Watkins said again.

Pollyread was hardly listening. The mention of uncle and auntie had confused her — and then astonished her when she realized who Miss Watkins was referring to: Trucky. Uncle Trucky! And Auntie Blossom, who was in grade four! She burst out laughing at the thought.

"What sweet you, Miss Gilmore?" Miss Watkins asked sharply.

"Nothing, Miss." Pollyread felt her face warm with embarrassment and laughter.

"You all will give the baby germs," Miss Watkins continued.

"No, Miss," all three girls cried together.

"We will wash our hands, Miss."

"And your face and every other part that might touch the pickney." Her voice was stern, but Pollyread knew that Miss Watkins's apparent embargo had been lifted.

"We not going to touch her, Miss," said Christine, the baby expert. "We only going to look see what she look like." She gave her teacher her most winning white-teeth smile.

Miss Watkins humphed. "You all be careful. Baby is not dolly."

"Yes, Miss," they all said as she turned and went back inside the school building.

Pollyread swept the school yard with her eyes one more time, looking for Jackson, and then ran to catch up with Christine and Aidrene, heading toward the school gate.

Confession, she thought, could wait. The guilt wasn't going to disappear. And Jackson should be there, to share the load.

"Evening, Mass Tom," the girls called in unison to Mr. Cowan, coming down the path toward them. Mr. Cowan, a small, slim man with sad eyes and a large domed head topped always by a felt hat that made it larger, lived alone just beyond Trucky's family. Every evening around this time, he could be encountered, freshly bathed and tidied in clothes that had previously served for Sunday church and funerals, strolling down the path that led past Standpipe to Stedman's Corner — and Shim's rum bar.

"Evening, little ones," Mr. Cowan replied courteously, inclining his head. He called all the children of Top Valley, even teenagers taller than himself, little ones. "I hear that some of you will be leaving us for the big city."

"Yes, sir," said Aidrene.

"Yes, Mr. Cowan," said Pollyread.

"Congratulations," said Mr. Cowan. "It's a big world out there." He nodded again as he went by them. "Make the most of it." Mr. Cowan spoke slowly, enunciating his words very carefully. Teachers at Marcus Garvey held him up as an example of clear speech. "Very clear," Trucky was heard to remark once. "When he in him rum at Shim's, you can stay clear over by Miss Clarice and hear him, clear-clear."

"We will, sir," said the girls to Mr. Cowan, even Christine.

Mr. Cowan nodded and smiled as he moved on down the path.

Pollyread felt a sudden cool wind blow through the

corridors of her mind. She had felt it before: yesterday at church. The singing, even her own voice, and Reverend Forsythe's preaching, had sounded in her head as though coming from a great distance, from the other side of Valley. An echo surrounded everything. And she saw the whole congregation and church at the same time, herself included in her light blue dress and white hair ribbons, as if looking down from the ceiling, like the occasional bird who flew in the open windows would have done. This had not happened to her before, in AME or anywhere else. And it was happening again now.

Something impelled her to stop and turn to watch Mr. Cowan walking down the path, with the feeling that this moment was special, unique (*unikew*, as Jackson liked to irritate her by saying), and would not happen again. As if — she wasn't sure about this, and fervently hoped she was wrong — she would not see Mr. Cowan again. But not because something bad was going to happen to Mr. Cowan. Something was going to happen to *her*.

Pollyread felt uncomfortable, as if her clothes were suddenly tight, and wondered whether she should really have gone straight home, Jackson or no Jackson, and confessed their crime to Mama and got it over with. But guilt was not the cause of these odd feelings, she decided. She didn't know what was.

Trucky's mother was at her gate, resting one powerful arm on top of a whitewashed gatepost and watching them come up the path. Taking a breeze-out, as Valley people would say.

"Well!" said Miss Gloria as they approached, looking at the girls with pretend ferocity. "I was wondering when we was going to see you." Miss Gloria (Miss G if you were her good friend, but children could barely imagine such familiarity) was a big woman, taller than her husband by a full five or six centimeters, and with shoulders and arms that handled hoe and cutlass with ease. Her face was black and broad and flat like a mask, a face that seemed ready for anything and expected the worst. When she was on the warpath, grown men with sense found a quiet corner elsewhere. But she was one of the storytellers of Top Valley, and little children were welcomed into a broad, soft lap on those nights when she was telling her Anancy stories. The three girls knew that warm place well.

"You soon turn Townie now," she gently mocked Aidrene and Pollyread. "Soon forget your poor country cousins." She smiled warmly at Christine, including her in the second, more noble category.

Even though they knew Miss Gloria was only poking fun, the remark left Pollyread tongue-tied. To "turn Townie" was among the worst remarks that could be passed at you. Growing up in Top Valley, its isolation part of the air you breathed, everything exciting or important seemed to happen elsewhere, in Town or abroad — and Town was practically abroad, so far were its ways from the ways of Valley. So the pride you felt about your home was mixed with awareness that it was only a small piece, and an unimportant piece, of a very big world.

At the same time, in the eyes of many adults like Miss Gloria, who was born in Valley, Town was Sodom and Gomorrah. "The abode of the prince of darkness and corruption," Reverend Forsythe thundered from his AME pulpit (though he was not himself averse to extended visits to the prince's lair). Town was where the young people of Valley went and came back ruined, the girls with bellies and the boys with attitudes and language that no one in Valley could tolerate. For all that sin and degradation, though, Townies went around with their noses in the air — "So them don't have to look down at the garbage and dead animal in the street," said Mama, who was a generally cheerful exile from the city where she had been born and raised. Townies behaved as though Town was the world, everywhere else in the island was behind God's back, and the people from such places an inferior species.

So Miss Gloria's teasing, while not at all malicious,

left Pollyread feeling awkward, as though she and Aidrene were inappropriately dressed.

"But see we come now, Miss Gloria," said Aidrene, growing her most dazzling smile like a black-and-white sunflower, and reaching on toetip to kiss Trucky's mother. Pollyread and Christine dutifully followed suit. Miss Gloria purred and chuckled.

"We proud of you," she said, one long arm around Pollyread and Aidrene, the other around Christine. "We will stay and pray for them in that Babylon," she said to Christine, giving her an extra squeeze.

"And we come," said Aidrene, her tongue dipped in syrup, "to look for your granddaughter."

Miss Gloria giggled. "Lord, him good, you see?" sounding more Keneisha's age. "Him just eat and sleep. No trouble at all." No one remarked on the switch: *Him* could be any living thing of whatever gender, on two legs or four; the listener would know the who and the what being referred to.

Miss Gloria opened the gate for them like she was raising a curtain on a stage. "Come make me show you him. But sh-h-h, I think them sleeping."

They followed her up the path in silence, Christine in the lead, and bunched up behind her solid figure when she halted in the doorway of the room that Keneisha shared with her younger sister, Blossom, who was nowhere around, and now the baby. It was shuttered and dark, a fan somewhere quietly whirring, brushing the baby smells of powder, urine, and bleach into Pollyread's nostrils. Thin strands of light from the half-closed shutters fell across Keneisha and her baby, curled like different-sized dark beans against each other on a bed, the peacefulness of the darkened cell blessing everyone.

As if sensing the presence of her mother and the girls, Keneisha opened her eyes. She smiled like she was bringing something very pleasant back from wherever she had been.

"Howdy," she said softly, fluffy tongued.

The baby, hearing her mother's voice, snuffled and cried out, sounding like a distant bird. Keneisha touched her baby's tiny face, her hand covering it. The baby gurgled and was still.

Keneisha beckoned. Moving as one, the girls tiptoed over and knelt beside the bed. The baby, whose hands and feet, fingers and toes were gently waving and wriggling in the air, turned her head toward Pollyread, who was between Aidrene and Christine, and looked at her. Pollyread had read somewhere that for the first two weeks of their lives, babies could see only vague shapes and colors, and recognized people by their smells and sounds. Well, *this* baby, though only a day old, was *looking*, at *her*. She didn't care what the books said: Those wet little eyes, shining like stars underwater, hooked on to her face. Not Aidrene's on one side, nor Christine's on the other — hers. The baby yawned, blinked twice, and smacked her mouth.

"She smile at me," Pollyread cried delightedly. "Miss Gloria, she *smile* at me." The baby's mother and grandmother laughed with Pollyread, who put one of her fingers in the baby's soft claw. The baby grasped and pulled it in the direction of her mouth. Pollyread felt a wriggling in her belly-bottom like a worm.

"Keneisha, I can hold her?" Pollyread asked timidly, her stomach wound as tight as the little fingers around hers. She had never felt so grown-up in her life. The baby was like one of those dolls she was always giving away, but this one she wanted to keep close by. Forever. "Please."

"Come wash your hands," Miss Gloria said from the doorway. The girls trooped outside, Pollyread understanding but impatient, to a pail of water on a table under a lime tree. A couple cut limes floated in the water. Each tried to get her hands into the pail first, splashing the others in the process. Christine finished first, and dashed back into the house while drying her hands on her school uniform, leaving Aidrene and Pollyread pouting at each other.

When they got back inside, Keneisha was sitting up and offering the baby, who seemed to Pollyread about the size of a loaf of brown bread, to a smiling and disgustingly relaxed Christine. Pollyread herself was tense and nervous.

"Put your whole hand under her back and neck," said Keneisha earnestly.

"I know," said Christine, who had probably handled more newborns than everyone else in the room put together — Miss Gloria was in the kitchen. Pollyread didn't particularly like dolls, and had never before wanted to have younger siblings, but now — right now, she would have given her eyeteeth, and perhaps even her Common Entrance scholarship, for the ease and confidence with which Christine gently swung the little bundle and crooned into her rapt face.

"It little-bit, eh?" Aidrene cooed. Aidrene herself was in the middle of a large family, but Pollyread didn't think she bothered much with those younger than herself. Still, she was edging closer to Christine, making sure to be next in line for the treasured bundle.

When Pollyread's turn came and the little bundle rested in her cradling arms, warm as dough against her chest, she wanted the moment to last forever. Nothing else mattered. Not Common Entrance, not Town, not even her guilt. Nothing. Everything that mattered in life, so far as she could tell, was resting warmly against her chest, a lucky charm of happiness.

Then the baby started wriggling, and opened her flower of a mouth to release a sturdy shriek. Pollyread was mortified. She had snoozed and gurgled in the arms of Christine and Aidrene, happy as anything, it seemed. Why didn't she like *her*? She was holding her as best she could, and she didn't smell any different to the other girls, she didn't think. And she had looked at her so — specially, just a few minutes before. She was sure of it. Pollyread's arms were stiff with embarrassment. She didn't dare look at Aidrene or Christine, in case their eyes were laughing at her.

Miss Gloria and Keneisha did laugh.

"She looking," said Miss Gloria.

"Looking for what?" asked Pollyread nervously.

"She hungry," Keneisha said.

"She looking for her mam's bubby," Miss Gloria chuckled, and Pollyread then realized what the bawling and the smacking of lips and the squirming against her chest really meant. And felt a sharp pang of disappointment that she couldn't nourish this little squiggling creature that simply wanted what she was entitled to and which Pollyread couldn't provide. She giggled, the air around her suddenly lightened by the baby's tickling. "Nothing here, pickney," she said down

161

into the little screwed-up face about to let go a further squall. "Sorry."

Miss Gloria rescued the baby, whose name Pollyread still didn't know, holding her comfortably in one hand as she helped Keneisha rearrange her blouse with the other. Baby and breast were finally brought together, the crying swiftly subsiding into sucking gurgles before the fascinated eyes and ragged breathing of the three visitors, knelt in chorus on the floor before Keneisha. Pollyread rocked back on her heels, her eyes and thoughts moving only the short distance between the two faces, Keneisha's and the baby's, inches apart and occasionally touching, forehead to forehead.

Running

Run. *Run like the wind.* Jackson heard those words pounded by his feet into his head as he ran. A character in some book had said this, but he couldn't remember what book or who. It might even have been an animal story from when he was younger. It didn't matter. What mattered, he told himself, was that *he* run like the wind.

At the same time, he wasn't sure why he was *running*. He wasn't running away from anybody; no one was chasing him. School was finished for the day. There were chores waiting at home, but they could be done when he got home.

The idea had been forming, like something growing from one of the tiniest seeds he'd planted in the ground, since he and Poppa had come down from Morgan's Mount. Empty-handed. And ignorant about what was being grown. On their land. *His* ground. Somehow the massacre in the backyard on Saturday night had clinched it for Jackson: all those broken, bleeding plants, while Jammy's up on Morgan's Mount were hale and hearty. It wasn't fair. And though Poppa spoke more than once of settling things with Jammy, there was no mention of going back up there.

Then, during science class today, when Miss Bovell was talking about genus and species, she had brought in several plants, ones that everybody in the class knew, to point out the scientific differences between them. A growling had begun in Jackson's stomach that was not hunger. A niggling, like an itch in a place your fingers couldn't quite reach. An itch that had made him squirm all through Miss Bovell's class and the next — thankfully the last of the day — with Miss Watkins. And which had propelled him, stealthily, first out of the classroom and then around the back of the building and over a broken-down fence that was meant to keep animals from straying onto the property.

He paused to draw breath. He was on the bank of Bamboo River without remembering how he'd got here. The weekend rain had made the river cheerful again. His schoolbag weighed a ton, but there was nothing to do but lug it along with him. Meanwhile, there was a pencil in his head, sketching in the way he had to go. . . .

In a blink, Jackson found himself on the other side of Bamboo River, as if someone had pushed him suddenly from behind, and he took off again, running. He didn't allow himself to think of anything beyond the next bush to be navigated or tree trunk to be hurried around. He sank into the sounds he was making and remained there, following a path his feet remembered taking a few months before with Bollo and Trucky, away from Bamboo River. It would have been easier to go the way he and Poppa had taken two weeks before. But that would have meant passing home. Mama . . . Cho-cho . . .

Run. Run like the wind.

Twenty minutes later, panting and sweaty, he was beside another gurgling stream of water. He couldn't remember the name people gave it but he knew where he was.

He followed the water to a jackfruit tree that he remembered Poppa telling him marked the boundary of Gilmore ground. The idea crossed his mind to cut one of the big fruit and carry it home for Mama, who loved jackfruit. Too heavy.

Jackson looked quickly around him, guiltily, as

though he had no right to be here. He had to remind himself that this was Poppa's land, and one day would be his. Around him, now that he'd stopped crashing through the bush, was silence, except for birds. He heard his heart thumping. Taking a deep breath to calm himself, his lungs filled with the sweet rich jackfruit aroma that nearly choked him. The little river at his feet seemed to be laughing at him. The sweat on his arms and face felt cold.

He looked carefully around him. He'd never approached the Gilmore ground from this direction before, and it looked quite different: bigger somehow. Or perhaps — yes, indeed, Jammy and his friends had started bushing the ground next to Poppa's. The seedlings there were smaller, more recently planted but in the same tidy rows. Despite himself, the farmer in Jackson was impressed at the industry and care that was evident. And it was evident still: A rhythmic, syncopated sound that he recognized as chopping drew his eyes to the top of the expanded clearing across the stream. There, two men were hacking away at bush and grass, the whump of the cutlasses jumping around each other like dancers. Even though the men had their backs to him, Jackson melted behind the jackfruit tree, telling his nose to ignore the cloying smell.

And tripped over something. Something that suddenly moved.

"Wha de rass!"

The explosion of words seemed to throw Jackson forward to the ground. His schoolbag fell on his back, winding him. He had tripped over a leg, a man's leg from the sound of the voice.

"Who you is?" The voice was like a dog's bark.

From two meters away, sprawled on the ground, fighting for breath, Jackson saw the red eyes first, then Rasta locks. Then gleaming teeth. And smelled him.

"Wait," Jammy said. "Don't you is Mass Gillie bwoy?" He was smiling. Jackson had accidentally kicked Jammy awake. And he saw why Jammy had been sleeping so soundly: a sumptuous brown-paper spliff still held between two fingers but now burning close to the flesh.

Jackson didn't answer. Jammy's smile irritated him.

"So is what bring you up here, bwoy?"

"I is not a bwoy." Anger made Jackson's voice strong and seemed to pull him up to a sitting position from where he could see Jammy properly.

"So, you is man?" Jammy teased.

"You is not man either," Jackson replied, though he remembered Poppa's remark about Jammy having pickney growing in a girl's belly in Town.

"You far from home to be so facety, bwoy." His scorn stretched out the repeated insult. "I-man sure Miss Maisie raise you better than that."

Mention of his mother fired up Jackson further. He remembered, though he hadn't been there, Jammy frightening Mama in the early morning. "Better than what? And how you would know better from worse?"

Jammy's shoulders stiffened and he scowled, as if focusing on Jackson for the first time. "What you come up here for?" he grunted. "You come to study? I see you bring you schoolbag."

Without thinking about a response, Jackson looked across at the rows of plants embedded in the Gilmore ground. *His* ground. And remembered the backyard, which he should have been at home replanting. His anger boiled up all over again.

"I come to tear up your plants. Just like you tear up our plants." He heard his own voice, like a stranger's, attacking Jammy. The threat of destroying Jammy's plants had not even occurred to him before this. He remembered Poppa's furious slashing at the plants the first time, and felt some of that same anger

168

suddenly enlarge his chest like hot air pumped into it.

"What plants?" Jammy's eyes were as fierce as Jackson's voice. And then they softened and slipped away from Jackson's. Jammy took a deep draw on the spliff and held the smoke inside a while. "Bird in the air have nest," he said dreamily, the words floating on wisps of smoke, "but I-man have no place to rest I head."

Jackson got to his feet and hoisted his bag onto one shoulder.

"Where you going?"

Jackson didn't answer. He wasn't sure.

And then he was. He remembered what he had come up to Morgan's Mount for in the first place. *Run like the wind,* Jackson heard in his head. He jumped as far as he could across the stream, landing in water up to his ankles, and scrambled over to the other side, struggling to stay upright from the unbalancing bounce of his schoolbag.

"Oi!"

Jammy's shout from behind him pricked Jackson to move faster. As he ran his eyes scanned the nearest row of seedlings for the winjiest one, which he hoped would also have the shallowest roots. He grabbed it close to the ground. Thanks to the weekend of rain, it came up easily in his hand. He hoisted his bag on his shoulder and took off. *Run like the wind.*

"Josephs!" Jammy called. "Ketch that little bwoy!" Jackson sensed Jammy getting to his feet but not running. Josephs must have been one of the two men bushing farther up the slope. If so, he could cut Jackson off easily by just running straight down the hillside to the river.

"Ketch him, Josephs! Pick up you foot and run, you lazy —!"

Jackson took Jammy's advice better than Josephs. He found strength in his legs he could not have imagined. And he knew this side of the hill well. The cries and curses of Jammy, and Josephs's shouts for him to stop, faded away, left behind as he scrambled up the hillside or drowned out by the bellowing and singing of breath in his own lungs, he didn't know which. But when he collapsed at the top of the slope against the big mahoe tree that divided Morgan's Mount from Top Valley, so exhausted at that point that he didn't care if Josephs and Jammy were just steps behind, he was alone with his burning lungs and jellied legs. He couldn't see very far back into Morgan's Mount, but he was fairly sure no one still followed.

He looked at the strange seedling in his left hand with a feeling of triumph. He'd got what he went for.

He didn't know yet what he was going to do with it. But he knew that the plant was important to finding out what Jammy was doing on Poppa's ground — his ground. If he could find out what the plant was. And he had a few ideas about that too.

Premonitions

She sweet, you see?"

"Who?"

"Abeo. Keneisha baby. She smell like hardo bread."

"Baby smell like bread? What kind of baby that?"

"New baby."

"Funny."

"You just feel to hold it all the time and smell it."

"Until it poop."

"So? Baby have to poop. It's natural."

"Not in my hand, it don't have to poop."

"So your baby not going to poop?"

"Which my baby?"

"Your baby. The one you and you wife going to have. It not going to poop? Them going to be special baby? Different from everybody else baby?"

"'Course not."

"So what mek?"

"It going to poop, yes. But it going to poop in its *mother* hand."

"You think so."

"I know so. I-man not going to be holding up any baby full of poop."

"I-man will see."

"Hmmm."

"I going to miss her, though."

"Who?"

"Abeo."

"What happen — she going somewhere? She just born."

"No. I going somewhere."

"Where you going?"

"Town."

"When you going Town?"

"Stupid — to school."

"Oh."

"You forget about Saint Giles?"

"I not going to Saint Giles."

"I hear them talking."

"Talking about what?"

"Mama is to talk to the principal. She went to Saint Giles with him."

"Really now."

"What you mean?"

"Nobody don't ask me? Suppose I don't want to go to Saint Giles?"

"Why you don't want to go to Saint Giles?"

"I didn't say I didn't."

"Oh."

"But suppose I didn't. Nobody don't ask me if I want to or not."

"I asking you."

"I don't know."

"I not going to see her growing up."

"Who?"

"She who brings happiness."

"Who that bring happiness?"

"Abeo, of course."

"I don't know what kind of happiness she going to bring."

"How you mean?"

"One more mouth for Miss Gloria and Mass Mose to feed. Besides, Keneisha too young to have baby."

"True. But plenty woman get ketch early."

"Them too fool."

"And I don't suppose man have anything to do with them getting ketch."

"Man fool too. Baby is madness."

"But is not the baby fault. They don't ask to be born."

"Maybe not. But baby is crosses."

"You was a baby once, you know."

"You too."

"I wasn't no crosses."

"Hush up in there!"

"Jackso."

"What?"

"I 'fraid."

"What you 'fraid for?"

"Town."

"Anybody with sense in his head 'fraid for Town."

"Not Town, not really."

"Then what?"

"Leaving here."

"You don't want to go?"

"Yes, of course I want to go. But . . ."

"But what?"

"I don't know. Abeo make me feel a way. And Mr. Cowan."

"Mr. Cowan?"

"Yes, when I see him this afternoon."

"What happen?"

"Nothing happen. It was the same as usual. He dress up going down to Shim's. Only . . . and it was the same thing with Abeo. When I watch Keneisha feeding her. Like . . . like I wasn't going to see them again."

"You mean like something going to happen to them?"

"Not exactly . . . more like something going to happen to me."

"Something like what?"

"Leaving Valley."

"Oh."

"You know when something special happen . . ."

"Like what?"

"Like . . . a rainbow. Just after it rain."

"Yes."

"The first time I see a rainbow, when I was little, after that I thought it would be there after every time it rain."

"And it wasn't."

"Right. Now, when I see a rainbow it make me happy."

"Me too."

"And sad."

"Sad?"

"Kinda. Because it going to be gone in a minute. And

the next one, whenever it come, going to be completely different."

"All rainbows look the same to me."

"Maybe. But you are not the same."

"How you mean?"

"You older."

"Older?"

"Yes. Maybe just by a few days. Or a few weeks. Since you see the last rainbow. But you is older than you was when you see the one before. So the rainbow look different."

"Well, is a different rainbow. It must look different."

"But is you just say that every rainbow look the same to you. . . . You understand what I saying now?"

"Maybe . . . but what this have to do with Keneisha and the baby?"

"This afternoon, when I was holding her . . . it was like a rainbow make me feel. Happy. I never see anything so pretty. And when I coming home, everything and everybody seem . . . special. Like I never see them before, and not going to see them again. By the time I reach home . . . I was crying."

"You crying now, yes?"

"A little."

"Hush."

"By the way."

"What?"

"Where you was after school? Everybody looking for you."

"Everybody like who?"

"Trucky and them was making up a side for cricket. And I was looking for you."

"For what?"

"To tell Mama."

"Tell Mama what?"

" 'Bout Cho-cho and the rain."

"You tell her?"

"No. But we have to tell her."

"I suppose so."

"Tomorrow."

"Maybe."

"Where you went?"

"Business."

"Business? What kind of business?"

"Plant business."

"Poppa send you somewhere?"

"No."

"So what kind of plant business?"

"Is a secret."

"You going to tell me?"

"Maybe."

"When?"

"Eventually."

"You mean you worried about something that don't happen yet."

"Kinda."

"And you feel sad."

"Yes."

"Even though is something you want to happen."

"Yes."

"Okay."

Fight

They were walking silently down to school, Pollyread ahead, when out of the sparkling morning air, a man's voice burst into Jackson's thoughts. A voice he knew. "Howdy, little missus."

Jammy was leaning against the cedar tree that stood sentinel to Miss Liza's yard, around which the path wriggled. They would have to go past him to get to Stedman's Corner, to Marcus Garvey Primary. They both paused.

"I couldn't be your missus, Jammy," said Pollyread without missing a beat. "I too young and you too ugly."

At Pollyread's facety remark, Jammy stepped out onto the path, blocking their way, scowling. He was dressed in the same clothes as yesterday. They were dirtier, and his eyes, framed by filthy dreadlocks decorated with leaves and twigs, were red.

"You mouth sharp, little girl," Jammy rumbled. "Mind you don't cut youself with it."

Pollyread, to Jackson's relief, said nothing in response,

but resumed walking. As she made to step around Jammy, he grabbed her arm. She yelped from the shock.

"Leggo me," she cried out, wriggling, trying to get away. "Leggo —"

"Take you hands off her," Jackson heard himself saying loudly as he came up to Jammy. It sounded in his ears like Poppa with a squeaky voice.

"You have big mouth too, eh, Jacko," Jammy said, and laughed. His eyes, caught in the bright morning sun, glinted brown and red. Close up, Jackson smelled the man's frowziness, sour sweat mixed with the sweet fragrance of ganja, and saw, as if there was nothing else in his sight, Pollyread's scrawny arm in Jammy's hand, which, in a flashing change of channel, became one of Poppa's sweet pepper trees that Jammy — Jackson was sure of it now — had smashed in the storm on Saturday night.

"Yes!" Jackson screamed, still hearing himself from somewhere far away, and then watched, as though it was happening on television, as he lined up Jammy's crotch like the goal mouth in a soccer game at Marcus Garvey, and swung his right foot for a free kick. Goal!

Jammy jackknifed and fell, clutching his groin with both hands. Jackson jumped over him and ran, pushing Pollyread ahead of him. They pelted down the twisting path, which was a dangerous thing to do, especially with their schoolbags like things alive on their backs. Sheer terror held them upright, feet barely touching the ground, and the terror increased when Jackson heard the grunts and roars from behind, which told them that Jammy was up again and coming after them.

They burst into the open space of Stedman's Corner, aware of Miss Clarice to one side of them opening up her stand, and Mrs. Shim on the other side raising the shutters on the grocery. Children were always moving across the square at this time of morning on their way to school, so no one was paying attention to them. Until Jammy appeared, roaring with anger. On open ground the twins, who were slowing down as they fought for gulps of air that seared their lungs, couldn't match his big strides. He caught up with them in the middle of the space and grabbed Jackson's shirt collar from behind, which brought Jackson down hard on the solid ground and Jammy falling on top of him in a suffocating pile of sweaty stinking flesh like a huge crocus bag of manure.

"Ketch you now, you little rude-mouth bwoy," Jammy panted into Jackson's ear, his breath rancid. "You and you sister think oonu better than everybody, well, I going show you."

Jackson, squashed under Jammy, felt the impact of something that crashed down on his captor, snapping Jammy's head into Jackson's.

"Whadde rass —!"

"Get up off him," Jackson heard Pollyread cry out. He could see only her shoes dancing excitedly, and then her schoolbag rolling off Jammy's shoulders onto the ground near Jackson's head. "Leave him alone!" Jackson saw a foot swing back and kick, heard Jammy grunt.

Jammy seemed to be considering which of them to beat up first. He held down Jackson with one hand and swung the other at Pollyread, who skipped out of reach.

"Let him go, you dutty dawg, you!" she shouted.

Then another voice cried out, "Jammy! Get up off the pickney." It sounded farther away, and then another pair of shoes came to stand beside Pollyread's, men's shoes with the toe caps and heels cut away. "I say to get up off the little bwoy, Jammy," Miss Clarice said. "You don't hear me?"

"Mind you business, old woman," Jammy said angrily, right into Jackson's ear.

"Who you calling old woman, bwoy? If you don't get up off that little bwoy right now, I going to mind me business with this beer bottle. Right in you head!"

There was a moment when everything seemed to hang in suspension, like a lightbulb about to be turned on. Jackson found himself wondering, for some reason, whether his school khakis were torn.

"I say to get up!" Miss Clarice shouted into Jammy's ear. "You deaf or what?" Jackson saw Miss Clarice's feet move apart as she stepped back. He didn't need to see her arm raise the beer bottle on high. Perhaps Jammy sensed it too. He eased himself off Jackson and stood up, followed by his squashed prey. Whose shirt was torn.

Immediately, Pollyread began fussing, dusting off Jackson's clothes before he could even think of it. "Look what you do, Jammy," she quarreled. "You have money to buy back this uniform?"

"Polly, hush you mouth," Miss Clarice commanded quietly, not taking her eyes from Jammy. Pollyread said nothing more, continuing to brush at her brother's clothes even as Jackson moved several yards away from a panting, dust-spotted Jammy. Who was glaring at Miss Clarice. Miss Clarice, more than twice Jammy's age and a foot shorter, stood her ground for the long moment it took for Jammy to look away from her.

"What business you have fighting with two little pickney, big man like you?" Anger and disappointment were mixed equally in her voice.

"Dem diss me," Jammy said, as though that were sufficient reason for any action he felt like.

"He grab on to me, Miss Clarice," Pollyread accused him.

"I tell her good morning."

"You have to hold on to her to tell her good morning?"

"No. But when I tell her good morning, she diss me."

"I tell him say him ugly," said Pollyread quickly, as though stating a fact.

Miss Clarice laughed. "She diss you in truth," she said. "You not that ugly. But you dirty. And you wutless."

Jammy chuppsed.

"And what you doing up these parts this early morning?" Miss Clarice asked, her tone serious again.

"I-man can roam where I-man like on Jah earth," said Jammy, crossing his arms across his sweaty chest.

"Don't bring that Rasta talk to me," said Miss Clarice dismissively. "You is not no Rasta, so speak English to I-woman. I been out here from daylight and I don't see you pass. You sleep out last night up so." She gestured with her arm in the direction from which the twins and Jammy had come.

"Me is big man," said Jammy angrily. "Me can sleep where me please."

"Maybe so. But you can't trouble people pickney as you please. Look what you do to the bwoy clothes."

Jackson looked down at his own clothes like a spectator. The top two buttons of the uniform shirt had been ripped off by the force of Jammy's grab on his

185

collar from behind, and the pocket hung like a flap. The trousers, thankfully, were merely filthy, less so now thanks to Pollyread.

"He can't go to school like that," Miss Clarice protested to Jammy. "If Shim did sell khaki shirt, I would make you go over there and buy one back right now."

"Me?" Jammy had regained some of his cockiness.

"You, yes. Who else is here I could mean? And is who tear the shirt?"

Jammy had no answer for that.

"If I was you," Miss Clarice continued quietly, "I'd make myself scarce for a while. When Mass Gillie hear what you do to him pickney dem, your corner will be so dark . . ."

Jammy looked scornfully at Miss Clarice and then at the twins. "I look like I 'fraid for Mass Gillie?"

"You don't have enough sense to be 'fraid for anything," she shot back at Jammy. "That is why you is always in some trouble or other." Miss Clarice snorted as though clearing something bitter from her throat. "Still, if I was you, I would take one of your little trips."

"I not going anywhere," Jammy declared. He tightened his arms across his chest and widened his stance. "I live here too."

Miss Clarice chuckled. "If Mass Gillie catch up with you today, you going live here forever and ever."

"How you mean?" asked Jammy suspiciously.

"In Riverbottom Cemetery." Miss Clarice thought this a great joke and cackled.

Other laughter came from behind Jackson, who, turning around, realized that they had an audience. People from under the poinciana tree, which served as the bus stop for transport going down. Men and women going to their ground. Some of the twins' schoolmates on their way to Marcus Garvey Primary. Twenty or so people. None of them fans of Jammy, as Jammy himself realized, looking around at the faces and picking up the voices. "What a way the bwoy shirt tear up." "No, Jammy do it!" "You never see how him hold down the pickney?" "Is a sin." "Big man like that." "Mass Gillie a-go kill him." "Unless Miss Maisie ketch him first."

Jackson glanced at Pollyread. Her eyes shone with more than the morning sun: She was enjoying Jammy's dressing down.

Jackson, his body beginning to feel normal again, and remembering his kick, felt a slight jolt of pity for Jammy. He shouldn't have grabbed Pollyread, but Jackson didn't think that was what he had planned to do. Jammy was a thief and a troublemaker, but he'd never actually brought violence to anyone in Valley, as far as Jackson knew. And Miss Clarice's roughing up . . . just what he deserved. But still . . . why was he waiting on the path for them? Because of Jackson's plant-gathering expedition yesterday? In which case, why did he speak to Pollyread first?

"Jacko," said Miss Clarice, reaching out to hold Jackson's shoulder, "take yourself home and make Miss Maisie give you a new shirt." Her voice was normal again, briskly organizing her fiefdom, Stedman's Corner. "Polly, you tell teacher your brother forget something important at home and have to go back for it."

"Yes, Miss Clarice," both said.

They walked away from Jammy, aware of his anger following them, glad to leave him to the small crowd of Valley people — and Miss Clarice.

Though carrying no backpack and sure to be late for school, Jackson didn't hurry up the path to home. He walked deliberately, eyes down at the path, ears turned backward, as Mama would have said, to listen. Just in case . . .

On the way up, he passed schoolmates on their way down, who looked at him curiously and asked the matter. He mumbled, "Fall down . . ." and hurried on. He didn't want to stop and explain to each one. He didn't want to say that he had kicked Jammy in his balls because he wasn't sure now that he should have done that. Jammy shouldn't have grabbed Pollyread, but maybe Pollyread shouldn't have been so bright with herself. But then what was Jammy, whose home was clear over the other side of Valley, doing up this side at this early hour of morning? Why was he waiting, as Jackson was certain he was, for them? Was it really Jackson that Jammy had wanted to ambush? Because of Jackson stealing the bush the afternoon before? Running it through his head, over and over, Jackson always came back to the dread vision of their wasted backyard in the early-morning light, the little trees and bushes savaged by a wicked force.

At the same time — and to his own surprise — he no longer felt furious at Jammy: He really wanted to know why he'd done it.

His head seemed to throb, inside and out. He had a headache, something he hardly ever had.

Poppa was walking toward the gate on his way to ground. Mama was standing in the doorway of the house, shaking out a duster. They both froze, their mouths falling open.

"What happen to him?" Mama called from the doorway.

"Look like him and the ground ketch up," Poppa replied, not taking his eyes from his son, whose steps had slowed.

Poppa was carrying his lignum vitae walking stick but not leaning on it. A smaller stick, one he used to poke holes in the soil to put seeds, was clasped together with the cutlass in his other hand. The old T-shirt he generally worked in, what was left of it, hung on his body like a strange second skin. Jackson saw the half smile on Poppa's face that asked: *Say something. Why you not in school?*

Jackson's throat was dry, and no words were to be found in his head. Poppa didn't agree with fighting. *Animals fight,* he told the twins. *There's usually another way.*

As he came close and smelled his father, Jackson felt something in him, a tightness he hadn't known was there, dissolve and rise up inside like hot water to overflow through his eyes, onto his cheeks, and into his mouth, sweet and salty. Embarrassed and suddenly angry with himself, he stood there stiffly and cried, silently, watching clinically as a teardrop fell into the dust between his scuffed shoes. He rubbed it out with his shoe but another one fell, and then another. One fell on Poppa's dusty right foot, all but bare in a misshapen flip-flop. Jackson was mortified.

He was aware of Mama coming down the steps into the yard and coming toward him. A subdued Cho-cho appeared and squatted close by, looking up at him.

"You fall down?" Mama asked.

Jackson shook his head, still not looking up.

"You was in a fight." Mama wasn't asking a question.

Jackson nodded. He heard a joint intake of breath, and gasped: "Jammy" before either parent could say anything.

"Jammy?" they said together.

"You and Jammy fight?" Poppa asked, unbelieving.

Jackson managed a shrug.

"No mind," he heard Poppa say above him, and felt his shoulder squeezed. "If you fight Jammy and still upright, you could cry." A little chuckle lifted his voice, and Jackson's spirits.

"What you fight about?" Mama's tone was not as gentle.

Jackson was about to say "Pollyread" when he looked up and saw Mama's fierce eyes and knew that would be the wrong direction to take.

"He was down by Miss Liza," he said frantically, tears forgotten, moving out of Poppa's warm arm. "Jammy. Behind a big tree."

"What he was doing there?" Poppa asked.

"He grab my schoolbag as I was passing —"

"What for?"

Jackson shrugged. "I don't know. But I give him a good kick" — another activity his parents didn't approve of — "and I grab back the schoolbag and run, and Jammy take out after me down the hill. . . ." As he told them the rest of the story, mostly as it had happened, Jackson found himself reliving the terror of the chase down to Stedman's Corner, and of being stifled by Jammy sprawled on top of him. Except that this time, in the retelling, he wasn't trying to escape from Jammy but to lead Poppa and Mama away from the beginning of the story, and Pollyread. Jackson didn't want to think about what would be the reaction if they knew that Jammy, for whatever reason, had put hands on Pollyread. His eyes bounced quickly from one face to the other.

"So where is Pollyread now?" Mama asked sharply.

"She at school," said Jackson, hoping to reassure.

"And where is Jammy?" asked Poppa.

Jackson shrugged. "Miss Clarice dealing with him."

"I going to be dealing with him when I ketch him," Mama snorted. "Jammy owe me money! He think he can just go around tearing off people clothes because he feel like it? Who never do a day's honest labor in him life!"

"Him owe me more than money," said Poppa, his voice soft and dark.

"Come," Mama said, pulling Jackson's dirty sleeve and turning back toward the house. "Come tidy up yourself." She led him away, quarreling with Jammy under her breath.

When Jackson came back out of the house, presentable again, Poppa was sitting on the big stone by the gate, smoking a piece of jackass-rope. From time to time he bought a coil of the strong-smelling tobacco down at Redemption Ground market. Mama only allowed it inside the house at Christmas and on his birthday. Mostly after the day's work, or if one of his friends came by and drinks were out, he'd cut off a piece and light up. The aroma was one the twins had known for as long as they could remember; it was the smell of calm.

"Soon come, Maisie," Poppa called out when he saw Jackson. "I going to escort young warrior here down to school. Before him beat up anybody else." He winked.

"Move lively, warrior," Poppa teased, and Jackson, hurrying to the gate behind his father, heard Mama laugh from the house.

"You not going to ground again?" Jackson noticed that his father was no longer carrying his usual things for a day in the field. And he'd changed his clothes.

"Change of plan," he said in a flat voice.

Finding Out

"**M**iss Brimley."

"Yes, Penelope."

There was no one else in the little library. Pollyread was glad of that. Cuthbert Bank Library was one of her favorite places in the world and Miss Evangeline Brimley, the librarian, a very special person. All the way down here from Marcus Garvey Primary, dragging a complaining Jackson along, Pollyread had prayed for privacy.

She took a deep breath. "You ever hear of rolling goat, Miss Brimley?"

The old librarian looked at both of them before responding calmly, "No, Penelope. I've heard of rolling calf, of course, but —"

"No, Miss," Pollyread interrupted, "rolling *goat*." She knew it was rude to interrupt adults, but Miss Brimley loved to talk and she didn't want her taking off in a direction that would only confuse things.

"Rolling goat?" Miss Brimley said with a smile. The old woman tried not to show it, but she was clearly puzzled by her young client's request.

"Is a duppy goat, Miss," Jackson chimed in.

"Ah," was all Miss Brimley said for a while, looking straight ahead. Then, quietly: "Have you seen this . . . animal?" Her eyes bounced from Pollyread to Jackson and back to Pollyread, where they rested.

They nodded. Pollyread didn't trust herself to say anything.

Miss Brimley was again quiet awhile. Pollyread thought she heard her own blood pumping its way around her body.

"Come," Miss Brimley said eventually. Thin shoulders lifted and bony hands gripped the edge of the table. In a moment, with the help of the knobbly walking stick that took her everywhere like a third leg, she was stepping off toward the back of the little library. The twins fell into step on either side of Miss Brimley's stick, in case she wanted to rest a hand on a younger shoulder. They were all now about the same height, the twins growing up, Miss Brimley growing down.

Miss Brimley always looked to Pollyread as though she was made of wood — breadfruit, Jackson had said once. Her skin was pale brown, like Mama's morning

196

coffee, and shot through with darker streaks. Her voice was brown too, and probably, Pollyread thought, her hair before it had turned the gray that the twins had always known. Miss Brimley was, the twins agreed between themselves, ancient. Poppa had made his first visit to Cuthbert Bank branch library as a boy younger than the twins, and she'd seemed old to him then. Miss Brimley's house, where she had been born, was one of the few upstairs buildings in the whole district. It had clearly been a splendid place once, when Miss Brimley's father, inheriting from his father before him, had owned almost all the land they could see between Cross Point above and Cuthbert Ridge below it. Pollyread knew this from Poppa, who had repaired the house at various times and restored some of the old furniture. Miss Brimley's mother was English and she had gone to school and university there. To everyone's surprise, Evangeline had returned to Cuthbert Bank.

"Books are what have kept me sane all these years, Mr. Gilmore," Poppa reported Miss Brimley as saying to him once, mimicking even her tone of voice: a little scratchy but businesslike. "If I am sane." (Pollyread, if ignorant of Miss Brimley's problem, could appreciate the remedy.) With her own money and initially with her own books, Miss Brimley had converted some outer buildings adjacent to her house into a lending library for the district. Eventually the island's library service had made it the Cuthbert Bank branch.

At the back of the library, behind the last bookshelf on that side of the room, was a small round table that was understood to be private. No one else sat there unless invited or instructed. It was where Miss Brimley had a cup of tea or a sandwich and drink, brought to her from her house that was across from a little garden that was Jackson's chief delight when coming to Cuthbert Bank. But there was no thought of flowers or herbs in anyone's head this time.

There were only two chairs at the table. At Miss Brimley's nod of the head, Pollyread sat; Jackson stood.

"So," Miss Brimley said, her voice soft to indicate that this was a private conversation, but matter-of-fact in tone, "tell me about this goat of yours."

And, gulping for words and understanding, they told her. Hesitantly at first, waiting for the other to speak first and then jumping in to elaborate or explain, they soon settled into the flow of their story. Pollyread felt relief rising in her, as when on a hot day she sank down into the cool waters — provided there *was* water, of course — of Bamboo River. She realized that she had not enjoyed keeping the goat a secret from everyone except Jackson. All the secrets she had, some kept even from

Jackson, shrank to the size of a guinep compared to this one. And as she heard the increasing lightness in his voice, Pollyread knew that he felt the same release.

"What you think it mean, Miss?" Jackson asked when there seemed no more for them to say.

Miss Brimley had listened in her own silence, not interrupting them. Occasionally, Pollyread saw her eyes drifting out the window to her little garden and the mountains beyond, but not because the old woman wasn't listening, more as though she was thinking, or remembering.

She smiled at the twins. "Heaven alone knows, Jackson," she said cheerfully. "It seems you definitely saw something. Clouds can make funny shapes, but never the same shape twice that I've ever heard of. And both of you saw the same thing at the same time. That's interesting too."

"You think is . . . obeah?" Pollyread asked. She felt the earlier tension nibble at her.

"No, I do not," said Miss Brimley, her voice suddenly stern. Pollyread stiffened.

"Obeah," Miss Brimley continued in a gentler tone, "comes from people, for doing things that will give one person advantage over another. People around here have tried it with me from time to time." She chuckled at the memory. "Once —" She cut herself off, frowning and looking off through the window. "But you don't want to hear about that."

The twins did, of course. Miss Brimley was full of wonderful stories that left you knowing there was more. "In the old days," Miss Brimley went on now, "they used to worship all sorts of things, and see omens and meanings in a lot of things that we don't pay much attention to nowadays. Most of us anyway."

"You mean," said Pollyread, hesitating between words, "when you was a little girl, Miss?"

Miss Brimley exploded in laughter, slapping the handle of her chair and almost barking in a voice that filled the whole library and escaped through the open windows into the sunlit afternoon. It was completely at odds with her scrawny old body. Still, Pollyread glimpsed, like bits of glass glinting in a pile of earth, sharp flashes of Miss Brimley when she would have been a little girl.

"I'm not *that* old, pickney, mercy me," she said, wiping her eyes. "No, I'm talking about l-o-n-g ago time, hundreds and thousands of years ago. Old Testament time. Baal and all those other gods and idols the prophets were always preaching about."

"Those were goats?" Jackson asked.

"Not all of them. But many were animals, and I'm

sure there were goats among them. They're wonderfully vigorous and lively animals, don't you think?"

Pollyread, thinking of the prankish energy of Mass Cleveland's goats, especially when one of them escaped into somebody's ground, had to agree. Their goat was lively too. And with a power like Bamboo River now, after the rains.

"Those animals were symbols of different things," Miss Brimley said brightly, struggling to stand. "I think I have a book that might help you discover what the goat stood for."

They helped her to her feet and she tapped off with her stick toward the shelves, then changed direction as two children and a woman came into the library, requiring her attention.

"I'll find it for you before you leave," she said to the twins. Then paused. "That new baby you told me about." Miss Brimley looked into the twins' puzzled faces. "It may be significant."

Jackson's and Pollyread's eyes collided like marbles. Abeo?

The Devil Plant

Jackson, I have some new things to consult with you about. But let me get these books for Penelope."

Miss Brimley called Jackson her "consultant gardener." (It was a word he heard on the radio sometimes, and kept promising himself to look up in the dictionary at home.) He knew from the tone in her voice that she was teasing him a little, but understood that she was complimenting him too — whatever consultant meant. Almost every time he came to the library, she would take him out into the backyard to show him her flower beds and her garden of herbs that grew in an apparently random ramble down the hillside behind her house. Jackson had helped her to plant the herbs the previous year, fulfilling very definite ideas Miss Brimley had about the casual effect she wanted to create. He would make suggestions to her about placement of plants according to sunlight and water runoff, passing on information that he hardly knew he had, so naturally had he imbibed it from working alongside his parents from when he was old enough to be trusted with his own knife for digging. There was an old man, Bampy, who had lived on the edge of Miss Brimley's land forever, and who was supposed to look after everything that grew, but was only interested in what could be eaten, and therefore sold. "Every year," Miss Brimley complained to Jackson, "his yam hills get closer and closer to my flower beds. If I die before that old rascal, he'll move them right up to the verandah. And there'll be string beans on my grave."

Jackson went over to the table where Pollyread was sitting with two books Miss Brimley had given her. On the way, Jackson stopped at the shelf that held the *National Geographic* magazines, his favorite reading at the library, and scooped up a few copies. Miss Brimley had been subscribing, she'd told Jackson, since she was his age, and she'd kept every copy, moving them over to the library when she was finished with them in her house.

Pollyread barely registered his presence, even when, as she appeared to be from time to time, looking directly at him. Eyes glassy, her mind was somewhere far. Thinking about Abeo, Jackson figured. Searching for symbols. Jackson held his own thoughts about Goat tight, in case they flew off into dark places. He turned his mind toward the pages in front of him, with their pictures of distant countries and strange peoples. Sometimes the people didn't seem so strange. Once he had been reading a story on Ghana, turned a page — and was looking at the market at Redemption Ground! The luscious fruits and vegetables sprawling over the edges of the hamper baskets much like those of Mama and Aunt Zilla and the other Valley women. Fussy shoppers aggressive in search of a bargain. Even the children running around! Pollyread and himself could have been in the picture. At home, as he had excitedly retailed his discovery over supper, Mama had smiled and said: "Well, is there we all come from. We bring it with us."

Other times, like now, it was enough to just flick the pages idly, letting the pictures flare at him like matches. One picture in particular flamed: a mountain that reminded him of Angel's Peak. He paused and spread his hands on the pages to hold the magazine open on the table. He started reading.

The mountain was in Colombia, which was a country not that far away, where they spoke Spanish (which Jackson would learn if he went to secondary school in Town). The whole article was about Colombia, which had cities even more sprawling than Town, mountains even taller than Angel's Peak, people of as many shades as he was accustomed to seeing here, and a bounty of plants and flowers tumbling off the pages.

And then he saw it. Jammy's plant!

He went stiff, staring at the page. "What happen to you?" Pollyread asked, finally noticing him. His turn to ignore her. But that was because his throat was tight shut, his body rigid.

The picture popped off the page at him. The same small bush with the yellow-green flowers set like jewels in clusters of light green leaves, oblong-shaped.

He scuttled over to the entrance, where everyone was required to leave their bags, shoved his hand into his backpack, and extracted his prize.

Back at the table — still not a word to his now intensely puzzled sister — he lay Jammy's bush beside the picture in the magazine.

The exact same thing!

"What is that piece of bush? Where it come from?" Pollyread demanded. Her voice rang out in the little library. A sharp "Sh-h-h!" came back from Miss Brimley. The rebuke bounced off Pollyread. "Where that bush come from?" she whispered, but so fiercely she might as well have shouted. Miss Brimley got to her feet with surprising swiftness and was coming toward them before Jackson could think of a response.

"What is causing all this noise over here?" Miss Brimley's walking stick underlined the sudden firmness of her voice. "Would you care to enlighten us, Penelope?" Miss Brimley's eyes seemed to be looking into her soul. And not much liking what she saw there.

"Is not her, Miss Brimley," Jackson said, bright as a new ten cent. "Is me cause it."

"Caused it? How?"

"This." He held Jammy's bush. "And this." He pointed down at the magazine on the table.

Three pairs of eyes looked back and forth between the bush and the page.

"Is the same bush," Pollyread cried.

"Yes," Miss Brimley said a moment after, her voice softer than before.

Jackson felt very pleased with himself.

Miss Brimley picked up the bush and brought it close to her eyes. She angled it in different ways and moved it closer to, then farther away from, her face. It was a point of pride with her that she didn't need to wear glasses, but the fact was that, as she herself put it, her eyes were growing dark.

"I don't think this is just my eyes, Jackson. This is something entirely new in my experience." Her fingers played with the oblong yellowish-green leaves with the deep grooves down the middle. She looked at him. "I don't think I've ever seen this before," she said after a while, speaking as though asking herself a question. "Where did you find it?"

Jackson waved his arm in the direction of the mountains. "Up Morgan's Mount."

Miss Brimley sighed again. "Ah." She looked down at the magazine.

"And you think it's the same plant as this one," Miss Brimley continued, a bony finger wrapped with stringy veins resting on the open page.

"It resemble." Jackson felt the words scrape his throat. Maybe he was wrong. Pollyread would never let him forget it if he was.

Pollyread herself was bent over the magazine, reading with an intensity that Jackson could feel.

Miss Brimley ignored her for the moment and held out the bush to Jackson. "Are there plenty of them? These plants?" He nodded. "Wild?" He shook his head. "Someone's planting them?" He nodded. "I see, said the blind man, adjusting his spectacles." It was a little saying of hers that made him smile.

Pollyread's voice cut in. "It name *erythro . . . throxy . . . throxylon coca. Erythroxylon coca*," she finished, looking triumphantly up at her brother.

"Cocoa?" His throat was still dry. He didn't understand. Jammy's bush didn't look anything like cocoa.

There was a tree in their backyard, shade for some of Mama's wild orchids. And cocoa grew plentiful in the district. Trucky's father had a grove of them on his ground. But cocoa leaves were much bigger.

"This is not *our* cocoa," Miss Brimley said. She sat down in the chair next to Pollyread. "Let me see."

Jackson, standing between the two chairs, was too far away to see more than a blur of words on the pages. Fidgeting while Miss Brimley and his sister read and turned pages, he was about to move off in frustration when he noticed Miss Brimley's hand press down hard on the page she was reading. Her back stiffened. Pollyread cried out, "Say what?"

"What?" he asked. Neither of them replied. Pollyread was watching Miss Brimley, whose eyes seemed to be looking clean through her to something far beyond. Jackson got the strange feeling that he was the only one awake.

"This," said Miss Brimley, "is not good." She was talking to herself, as though Pollyread and Jackson were not there.

Jackson asked, "What is not good?"

For a moment he thought no one had heard him. Then Pollyread said, "Is cocaine."

"Cocaine? What about cocaine?" Jackson heard irritation in his own voice. "Cocaine is not something that grow." He knew about cocaine, a terrible drug that people in Town and foreign used and killed themselves with.

"It make from coca," Pollyread said, her own impatience beginning to show. "It say so here." She indicated the magazine on the table with her chin.

"Lemme see." Pollyread got up from her chair to allow him to sit down. In the next chair, Miss Brimley was sitting quite still, no longer reading.

Jackson began at the top of the page that was open, and soon was skipping words and then lines, his eyes looking for the words "coca" and "cocaine." Eventually, as Pollyread and Miss Brimley had done, he found them. But a weird thing happened. Despite his efforts to pay close attention, some of the words of the article faded and blurred, while others were sharply in focus. His thoughts were jumping on those words like they were stepping-stones across a turbulent river: "narcotic" . . . "addiction" . . . "crack" . . . "lifetime" . . . "death" . . . On the other side of *this* river was darkness.

His chaotic thoughts were broken into by Miss Brimley gripping her stick and getting to her feet, slow but firm in her movements. "You have to tell your father about this," she said, sounding grim. "This is a devil plant."

Miss Brimley's stick tapped insistently on the wooden floor. "Do you hear me, Jackson Gilmore? You must go straight home and tell your parents about this. Take the magazine." She looked sternly at Jackson first, then Pollyread. "They will know what to do."

On cue, it seemed, a horn sounded. "Roadman," Pollyread called out involuntarily.

"There you are, then," Miss Brimley said with a little smile. Then, unexpectedly, she started fussing nervously. "Is he close? I'm not hearing as good as I used to." She sounded suddenly like a frail old lady, which neither of the twins had ever thought her before. "Oh, dear," she muttered to herself, the devil plant and the goat and everything else completely forgotten. "Where did I put them?"

Pollyread asked, "Put what, Miss?" but Miss Brimley paid her no mind, instead turned a full circle around herself, eyes glazed. Finally, she said, "The books," more to herself than to Pollyread, "where . . . ?" And then, with an emphatic bang of her stick on the floor, "Ah!" and she tap-tapped her way toward the entrance to the library.

Jackson, meanwhile, ignoring the confusion around

him, had grabbed his piece of bush and the *National Geographic* magazine and was right behind Miss Brimley, leaving a slightly bewildered Pollyread to catch up.

Miss Brimley smiled broadly as she said, "Here they are," and took two books out of one of the drawers underneath her table. She was, to Pollyread's relief, her old self again.

She held out two books, one in each hand. "Congratulations," she said. "I wanted to add ours to the heaps and heaps you've no doubt been getting from everybody."

They spoke in chorus, uncomfortable but pleased. "Thank you, Miss Brimley." With all the excitement of the past hour, everything else had flown clear out of their minds.

"We want to have a celebratory tea party," said Miss Brimley, "but we'll have to do it another time. Miss Walters had to go to Town this last weekend, and I didn't know when you'd be coming down to visit us." Miss Walters had lived here with Miss Brimley for as long as all but the very oldest heads could remember. She wasn't, as far as Pollyread knew, any kind of relative. The important information about Miss Walters was that she made the most delicious cakes and tarts of anyone living between Valley and Town.

Both she and Miss Brimley were thin as bamboo, but generations of children had been fattened from Miss Walters's oven.

Pollyread looked down at her book: *Selected Poems of Louise Bennett*. She glanced across at Jackson's: *New Day*, by V. S. Reid.

"Thank you, Miss Brimley," they said again in raggedy chorus.

"I hope," said Miss Brimley, "that you'll thank me even more many years from now, when I'm gone. You will both travel very far," she said, quietly but firm-voiced, "like I did. And I don't think you'll be coming back — these are different times. But always take these books with you. Not for me. For yourself. They will help you chart your course because they will help to root you in your home."

Here it was again, that feeling like a fingernail scratching the bottom of her stomach. Like everyone was sending her away — and Miss Brimley forever! For a moment, the bright afternoon seemed to darken.

"Now run along and catch your wretched bus," said Miss Brimley briskly, turning them toward the door. "I think I hear a rattling sound coming this way. Like rolling calf." She chuckled. "You must come back and tell me more about that goat of yours."

Pollyread didn't know what prompted her, but she kissed Miss Brimley's cheek. It was cool and smelled of baby powder and lime juice. Miss Brimley was as surprised as she was. "Oh, dear," she said with a little giggle. Jackson, Pollyread noticed, seemed uncomfortable, which she was sorry for causing but at this point couldn't help. Miss Brimley put a bony hand on Jackson's shoulder and squeezed. "And don't forget to tell your parents about that plant. And," she turned to Pollyread, "I'll send to let you know when we'll have that tea."

A raucous blast from Roadman's horn, quite near now, set the twins scampering for their bags.

"And take this with you," Miss Brimley cried, thrusting a book at Pollyread. "Normally I don't lend out reference books, but under the circumstances . . ." Her chirruping voice faded behind the twins as Pollyread grabbed the book with a shouted, "Thank you, Miss," and they pelted out into the road.

Reports

The whining and growling of the minibus swallowed all other sounds in the air — birds, breeze, the twins' voices, eventually their very thoughts. When it had obliterated everything else, Roadman, named after its owner-driver, lumbered around a corner, moving slowly because of its sardine-packed load and tilting like a drunken elephant. It ignored the twins' waving hands and growled on past them, blessing them with foul exhaust fumes and dust. As they coughed and spluttered, resigning themselves to the long uphill walk home — at least until Santos, the other minibus plying this route, gave them another chance at a ride — Roadman screeched to a halt thirty meters on. For a moment nothing moved, including the twins. And then, of all people, Poppa leapt out of the bus as though someone had thrown him. His clothes, crushed and sweat-streaked, were his Sunday best: He had been to Town. For something very important.

"What you all doing down this way?"

"Library, Poppa," said Pollyread, finding her voice.

"Is so late you coming back now?"

"It not so late, Poppa. And Miss Brimley keep us."

"We have something —" Jackson began, before Roadman's horn blasted his words to pieces.

"Come," said Poppa, waving his arm and turning back to the bus.

Pollyread groaned aloud as they tracked behind him. It looked like a solid piece of machinery with parts of wriggling humans embedded. There wasn't a chink of space to be seen within Roadman.

Jackson found a breathing space in the bus, under Poppa's armpit and centimeters from the damp breastplate of a large woman whose face he couldn't even see. Pollyread was somewhere close, perhaps under Poppa's other arm, but he couldn't search for her without his face bouncing the woman's sweat-stained chest. As it was, the jolly-riding of the bus, as Roadman took it around and, unavoidably, through the potholes, brought him perilously close to embarrassment several times. He was hardly aware of the green hillside flashing by outside.

"One stop, driver," someone called out, and Roadman-the-bus came to a juddering stop, rearranging the bodies inside willy-nilly. Poppa held on to his children as people were reshuffled by the need to release one or more bodies. Then off again, with a rasp of gears and a belch of exhaust in all directions that the inmates inhaled as they passed through it.

"Roadman," Poppa shouted, startling Jackson. "One stop." They hadn't properly reached Cross Point, much less Stedman's Corner.

Poppa looked down at him. "You and Pen go on up. Tell Mama I soon come."

Jackson caught a glimpse of where Roadman had stopped: right opposite the Cross Point police station. Was this where Poppa was going? Before he could think to ask him, Poppa was through the bus door, one of several passengers bouncing and jostling their way down the steps. The doors clanged shut and the bus lurched forward again.

Now able to see each other around the body of the woman, thick and solid as a tree trunk, Jackson and Pollyread looked at each other: Something had to be done.

"Roadman!" Pollyread shouted.

"What?"

"One stop here!"

"Please," Jackson added loudly.

"Wait," Roadman called from the front of the mini-bus. "Next stop."

"I need to pee-pee," Pollyread shouted.

"Hold it," came the immediate reply.

Before Jackson's astonished eyes — and to his complete embarrassment — Pollyread squeezed her eyes tight shut, then blinked twice quickly, then erupted in a caterwauling that made his neckback shiver. *"Whaiiie!"* she screamed, grabbing her head.

It was like letting loose a flock of parrots in the bus. Everyone — except Jackson — started talking at once, some beseeching Pollyread to hush up, some trying to shush her, the loudest voice shouting at Roadman to stop the blankety-blank bus and let off the blankety-blank pickney.

Roadman agreed. Abruptly. If Jackson hadn't managed to grab her, Pollyread, still screeching, would have fallen into the little space that had cleared around her and into a bankra basket that held a dozen or so little yellow puffs of week-old chicks that would be somebody's livelihood in a few months. Behind them, the door flew open and in a few seconds they were out on the bankside inhaling the stinking diesel exhaust of the disappearing minibus.

It took Pollyread two swipes of her sleeve, one to

each cheek, to dry the few drops of crocodile tears on her face; her eyes weren't even red.

Without a glance at Jackson, she set off in the direction from which they had just come.

They both knew what this act of rank disobedience might mean.

Rank — usually pronounced "renk" — was Mama's word for things, and people, that she strongly disapproved of. She would probably regard her own children, after their sweaty walk from Marcus Garvey to Cuthbert Ridge and their sojourn on the bus, as smelling renk. But that would be the least of their renkness because it wouldn't be their fault. Disobeying a direct parental instruction, on the other hand, was about as renk as a child could get, in skin or soul.

But there was no going back now. Except back to the police station where Roadman had let Poppa out.

The Cross Point police station was an old cut-stone building raised off the ground so that — the legend said — prisoners could be chained underneath. Not even the oldest person in the district could remember this happening — in fact, there was a concrete-and-zinc oven of a lockup round the back — but the story had sufficed to wrap the quite attractive building in an aura of dread. The solid wood front door looked as though if it shut behind you, you'd never be readmitted to daylight and home — never mind that the door was never shut, even late at night.

Pollyread's firm step slowed as they got closer to the station. Jackson drew alongside her.

"You tell Poppa," she said. "Miss Brimley said you was to tell him."

"And you will tell him how we get off the bus?"

"Why is always me?"

Jackson didn't respond. They were practically at the foot of the five steps that led up to the station entrance. Jackson listened carefully but heard nothing except the country sounds around them, and even they seemed quieter than usual. *Too late now,* he thought, and walked up the steps, Pollyread one step behind.

"Can I help you?"

The young policeman sat behind the counter on a stool almost as high as the counter, resting his elbows on the biggest book the twins had ever seen. They marveled anew at it each time they visited the station. It was called simply the station book, and every station in the island had one, so Corporal Letchworth said anyway. Everything official that happened inside the station was recorded there, inscribed by one of the several pens that decorated the pocket of this young policeman's uniform shirt. He was new to the twins. Where was Constable Ranglin, who had been there behind that counter from they'd known themselves? This was going to be *really* difficult, Jackson thought.

"We're looking for our father," Pollyread said, trying to sound official.

The young policeman's head was like a black egg, his nose and lips barely protruding, his oblong eyes only slightly indented. His skin glistened. His lips parted sufficiently to display tightly packed white teeth as he said, twice as official as Pollyread: "Are you here to make a missing persons report?"

Jackson felt his sister bristle beside him and jumped in before she found her next set of words, which were likely to be sharp-edged. "Mr. Gilmore. He come to see Corpie about a business."

The policeman's words pounced on Jackson. "What kind of a business?"

"Police business," Pollyread said.

"I am police," said the young officer. "What is the business?"

"He never tell us," said Pollyread, not giving an inch. "He only tell us is police business." Jackson's breath caught in his throat: Poppa had told them no such thing.

Not even that he was going to the police station to talk to Corporal Letchworth. He could be anywhere in Cross Point.

The policeman removed one of the five or six pens that decorated his shirt pocket like an extra set of teeth. He removed the top and, with a theatrical flourish, brought it to rest, poised like a knife, above the big book in front of him. "What you name?" His voice had deepened, becoming even more official. He looked at Pollyread with bright eyes, his pen hand moving above the page as though stirred by a slight breeze.

"Why you have to know we name?" Jackson's own voice startled him.

Pollyread glared at the policeman. "We don't do nothing."

"I am police. I can ask you anything!"

"Not if we not here," said Jackson, grabbing Pollyread's shoulder and pushing her toward the door. Behind them the policeman growled.

"Halt!"

In truth, Jackson reflected afterward, his legs had been none too strong taking him out of the station and down the steps. And probably Pollyread was as frightened as he was at their boldness. Stopping halfway down and holding on to the nearest railing was a relief.

"You want me to place you under arrest? Eh?"

"For what?" Pollyread muttered under her breath.

"Eh?"

"Who you arresting, Constable Phillips?"

The twins were still facing out onto the road that ran past the station. The voice, big and imposing, came from deeper inside the station and turned them around as though it were Corporal Letchworth's hand. Constable Phillips, who had grown taller by some means to shout his command at the twins, was subsiding back onto his stool, pen still in hand. Corporal Letchworth was walking out of the darkened interior of the station where the offices — and the cells — were located. Jackson felt a flutter of relief. For just a moment. Because behind Corpie was Poppa. Whose eyes flickered with warmth as he saw his children. Then shut down cold like a door slammed.

"That is what they teach you at police college, bwoy?" Corporal Letchworth's voice was a knife. "To arrest pickney?"

"Them diss me, sir." He was glaring at the twins as he spoke.

They were looking neither at the constable nor at Corpie but at Poppa's face. And he was watching them. There were no questions in his eyes, just the accusation: *You disobeyed me.*

"How them diss you?"

"They wouldn't tell me what they name."

"You have reason to ask them them name?"

"They come to make a report about them father."

"What the father do? Beat them?" Jackson's quick glance at Corporal Letchworth told him that his aggressive attitude to the younger policeman was only partly serious.

"He missing," Constable Phillips said, still staring at the twins. They had stepped back into the station now.

"We never say he missing." Pollyread's voice was defiant.

"Hush, child," Corporal Letchworth said quietly. "Show respect."

"We said he come here," Jackson chimed in, "and that we come to find him."

"That is what *I* am saying," the young man insisted, "that he missing."

"And now he is found," Corpie intoned like a preacher. "See him here." He indicated Poppa.

"That is what we was telling you," Jackson said.

"Jackso, be quiet." Poppa's voice was quiet but firm. "The constable wasn't here when I come through to Corporal Letchworth, so he never see me. He just doing his job."

In the moment's quiet that followed Poppa's rebuke, Jackson felt as though he had been put on a stage with a strong light shining on him. He needed to explain why they were here, and before Poppa asked him. He felt giddy from all the excitement and anxiety of the past hour. Summoning all his strength to hold Poppa's eyes, Jackson said, "I have something to tell you. Important."

"Very important," Pollyread said.

"What?" The line of Poppa's mouth softened. "Something happen at school?" He looked from one to the other.

"No, Poppa," Pollyread said quickly.

Jackson said, "Jammy," and saw both Poppa and Corporal Letchworth quicken.

"Jammy?"

"What 'bout Jammy?"

Jackson took a deep breath. "He growing drugs."

Corpie exploded. "Drugs?"

"Drugs?" Poppa's frown returned. His eyes told Jackson that, for all the sense he was making, Jackson might have spoken in French.

Jackson could only nod.

Corporal Letchworth took a half step toward Jackson. "Jammy growing ganja?"

"But is not ganja I see growing up there," Poppa said. The farmer in him was thinking aloud.

"If is ganja he growing, you can't protect him, Mass Gillie." Corporal Letchworth was sounding official now.

"Worse than ganja," Pollyread piped up.

Poppa looked from one twin to the other, still mystified. "Worse than ganja?"

"Coca," said Jackson.

The three adults bounced puzzled glances off one another, and then all looked intently at him.

"Like cocoa tea?" Corpie asked. He sounded like his son, Dylan, in class. "That kind of cocoa?"

"Chocolate?" Constable Phillips asked.

"No," said Pollyread in her teacher voice. "To make cocaine."

The adults looked at her as if she was crazy, especially Poppa.

"Cocaine?" Corporal Letchworth's mouth opened in disbelief. "Here?"

"But you don't grow cocaine," Poppa said, his words overlapping the corporal's.

"I never know you can make cocaine from cocoa," Constable Philips said, his eyes widening in amazement. "Blow-wow."

"C-O-C-A," Pollyread spelled it out, trying to keep a straight face. It was a lovely feeling, knowing something important that adults, even Poppa, didn't.

"Like Coca-Cola that you drink?" Constable Phillips was even more confused.

"No," said Pollyread. "It spell same way. But Jammy not growing Coca-Cola." At the image of cans and bottles growing out of the ground, Pollyread couldn't help but smile broadly, which didn't please the young policeman.

Beside her, Jackson wrestled with his schoolbag a moment and produced the piece of bush that had started the whole confusion. "See it here." He held it up like a trophy.

Poppa took it from him and examined it closely, the two policemen waiting silently for his verdict. "Yes," he said, "it look like what I see up there. But how you know is — coca?"

Like a magician, Jackson pulled the *National Geographic* magazine out of his bag. He had even marked the pages with one of the coca leaves. Pollyread was impressed.

The station house was quiet for a moment as Poppa and Corpie stood shoulder to shoulder reading the magazine, which Poppa held. Corporal Letchworth's breathing grew louder the more he read, and became

226

ragged as his inner agitation grew. Poppa, in contrast, was like a tree beside him.

"That bwoy!" Corpie flung his arm at the ceiling as though brushing Jammy away. "He gone too far this time." He was practically shouting. "Cocaine! In this place. I going to —" Corpie stuttered into silence.

Poppa seemed oblivious of him. Holding the bush up, he was looking directly at Jackson. "How you get this bush?"

Pollyread held her breath. She wanted to know also, but Poppa's interest was more than just curiosity.

But to her surprise, Jackson grinned. "I tief it." His eyes glinted with pure mischief. Which made Pollyread anxious because she didn't think Poppa was in the mood for mischief.

Indeed, he was dead serious as he looked at Jackson. "From who?"

Jackson tossed his head in the direction of the mountains. Poppa understood immediately and, to Pollyread's further amazement, smiled.

Corporal Letchworth gave an explosive laugh. "Tief from tief, God laugh."

Everyone smiled except Constable Phillips, who looked puzzled.

"When?" Poppa asked.

"A few days ago."

"You sister went with you?"

Pollyread answered promptly, "No, Poppa, he go by himself. I didn't even know until today." She wasn't sure when the wind might change, and wanted everyone to be clear about her innocence in this matter.

"Gillie." Corporal Letchworth was looking grimly at Poppa. "This is serious business Jammy get himself involve in. Not like squatting. Or even what him do to your backyard there. This is heavy matters." The big policeman paused. "Criminal matters."

Poppa seemed suddenly sad. "Is what that bwoy get himself into now, eh?"

"Him is not bwoy any longer," said Corporal Letchworth. "The court not going to treat him as no juvenile."

"Jammy don't have enough sense to know about coca. Someone put him up to this. I sure of that." Poppa seemed more to be talking to himself than to those around him. Pollyread was puzzled at Poppa. There was a complete absence of outrage and shock such as Corpie had expressed.

Ignoring Poppa's musings, Corporal Letchworth took the piece of coca bush from him and handed it to Constable Phillips. "Constable, put this in a plastic bag and seal it."

"Yes, sir," said the young constable, relieved to be part of the action again.

"And get it down to the forensics people in Town. Tell them we need an identification right away. Tell them what we think it is, but we need official confirmation. Right, Constable?"

"Right, sir." His puffed chest of pens told Pollyread how thoroughly pleased he was to be entrusted with such an important task.

Corpie turned back to Poppa and the twins and shrugged. "But them boys at forensics have so much dead people dealing with, they might take them sweet time with a piece of bush. We need a faster certain." He grinned. "And we certain that he squatting on your ground, Mass Gillie. The court say so." He waved a long envelope that Pollyread hadn't noticed him holding. He must have brought it out with him from inside, where he'd been talking with Poppa. "We have him for that. Come."

Everything and everyone else was forgotten as Corporal Letchworth, reminding Pollyread of Cho-cho when he picked up a scent, marched through the station and down the steps. The three Gilmores, Pollyread and Jackson thoroughly confused, straggled behind him. At the bottom step he stopped abruptly, turned, and nearly knocked the twins over as he barged back inside.

Minutes later, he came back. He seemed to Pollyread to have changed slightly, to have grown even bigger in some way. And then she saw why: a pouch over his shoulder and across his chest from left to right, like a little purse, out of which poked the handle of a revolver.

Eviction

It was Poppa's fault, Pollyread told herself.

Poppa had told them to go inside and stay at home, as he and Corporal Letchworth had marched on up the path toward Morgan's Mount to "fix Jammy's business," as Corpie had said outside the station. That business, she knew, and the fixing of it, had to do with the large envelope Poppa had given to Corpie in the station, and which Poppa once more held firmly in his hand.

She had business with Jammy also. His frightening her on the path, whether or not it was for pushing down his sister. And squashing Jackson at Stedman's Corner. And, worse than all that, worse even than the depredation of the Gilmore backyard, frightening Mama that Sunday morning. Definitely scores to settle.

"No, little one," Poppa had said, gently but firmly, in response to her plea to go on with them. "Not this time. This is dangerous business. Jackso, bring my stick and the cutlass."

And he'd dismissed them inside to stay and help Mama, who wasn't even aware of what had happened that afternoon.

Pollyread had been livid. Jackson too. They had lain in their beds stiff as boards with outrage and disappointment. The world was happening, dramatic events of great moment, without them.

"You want to go to Morgan's Mount?" Jackson's voice had been a whispering breeze.

She didn't twitch; she didn't even blink.

"You hear me?"

Silence.

"Well, I going," he said, and swung his legs over the edge of the bed to sit up.

"What you mean?" she whispered, raising herself slowly to sit opposite him.

"I going," he said, looking at her with eyes as flat and certain as his voice. "You can come if you want, but I going."

"How?"

"The back way."

Pollyread didn't know any "back way" to Morgan's Mount but didn't doubt her brother, who wandered all over the place.

They looked at each other.

"What we going tell Mama?"

"We going for water."

"The barrels full."

Jackson didn't answer; he knew that. But it was as though everything was set out already. What they were talking about was something that had to be done. And he had to do it.

"We'll get into trouble," Pollyread said, speaking to him in her teacher voice.

"We in trouble already."

No mention had been made on the walk up from Stedman's Corner of the earlier act of disobedience, but both twins knew that that was only because Poppa didn't believe in talking family business in public. When he returned from Morgan's Mount would be time enough.

"You 'fraid?"

"I 'fraid, of course," she said sharply. "You 'fraid too."

Jackson didn't have to answer. They looked at each other a long moment more. Then, without another word, they got up and turned their backs to each other and changed out of their school uniforms. All the while they were listening to Mama's movements in the kitchen.

They crept out of their rooms and down the steps. Jackson fetched his baby cutlass and planting stick and, to Pollyread's annoyance, handed her a water container. He fixed Cho-cho with a glare that made the dog to understand that he was not to move. For once, Cho-cho obeyed.

"Soon come, Mama," Jackson called out as they ran to the gate.

"Where you going?"

"Standpipe," cried Pollyread, at the gate by then.

The sound of her voice throwing the lie at Mama rattled still in Pollyread's head as she thrashed through the unfamiliar bush.

Down the path a little way, out of possible sight of Mama, Jackson had turned off to follow a smooth-worn track that wriggled around the rocks and trees down to Bamboo River.

Pollyread followed without a word, feeling herself sink deeper and deeper into a quagmire of anxiety. She was nervous about the aftermath of this expedition, knowing that the worst part would not be the punishment, which she thought less about the more certain it loomed in her own mind, but the disappointment that would take up residence in Mama's eyes and voice when the deception was revealed. Mama, Poppa too, would be ashamed *for* them, and probably angry with themselves as though it was somehow their fault that the children they'd raised so lovingly had turned out to be disobedient, sneaky, lying pickney.

Added to the disobedience of earlier, it was shaping

up to be a dramatic and tragical evening of reckoning. Still, nothing except rope tying her to the ackee tree would have kept her at home.

They were beside Bamboo River now, a twist of tumbling water freshened by the recent rains, green-rimmed rocks like turtles' backs and weedy-looking plants wriggling lazily in the water. Jackson led them a while up their side of the river, his worn rubber sloppies and stick in one hand, cutlass in the other, and then leapt onto a rock, and then another, and another, and was on the other side of the river. He turned to look back at her, still on the other side.

He was waiting on her to say something — or to come across. Their eyes leaned against each other.

"You know where you going?" asked Pollyread.

He grinned confidently. "Sure."

Pollyread took off her sloppies and hopped on the same stones across the river.

They didn't speak again for a while. The farther they moved away from Bamboo River, the ground under their feet sloping ever more steeply, the more Pollyread felt her guilt and fear fall behind. It was as though the leaves on the branches, as she pushed through them, brushed away her hesitation.

She was aware, the farther they went from home, of the skylight fading toward dusk and eventual darkness.

A time when children, especially children away without permission, should be heading *toward* home.

"Jackso."

He grunted.

"We soon reach?"

He grunted twice. Yes.

"It soon dark."

Not even a grunt.

Now they were moving sideways, it seemed to Pollyread, crablike up the hillside. It was like marching in place, with the scene around them moving past. They were going parallel to a little stream, not Bamboo River anymore but one that probably joined Bamboo farther down. They were walking against the flow.

"Sh-h-h," Jackson suddenly hissed, half turning his head toward her. Pollyread bumped into his bottom as he crouched over; she crouched too.

She didn't hear anything unusual, but waited, trying to quiet her breathing, listening for whatever had stopped Jackson. And eventually she heard something, sounds that weren't being made by birds but were coming from the air. Human voices. Men. Not close, but not that far away either.

The voices, when Pollyread focused on them,

were coming from below where she and Jackson were crouched. Words and phrases floated past them like mosquitoes, including cuss words, thrown not in anger but in the rhythm of everyday speech between the men — there were at least two voices. Nothing made sense to her. And she couldn't see anything much. They were surrounded by trees and bush. But there seemed to be a clearing farther down, where the voices were coming from.

Then they heard another voice, from somewhere else, perhaps above them.

"You there!"

There was no mistaking that voice. Corporal Letchworth. Jackson stiffened.

"What you doing there?" Corpie demanded.

"Who want to know?" the challenge came right back.

"Police!"

"R —!" A different voice.

The twins had inched nearer to the edge of the clearing now and peered out from behind a large tree.

The little stream below divided the scene into two halves. On the far side of the trickling water, the slope gray-blue in the fading light, were the two men whose voices Pollyread had first heard. On this side were Corpie and Poppa. The twins were fifty or more meters away from either group. The adults were glaring at one another.

The two men across the stream were shirtless, each with a cutlass in hand, halfway up the slope among the knee-high shrubs that Pollyread now knew to be coca plants. She wondered for a moment whether Jammy, who was nowhere to be seen, had told them what they had planted and been tending so carefully. Probably not. They faced Corpie and Poppa on the other side defiantly, their chests blue with sweat.

"You trespassing," Corporal Letchworth called to them.

"Says who?" asked one loudly. "This land don't belong to anyone. I-and-I —"

"It belong to me," Poppa shouted, slapping his own chest loud enough for Pollyread to hear. "You don't have no permission to be doing what you doing there. Or to be on my land any at all."

"You have paper to say is your land?" the man taunted.

From the corner of one eye, Pollyread had noticed the other man, the one above, moving farther away from his partner while the shouting match was going on. He'd picked up a crocus bag and was inching away up the slope.

"He have paper," said Corporal Letchworth, "to put you in jail if you don't get your backside off that land right now." The policeman, followed by Poppa, walked down the slope toward the stream. "What you name?"

"I-man don't have to tell you."

"If you don't tell me now," said Corpie menacingly, "you can tell me down at the station."

The man thought for a moment. "Bailey."

"And what your brethren name?" Corpie gestured to where the smaller man was edging his way toward some thick bush at the top of the field.

Bailey looked hard at his partner. "Josephs," he said angrily.

Poppa laughed. "Josephs have more sense than you. He looking after himself."

"Furthermore," Corporal Letchworth said loudly, "you are growing a forbidden substance."

The man laughed mockingly. "Cocoa is forbidden substance? In this country?" He kissed his teeth. "You think I-man is idiot."

Pollyread could see a little smile tilt one corner of Corpie's mouth. "Whereabouts you come from, bwoy?" His tone was almost conversational all of a sudden.

"I am not no 'bwoy,'" Bailey protested, throwing out his chest.

"I have pickney your age," said Corpie, stepping across the little stream onto the other side. "You is bwoy to me. And I am asking you where you come from."

"Not from round these parts," Poppa said, mocking Bailey, "or him would know which cocoa is really cocoa."

Pollyread could see some of the stiff defiance leave Bailey's body.

"Where Jammy?" Corpie demanded suddenly. About twenty meters now separated Corpie and Bailey. Josephs was almost at the line of bush. Poppa, Pollyread noticed, was staring up the slope at a wooden shack that she didn't remember being there when she had come sometime last year with Jackson and Poppa. There was no sign of life there.

Bailey didn't answer.

"He sleeping while you out here working?" Corpie mocked.

"Him gone to Town."

Corporal Letchworth laughed. "If I was you, I would follow him."

Bailey shrugged.

"I-man is right here!" From the hut that stood farther up the far slope, Jammy appeared, stretching as though he'd just woken up.

"Ah-h-h," Corpie sighed loudly.

240

"Babylon, what you come to bother I-man for?" Jammy's tone, Pollyread thought, was what Poppa would have called insolent.

"Not a bother at all, Jammy," Corporal Letchworth responded with a cold smile. "It is a pleasure."

"Not a pleasure for I-man."

"I don't really care what it is for you, Jammy. And you can stop this I-man foolishness. You is no more Rasta than I-man."

"Man free to call himself what he want."

"Man not free to occupy other people land, though."

Jammy laughed. The sound chilled Pollyread: It was the laugh that he had thrown at her on the path, just before grabbing her.

"I see you come back behind Babylon skirt, Mass Gillie," Jammy taunted.

Poppa stepped around Corpie toward Jammy but the policeman held on to Poppa's arm. "Easy, Gillie. Don't let this idiot cause you to make trouble for yourself."

"I did tell you, Jammy —" Poppa began.

"Don't tell him nothing, Gillie," said Corpie.

Poppa ignored Corpie as he waved the envelope he was carrying at Jammy. "This is an order from the court," he shouted, his voice changed, official-sounding. "It say you must get off this land. Now."

"And on top of that," Corporal Letchworth intoned,

241

sounding even more official, "you are undertaking illegal activities on said land. Criminal activities. For that, you have to come with me."

Jammy didn't answer and didn't move. Pollyread noticed a bird hovering high above the men. A little prayer escaped her mind that the bird would drop a load on Jammy's head. Pollyread found herself thinking of Sharon, his half sister, and their recent brief encounter. Jammy's face, even from the twins' distance, had that same slatelike emptiness of expression.

Jammy looked at the ground a long time, ignoring the other people on the hillside as though they had suddenly vanished. Then turning, still without saying a word, he walked slowly back into the shack from which he had emerged.

Everyone waited. Corporal Letchworth, after half a minute or so had passed without sign of Jammy, took a couple steps up the slope toward the shack. As if cued by the policeman's move, Jammy came back out, wearing a tattered shirt and a tam under which his locks were gathered, and carrying his own crocus bag. He looked toward Bailey and Josephs, the latter quite far away by now.

"Come, brethren. Babylon and the system beat down black man again. The birds of the air have nest, but —"

"Don't say another word!" shouted Corporal Letchworth the churchman. "In your mouth the Bible sound like garbage."

This time it was Poppa who restrained Corpie, who had taken two more steps toward Jammy before Poppa grabbed his shoulder. Pollyread saw Corpie's right hand come to rest on the revolver at his waist.

"You a-go shoot I down as well?" Jammy jeered. By now only three or four meters separated him from Corpie and Poppa.

"If I have to," said the policeman. "Don't make me have to." His voice had calmed.

"I don't 'fraid to dead, you know," said Jammy, as though debating the policeman. "This vale of tears don't hold nothing for me except what you see here. I can dead and leave all this without a look behind me." Then he looked directly at Poppa. "But I not going far," he said, his voice firm and clear. Pollyread braced herself, grabbing Jackson's shoulder and digging her fingers into his squirming flesh. "You, Mass Gillie — you not going have no peace from me."

"Mind who you picking fight with, Jammy." Corpie laughed mockingly up at Jammy before Poppa had a chance to do or say anything. "I hear say Mass Gillie pickney beat you up and send you running like mongrel dawg. Them Poppa might just finish you off this time."

Pollyread felt Jackson freeze. She felt exposed, out in the open of a sudden, and wouldn't have been surprised if Corpie had turned and pointed to them. But no one moved. For a moment.

And then, with a roar of rage that propelled him through the air, Jammy launched himself at Corporal Letchworth and landed on top of him, the two of them tumbling to the ground. After a moment of furious struggle, Jammy was up again and running with something bouncing from his hand. It was not his crocus bag, left beside Corpie on the ground, but the little canvas pouch that had been across the policeman's shoulder.

"Stop him!" Corpie cried out, struggling back to his feet. Poppa, momentarily frozen by the surprise attack, sprang after Jammy, who by now was several meters in front and propelled by frenzy.

And heading, Pollyread noticed immediately, toward them.

Before this registered properly, he was right there, a few meters away, and saw them. His eyes widened at the same time as Jackson and Pollyread, with a single thought, threw at him what they had in their hands:

244

Jackson his planting stick, Pollyread her previously encumbering water bucket. Jammy, with a flurry of bad words, came crashing to the ground right beside them. And Poppa, seeing them for the first time, stopped dead in his tracks, his mouth hanging open — *catching fly*, as he himself often described it.

Poppa and the twins staring at each other gave Jammy the chance he needed to scramble to his legs and scamper up into the hillside into the woods behind them.

"What —?" was all Poppa could say, as though he knew no other words.

The twins got shakily to their feet. Pollyread, her legs weak and painful from being so long in one position, felt ready to collapse again. She held on to Jackson's shoulder. She couldn't look Poppa in the face, so she focused on Corporal Letchworth, running up behind Poppa and past him. He seemed intent on going after Jammy, and then was distracted by something on the ground beside the twins and stopped. Pollyread looked down.

Corpie's gun.

She took a step back in recoil. She had never been this close to a gun before, and although it was just lying there on the ground, the images of what guns did flashed around in her head like a light show, frightening her into immobility. Corporal Letchworth stepped nimbly around her and picked it up. He brushed it off like he would a baby, Jammy apparently forgotten.

"What you pickney doing here?" Poppa's angry voice scorched Pollyread's thoughts. "Didn't I tell you —?"

Pollyread felt two sets of eyes pinning her and Jackson to where they stood. For some reason, she looked around for Bailey and Josephs, but they had disappeared.

"How you reach up here? You follow me?"

"No, Poppa," said Jackson quickly, relieved to be able to utter a simple truth.

"So how you reach?"

Jackson waved his hand in the direction Jammy had gone. Just at that moment they heard his voice falling on them out of the darkening air.

"Babylon! Mass Gillie! You going see me again. And feel me fire."

Corporal Letchworth spun around and pointed his gun in the direction of the voice. "Feel that fire, you —" He fired the gun three times into the trees, varying his aim slightly with each shot. Pollyread felt Poppa's arm press herself and Jackson to the ground. Her hands flew to her ears but even so, she heard the bullets burst through the leaves, and then tearing sounds as Jammy scuttled farther out of harm's way.

Poppa's heavy breathing filled the silence that rolled back down the hill.

The three of them were stiff on the ground, but Corporal Letchworth was chuckling. "It never ketch him, but him feel it all right," the policeman said, pleased with himself.

How did Corpie know that he hadn't shot Jammy? Didn't he care? Pollyread felt, beneath the shock and confusion, a trickle of concern — for, of all people, Jammy!

"I still waiting," Poppa said sternly, looking from one to the other of his children as though the interlude of taunting and gunfire had been an unnecessary interruption.

Neither of them had an answer, quiet or otherwise, that would turn away wrath. There *was* no such answer. Pollyread looked finally into her father's eyes because to have avoided them any longer would have been insulting and angered him further. The fury she'd expected to see was there, like a little flame that danced between his flared nostrils and questioning eyebrows.

"Don't be too hard on them, Gillie," Corporal Letchworth said soothingly. "If it wasn't for them, it would be Jammy firing gun down at us instead of the other way around. My gun."

Having come to their rescue, however, the still-chuckling policeman then deserted them. With a pat of Poppa's shoulder as he passed him, Corpie went back down the slope toward the river, leaving an angry, puzzled father to deal with his wayward children.

Reckoning

The twins had walked down from Morgan's Mount in their own haze of anxiety, not speaking even to each other. Poppa and the policeman were walking behind, Corpie's boots thudding ominously on the path down to home. Jackson was very conscious of the water container swinging from Pollyread's hand, empty, banging against her knees, reminding them of their misdeeds with every step. The cutlass and planting stick hung heavy in his own fingers.

The first round of interrogation was behind them. But only the first.

"Is whose idea this was?" Poppa had asked, looking from one to the other. They were still by the tree where they had tripped Jammy. Corporal Letchworth had gone back to the other side of the river and was searching Jammy's hut. "You, Pollyread?"

"Was my idea, Poppa," Jackson jumped in before his sister could answer. "Is me bring her here."

"You didn't bring me," Pollyread protested. "If I didn't come, you would still be home now."

"Not so," Jackson said forcefully. "I knew Poppa wasn't going to let us follow him up here, so I make a plan."

"But you wasn't going to come without me."

"You did 'fraid to come." Jackson's tone was mocking. "Is me convince you."

"Jackso, you can't convince me of anything, and you know it. And you is putty for me."

Jackson felt light-headed. The mixture of nervousness under Poppa's merciless stare and the excitement of the long afternoon made him feel almost giddy on the path.

"Putty?" he shot back, stung by Pollyread's taunt. "You did tremble like a breeze was blowing you 'bout the place."

He realized, looking closely at Pollyread, that she wasn't any more angry at him than he was at her. They were throwing words at each other to distract Poppa, and to delay the inevitable moment of reckoning. It was a hopeless case, they both knew, but it was as though they were in a school play with one of those strange unfunny scripts that Miss Parkinson wrote for grade six every year. They had to play their parts.

"Lie."

The word was like a whip-crack in the cool evening air. They never called each other liars, because they didn't lie to each other. They might keep information to themselves, or deflect a direct question with an indirect answer. But they didn't lie, so they never used the word to or about each other.

"So tell me," Poppa intervened, almost polite, "who must I punish first? Or the most?"

No more than a couple meters apart, Jackson felt as though wires joined him and Pollyread, and as though Poppa's unexpected question had suddenly cut them. They looked at each other and then down at their dusty feet.

Poppa surprised them again by laughing. Not loudly, but the sound was like a warm brush of wind. "You two are a tonic. Come. We can settle this at home. Dark soon come down." He half turned toward Corporal Letchworth, who was coming toward them with a crocus bag of things in his hand and, Jackson noticed, an entire coca plant, pulled up by the roots. Then Poppa turned quickly back to face them squarely. "But this matter is not finished." There was no hint of humor in his voice or eyes now. "Understand that," he said.

"Yes, Poppa," Jackson said, speaking for both of them.

Judgment day was nigh, thought Jackson, who usually left biblical phrases to his sister. For what awaited them was a full recitation to Mama over supper.

Explanations

But it could have been worse. A lot worse. Given all the circumstances, it was probably as good as it could have been.

Poppa began the story — what Pollyread afterward called the saga. Poppa was not the best storyteller in Valley. Even his beloved Maisie would tease him, with a gurgle of impatience, *Hurry up nuh, Gilbert. . . . You want to hear or you don't want to hear?* Poppa would respond sharply and they would fall silent, the twins and Mama bouncing little smiles off one another as he collected his thoughts for the next elaboration of whatever had to be told.

This time, however, they all listened patiently. Poppa had information that not even Corporal Letchworth, who had accepted Mama's invitation to supper, knew. So while the rest of them ate, they followed his story down to the courthouse in Town with Mr. Montgomery, a lawyer he'd done work for over the years, dressed up in his fancy court clothes in front of the judge sweating in his wig. The matter was dealt with very quickly because Mr. Montgomery had made sure that the judge had all the papers. (Besides, there was no one objecting because Jammy didn't know what was being done — and wouldn't have dared to show his face in courthouse, Corpie added with a cold laugh.) Poppa had come away with the envelope he had shown to the policeman, with which to "fix" Jammy's business. An order for recovery of possession, it was called. Poppa rolled the words around on his tongue and put them on the supper table like a present. It meant that it was temporary, that Jammy could challenge it if he wanted. But around the table it was agreed that he was very unlikely to do that.

"And what hurt me," Poppa said, looking at Corporal Letchworth with sad eyes, "is that I try and talk to Jammy." This got everyone's attention. "I try and reason with him. Show him the error of his ways."

"There is no reasoning with that fellow," Corporal Letchworth said. "He have to feel. Like this evening," he chuckled, looking at the twins.

Mama asked, "When you talk to him, Gil?"

"Last week," Poppa said. "I take a whole morning of my time to go up there and talk to him. Them was still sleeping when I reach. In the big sun hot." He shook his head in disapproval.

"What you expect? Them is not serious farmer." Corpie snorted with disdain.

"Them farming serious things, though," said Poppa. His eyes were bright with sudden anger.

"True thing," Corpie sighed as he took a sip of his drink. "I have to organize somebody to watch that place, see what else them doing up there."

"What Jammy doing up there?" Mama, for some reason, was looking straight at Jackson, as if he alone knew. Her voice and eyes were sharp.

"Cocaine." The word was out of his sister's mouth before Jackson had time to think how to answer Mama.

"Cocaine?" She looked at Pollyread, but briefly, and came back to Jackson. "You mean —?"

He could only nod.

Jackson had once heard Mr. Shim say, in answer to a question from one of his tipsy customers as to why he was always so quiet in the midst of the noise and carryings-on in his establishment: "I am like cockroach. I stay close to the ground, no one notice." A cockroach seemed a good thing to be just now.

But Pollyread couldn't leave well enough alone.

When Mama said, "But cocaine is not something you grow," still looking at Jackson, Pollyread chimed in, forever the teacher, "It start with a plant, though."

At which point, fortunately, Poppa got back into

the story. And managed to explain things to Mama without mentioning Jackson's solo expedition to Morgan's Mount to collect the evidence.

"So Jammy planting poison," Mama exclaimed. "The bwoy need a big lick in him head."

Corporal Letchworth humphed. "Him going get more than big lick when I ketch him."

"You have to ketch him first," Pollyread said, slightly miffed by being eased out of the storytelling.

"Don't worry, child," Corpie said, "me will ketch him. He always come back to these parts. The bwoy don't have more sense than a mongoose."

How, Jackson wondered, had Jammy ever thought of bringing this plant, which grew way up in the Andes, according to the magazine, a thousand or more miles away, to a little plot of land behind God's back? If it had not been that the plot of land belonged to the Gilmores, and that what Jammy was growing was poison, Jackson, as a planter himself, would have been impressed. Still, in a funny way, and though he knew he couldn't say it even to Pollyread, he admired Jammy's initiative. But where had he got the coca plants?

"Jammy trying to set himself up as a Don-man," said Mama with a dismissive laugh.

"Him laugh after me," Poppa said, his mind still up

on the distant hillside with Jammy. "Tell me is young people time now. Is dem to run things, him say. And the two jagabat bwoy with him laugh and say is so it must go now. Is that make me vex!"

"Look at this, eh?" Mama shook her head slowly as she spoke. "This is what Miss Mildred pickney come to."

Corpie challenged Mama's view. "Him bring himself to it, Maisie. Mildred is a decent woman. Her other pickney dem don't give trouble. Jammy born giving trouble."

"He wasn't always like that, Philbert."

Jackson and Pollyread looked at each other, ears wide open now.

"True. Him was a good little bwoy," Poppa said, suddenly calm himself.

This was something new: Mama and Poppa speaking warmly of Jammy. *Curiouser and curiouser.*

Jackson had never thought of Jammy as a little boy, much less a good little boy. He had always been much bigger than the twins, and always the "bad bwoy" of the district.

"Well," said Corporal Letchworth, "I have to deal with what come at me. Never mind what him was, that Jammy is a criminal now. I used to try to reason with him, you know, Maisie? Not once. Not twice. But the bwoy just own way. Him head hard like calabash."

There was a moment of silence as they all considered the hardness of Jammy's head.

"But the bwoy fast," Corporal Letchworth resumed with a little laugh at himself. "He bounce me down and grab my gun before I know what happen."

"Gun?" Mama's eyes opened wide. "When was this?"

"Just this evening." The policeman sounded almost casual.

Jackson's belly tightened. He felt the world tilting toward darkness.

"This evening?" Mama was genuinely baffled. Poppa hadn't yet supplied vital links in the story chain, so this talk of guns was very confusing.

Not for long, Jackson thought gloomily.

"Him was out to shoot you?"

"Is your warrior children disarm him."

"Disarm?" asked Mama, hand going to mouth. "How you mean?" So caught up was Mama in the mention of guns and disarming that she didn't seem to realize yet that her warrior children had been where they weren't supposed to be. From all appearances, the twins had simply returned from the standpipe at the same time as their father and the policeman after a chance encounter on the road. Mama hadn't noticed that the water bucket was empty.

Jackson had been watching his father, partly to avoid meeting Mama's eyes. Poppa had, for the moment, resumed the meticulous slicing of his food and his careful chewing. His brown impassive eyes rested on the speakers, one by one. Now he put down his knife and fork and looked directly at Jackson. As Mama already was.

"You mean," Mama began, "that you two pickney was up there with Corporal Letchworth and your father?" The formality of her speech was preparation for the sentence Jackson knew would be pronounced sooner or later.

"Jackso trip him up," said Pollyread brightly.

"Pen too," Jackson added, driven to say something.

"He throw the cutlass at him," Pollyread cried.

"What cutlass?"

"And she throw the bucket."

"Bucket?"

A heavy silence.

"A water bucket," said Poppa.

"What water bucket —?" Mama's hand returned to cover her mouth and her eyes opened even wider, as understanding finally bloomed. "I thought you was going to Standpipe. You was —?"

"Yes," said Poppa. "We didn't know —"

Corporal Letchworth cut him off. "Good thing too," he said, winking at Jackson, whose face was frozen. "If them wasn't there . . ." And he briskly related what had happened.

Jackson stared unwaveringly at the dish of boiled bananas that was halfway between himself and Pollyread. He knew that if he looked anywhere else, even at Pollyread, everything would humpty dumpty. All his transgressions — Common Entrance, bringing Cho-cho inside, sneaking up to Morgan's Mount the first time to get the coca plant, then sneaking up there again this afternoon — descended on his mind in a foul-smelling cloud.

"Well, Mister Man?" Mama's voice was soft, but not tender. "And you, Miss Lady."

Jackson continued to stare at the green bananas. There was a piece in his mouth right now that tasted like wet newspaper.

"Cat get your tongue?" said Mama, anger curling the edges of her words.

The rearrangement of the table to accommodate the policeman placed the parents next to each other, and in the corner of a watery eye Jackson noticed Poppa's hand reach out and cover Mama's and squeeze.

"Well," Poppa sighed, "maybe if they wasn't there, worse things would have happened." He spoke carefully.

"Jammy is a desperate man. And a desperate man with a gun — who knows what terrible thing he might have done."

A moment's silence while Poppa's words settled.

"True word," said Corporal Letchworth. "Perhaps they were there for a reason."

"They were there," said Mama forcefully, "because they hard of hearing and only understand English when it suit them. If I did disobey my father like that, you think I would be able to sit on a chair now?" No one responded: The tone of the question gave its own answer. Jackson knew that Mama was not about to make their bottoms un-sit-downable-upon, but that wasn't any comfort at the moment.

"My daddy too," said Poppa. But there was a lightness in his voice that gave Jackson a ray of hope. "But maybe they save our lives too. Who to know?"

Mama grunted, not entirely convinced, nor entirely forgiving.

Poppa put a forkful of food in his mouth.

Corporal Letchworth slurped his drink and swallowed noisily.

Slowly, Pollyread lifted her mug of cocoa and sipped delicately from it.

Jackson, to his own amazement, heard himself say: "Another thing, Mama." *What are you doing?* His own voice banged inside his head. He felt Pollyread's eyes like searchlights from across the table.

"What other thing, Mister Man?" One shoulder lifted, as if in preparation.

"Cho-cho," Jackson croaked, and his sister's eyes swiveled heavenward in anticipation of disaster. Despite the warning in his head, Jackson thought he was doing the right thing, and was determined to proceed. If only he could find his voice.

"Cho-cho was up there too? I thought —"

Jackson croaked at the same time as Pollyread rescued him. "Not up there, Mama. Here."

"In the house?" Mama, forehead rippling with confusion, bent over and looked under the table. She straightened. "But Cho-cho always in the house." She looked at Jackson as if her son might be a little soft in the head. Pollyread's eyes said: *You start it, now you finish it.*

"Him was in the house that night," Jackson said in a rush.

"What night?" Poppa chimed in, suddenly interested.

Jackson didn't dare pause — he'd probably choke — so he rushed into his story of the thunderstorm, which recreated itself in his head. The thunder and lightning of the twins' misbehavior rumbled and flashed behind his eyes; the words poured out like heavy water flushing through his conscience. He fixed his unblinking gaze on the table in front of him. Hands. Four pairs of hands resting on the dining table. He told his jumbled tale to them, the words clattering onto the table like marbles, all colors and sizes, making different sounds. To his surprise the fingers made no effort to catch the words. Finally, the last one rolled off into the surrounding silence.

One set of fingers, Poppa's, had started to drum on the table. Jackson knew the signal. Trouble. But he felt lighter. He hadn't known what he was going to say, or even that he was going to speak at all. But the words that had tumbled out of him, which had now evaporated into the air like mist in sunlight, had been bundled up inside him for days. And now he felt . . . like a balloon.

The drumroll of his father's fingers merged with another rumbling, which grew like a wave and overwhelmed Poppa's annoyance. Mama. Laughing. Cackling.

"Philbert . . ." Jackson finally looked up. Mama was gasping for breath, everyone else watching her closely. Pollyread's fingers were pressed over her mouth. "Is a good thing . . . he not in court . . . giving statement. He would confuse . . . the judge . . . everybody." Mama wiped away tears of laughter.

"Well, he don't confuse me," Poppa said, stern as a piece of board. "I know exactly what he saying. That dawg —" Right on cue, Cho-cho scrambled out from under the table and stood on his hind legs to put his front paws on Poppa's leg. Poppa looked down on the dog as though a small spaceship had landed on his thigh. A squeak escaped between Pollyread's clamped fingers. Then Mama noticed Cho-cho and her laughter inundated the table. Corpie added his hearty growl, and Poppa eventually threw up his hands in despair and allowed himself an embarrassed smile. Jackson alone kept himself serious, waiting. Just in case.

The policeman pushed back his chair. "Well, my work don't finish for the night yet. Sister Maisie, thank you kindly for an excellent repast. Don't be too hard on the little ones," he added, bathing the twins with a broad smile, "they did mean well."

Mama's laughter drained away, and her eyes brushed the twins with shadow as she grunted noncommittally.

The adults stood up.

"Poppa?" Pollyread called softly.

Poppa, on the way to the door with Corporal Letchworth, turned to look at her.

"When you come back, I need you to help me write my speech," said Pollyread, with a little smile twitching the corners of her mouth.

"Speech?" Mama and Poppa spoke together.

"For Monday," said Pollyread in a little voice. Normally she would have preened in the center of this pool of attention, but Jackson understood her air of reluctance: She was testing, like Cho-cho sniffing the air, to see how far they had emerged from under the cloud of parental displeasure.

"What is happening on Monday?" asked Corporal Letchworth.

"Prize giving," Jackson ventured.

"Ah yes," said Corpie, remembering. Nova, his daughter, one of the bright sparks of grade five, would almost certainly be getting a prize.

"You giving a speech at the prize giving?" asked Mama, sounding a little distracted, still chewing over the strange stories she'd just heard. "You didn't tell anybody that?"

"She is valedictorian," said Jackson, proud of his sister — and relieved at the apparent success of the distraction.

There was a collective intake of breath and then a brief cloudburst of congratulatory clapping and laughter. Mama, back fully with them now, beamed. "You need to take out you best shirt and wash it tomorrow. And put it out in the sun. I will be down at market. Your good shirt need to mend, Jackso, I don't know what you do with you clothes. I will do that when I come back."

"Yes, Mama," they chimed together.

"You know what you going to say?" Poppa asked, delight and pride bubbling in his voice. The sun rose again in Pollyread's eyes. Jackson relaxed a little.

"Sort of," Pollyread replied. "But I need you and Mama to help me polish it."

Jackson, once again, had to acknowledge a grudging — and in this case welcome — admiration for his twin's technique in parental manipulation. Pollyread probably knew exactly what she was going to say. Finding things to say was never her problem. Miss Watkins had told her two days ago about being valedictorian. But she had not told their parents, and had sternly sworn her brother to silence about "her" news. It was as if Pollyread had instinctively known that the value of such news was going to be enhanced by *when* it was shared, and had decided that *this* was the moment. Bringing in Mama and Poppa before a word had been written down was a means of completely dispelling the last traces of the pall that had hung over their heads throughout the evening. Jackson heard in his mind the ba-DAM of the winning domino slammed down on the table in the corner of Shim's rum bar, where the men played most nights. His sister, he had to admit, was a master — mistress, she would insist.

Vale

The library of Marcus Garvey Primary was in the old building in which the parents of many of today's children, Poppa included, had themselves attended school. It now housed the principal's office, teachers' common room, and library, which was actually a large cupboard where supplies such as boxes of chalk and exercise books and ledgers had once been kept. Those things were now piled in a corner of Miss Phillipson's office, threatening to topple at any moment if someone stamped too hard on the old wooden floor. Probably, in the days when the old building had been a dwelling house, this space had been the pantry. Shelves ran along each wall, and there was room for a narrow table that Miss Phillipson had brought a few years before. "The man whose name adorns this school was a writer and printer," the principal would declare from time to time. "We honor his name with these few books as we have here." Few enough they were, and Miss Watkins was their zealous guardian.

She had Pollyread look up the word *valedictorian* in a battered dictionary. Its root word was the Latin *vale*, farewell. The valedictorian, therefore, was the person who said farewell. Pollyread liked the word *farewell*. It had more substance to it than *good-bye*, was more grand. Everybody said good-bye and for all sorts of little things, like going down to Town or going home after a visit. Leaving Marcus Garvey Primary for the last time, to move to Town and onward into the wider world, was surely something worthy of a farewell, one with a tragic wave and a little eye water. As in "vale of tears," which old people were always talking about "soon shuffling off." *A perfect fit,* Pollyread thought.

"You will be speaking on behalf of your classmates," Miss Watkins had cautioned right away at their first little conference in the library.

"Yes, Miss."

"So you need to ask them what they want you to say on their behalf."

"Yes, Miss."

"What they would say if they had the chance to speak."

"All of them, Miss?"

"Penelope!"

"That would take a very long time, Miss."

Miss Watkins knew her star pupil well: She had

followed this road of words many times before, sometimes right into a brick wall or a swamp.

"You know very well what I mean, Polly," she said sternly.

"Yes, Miss."

Pollyread was going to miss Miss Watkins. There would be new teachers at St. Giles in Town, and surely a few of them would be nice, and interesting, and helpful. But none of them would be Miss Watkins, who was all of those things and more. She *liked* Pollyread, and wasn't afraid of her nimble mind or her sharp tongue or her cunning ways, because Miss Watkins was like that herself. Pollyread had read once in a book about someone "who wore his authority lightly." Poppa had explained that it meant someone whose authority and power did not need to be thrown about to impress people; people recognized it right away. Miss Watkins was like that. She wasn't like some other teachers at Marcus Garvey Primary who tried to intimidate the brighter children because they asked questions that those teachers didn't always know the answers to. Pollyread wanted to talk about those teachers in her valedictory speech. Not by name, of course, but so that everyone would know. But she knew she couldn't. It would only get Miss Watkins into those teachers' bad books for encouraging such facetyness. Besides, her parents would be embarrassed. But, Pollyread thought wistfully, she would be a heroine to her classmates. . . .

Now she was just one of the 327 students sitting in assorted chairs and benches in the cooling quadrangle of the school yard — for the moment anyway. Soon, too soon, *her* moment would come. Hopefully it would come before the rain. They sat under a vault of blue sky — *God's bald head,* as Pollyread thought of it — but it was fringed by dirty gray clouds that were heavy with the near certainty of rain. Rain was always welcome in Valley, and you didn't curse it in case it kept away out of pique. But there were times, and this was one of them, when your life was hostage to the clouds' whimsy. This afternoon, children and adults, students and teachers, families and well-wishers, threw eyes and anxious prayers at the sky.

Pollyread was in two minds about whether she wanted God to wait until she'd finished her *vale* before pulling the clouds over his bald head. She wanted her moment up on the stage, in the spotlight. But she knew that many people present felt that she enjoyed the spotlight much more than was proper for any "little" girl. That was their business, and not the source of her uncertainty. But today's spotlight was bigger than any she had ever had before, bigger even than Common Entrance.

That morning, surprise though it had been, was in front of just the school. And the surprise of it had helped: She'd just said things as they came into her head.

This time, however, she had known about today for a week. She had a speech written out. Miss Watkins had coached her on it, and typed it out on a typewriter she had at her home. The two folded sheets were in the pocket of Pollyread's school uniform, crackling every time she moved. And most of the people who lived in Top Valley were gathered, and many from Cross Point and as far down as Cuthbert Ridge. As the school had marched in to the loudspeaker playing "Land of Hope and Glory," she'd noticed Corporal Letchworth and his missus, sitting beside Mama and Poppa and similarly dressed in Sunday AME clothes. She'd also seen Constable Phillips and another policeman whom she didn't know looking out of place in uniform on the edge of the crowd. In case Jammy showed up, she figured. He had two siblings at Marcus Garvey, though she doubted that he had any interest in seeing them get prizes, if they did.

Everything was in place. All the parents, those whom she knew wanted her to give a good speech, and probably some others who didn't. (*Don't pay mind to bad-minded people,* Mama had tried to teach them.) It was a ceremony, a ritual she had taken part in every year from grade one through to grade five. Like a familiar dream. It went on too long, and the speeches were boring, and the sun was hot, and a couple times she remembered there had been showers, causing consternation and the rearranging of things. But all that was past. Today was real. And would be the last prize giving. In fact, it would be the last day that she would be a pupil (*inmate,* she sometimes thought) of Marcus Garvey Primary. After this afternoon, the world would change forever. Inside her, she felt it changing already.

And that was why she felt nervous. Everyone — her classmates, her parents, the teachers, Miss Watkins, and even Miss Phillipson, who had been very friendly over the past week, perhaps because she knew it was her last week of Pollyread — was looking forward to another perfect prize giving. And she, too-big-for-her-boots Penelope Elizabeth Gilmore, might spoil it for them.

So maybe it *was* time for Massa God to intervene. Pollyread looked up at the sky. His bald head was still very much there, beaming blue down at them. But smaller. The fringe of clouds was a little thicker now, and ragged. Perhaps . . . she didn't dare even *think* the full thought, in case she put her goat-mouth on the proceedings. (And where was Goat, she wondered.)

*   *   *

273

Grade four did a calypso as their contribution to the afternoon's entertainment. One of Miss Singh's daughters, Sintra, was the lead singer, dressed as a market woman and carrying a little basket on her head with an ease and skill that Pollyread envied. Sintra would be, Pollyread reflected, the next "star" at Marcus Garvey Primary, because after the calypso, dressed in her rainbow blouse but school uniform skirt, she collected several prizes.

Grade five's performance, an Anancy story dramatized, with Revival singing at the end, went on too long. By the time Vince "Trueblood" Parchment, Jammy's younger brother, who played Anancy, had wiped the last speck of porridge from his mouth, God's bald head was like a dainty little blue saucer adrift on a huge iron-colored tablecloth.

An eye on the relentless clouds, Miss Watkins hurried her grade sixers onto the stage. "Just stan' up anywhere," she hissed over and over as they filed up onto the little stage, tripping over one another's feet. "And talk clear!" They did three poems by Louise Bennett. Miss Watkins had made them into a little play, with different students starring. Pollyread and Jackson were in the chorus. Aidrene Albert, show-off AA, champion elocutionist of the district, led the first poem, Jeremiah "Bus Driver" Darby the second. But it was

Christine Aiken — shy, hang-back Christine, adorned in bandanna cloth, her lips, finger- and toenails bright red — who had the crowd clapping in time and banging on their chairs by the end, her energy and flair in the last poem carrying her classmates to an excellence of timing and intonation not achieved in rehearsal and bringing a wide smile of prideful delight to Miss Watkins's face.

Various members of the board had given out the prizes to different grades. Now the sixers were to be honored by the chairman himself, a tall, serious reverend who had not found Christine's antics amusing. He came onto the stage on one side while the sixers went off on the other, back to their seats.

Jackson's quartet got the cup, a large one, for the best agricultural project of the year, a little herb garden that Jackson had designed and supervised, driving his less work-inclined friends like (they claimed) a slave master, and ending up doing much of the work himself anyway. They had a fine time giving one another high fives as they bounced back onto the stage and Bollo held the cup aloft as though he had been personally responsible for the triumph. Their parents drowned out all others with their clapping.

Aidrene won the prize for speech. She was destined for Town the following week to compete against eleven-year-olds from all over the island in the national speech championships. One of Uncle Josie's small buses was already booked for the day to collect a busload of Marcus Garvey children, including Pollyread, to be there to cheer AA on, led by Miss Watkins.

Tafiri Smith, to no one's surprise, won the prize for art. He was a quiet boy, except on the soccer field, where, dreadlocks flying, he was a fierce and talented striker, the star of Marcus Garvey's team. The eldest child of a couple who farmed just below Cross Point, Tafiri led a troop of neatly turned-out siblings to school every morning, one in every grade. A cry of "Righteous!" came from Tafiri's father as his son collected his prize, art supplies.

Jeremiah Darby, to the surprise of many, won a prize for "most diligent student." He was the class clown, but only when there wasn't any work to be done. When there was, his head was bent closest and most steadfastly to the desk, and not only because of his thick-lensed spectacles. Jeremiah did his trademark bob-and-weave bus drive up to the stage; even Miss Phillipson smiled.

To almost everyone's surprise, including her own, Christine Aiken won a prize for "most helpful student." Expecting to take no further part in the proceedings, she hadn't bothered to change out of her costume, and came onto the stage barefoot, pulling down her bandanna skirt. From the back of the crowd, her mother beamed. She couldn't applaud, as she held a child in each wiry arm. They clapped their sister for her.

"And the final prize," Miss Phillipson announced, "is for the best overall student in grade six. Our Common Entrance scholarship winner — Penelope Gilmore."

Pollyread felt herself drowning in the applause, and numb. Not with shock or surprise — Miss Watkins had told her from days earlier how the program would be organized. But the long afternoon of prize giving and performances and speeches had left her drained of energy, almost sleepy. Still, Mama and Poppa would be smiling broadly and puffed with pride, so she put a small plastic smile on her face as she went onto the stage.

The smile on Miss Phillipson's face seemed genuine. That did surprise Pollyread. She thought that the principal was probably just relieved to know that Pollyread, finally, was moving on out of her life. Pollyread, feeling a little guilty for her wicked thought, stretched her own smile as she took her prize — she glimpsed the words A–Z of between the strips of decorative ribbon — and shook the principal's cool, small hand, and then took the book from the chairman of the board's larger, rougher fist.

"Thank you," she whispered.

"Penelope, as you know," Miss Phillipson said, turning back to the audience, "is also our valedictorian. And she will now say a suitable good-bye on behalf of all the grade sixers." Miss Phillipson smiled as she emphasized "all." Miss Phillipson adjusted the microphone to Pollyread's height, then retreated to the chairs at the back of the stage, followed by the chairman.

Pollyread looked pleadingly at Mama, whose white church hat made her easy to find near the back of the crowd. Mama pointed her thumb at the sky in a blessing of encouragement. Poppa, standing with the men at the back so that the women could sit, waved his hand and grinned. Pollyread looked up at the sky. Massa God winked the last little piece of blue at her. Cloud obscuring the mountains around, enclosing their world. A distant rumble of thunder like furniture being moved around an immense house.

Pollyread pushed her hand into her uniform pocket and wrestled the piece of paper with her speech out, unfolded it. Saw the lines and lines of letters that were supposed to be the words that Miss Watkins had painstakingly typed out for her to say — and understood not one of them! It was as though she were a baby again, when she'd put down Poppa's books on the floor and stare at the black markings, certain that great secrets and delights dwelt therein, because Poppa enjoyed staring at them but, frustratingly, having no means of tasting those delights, even when she licked the page.

She looked up from her sheets of gibberish to see if anyone else had noticed her confusion. Her audience, faces she'd known all her life, was a vast quilt of colors. She recognized the colors, but not the faces! But she sensed their collective expectation.

"Friends. Romans. Valley people." Pollyread heard her own voice like a stranger's elsewhere on the stage, or like the words had come out of the sky — surely that was where they had formed, and then fallen into her open mouth.

Pollyread heard a sharp breath taken in behind her. Miss Phillipson. And titters — teachers. The quilt of people in front of her rippled with laughter.

"Once upon a time . . ." Her voice was swallowed by a pounding inside her head. Voices in the audience hooted with laughter like flapping birds. If her feet had not felt like cement pylons, she would have bolted from the stage and kept running forever. Then a muted but firm voice behind her said: "Take a deep breath, Penelope." Accustomed for years to obeying that voice, Pollyread filled her lungs with what felt like fire, and blew it out. The world seemed to vanish for the moment. Only that voice was real. "Now," said Miss Phillipson, "take another one." And Pollyread did. And balance was restored. The faces, no longer laughing but still filled with lively expectation, came into focus again. She even glimpsed Mama's — worried, willing her strength and calm. She looked down at the paper she was holding and saw words, just words, not blurries or blobs, which had a moment ago resembled bird droppings. For good measure she took another deep breath of air that was clean and cool with promise again.

"Sorry," she said, and sighed. "Once more from the top."

"Reverend Giddishaw," she read out from her paper, "Chairman of the School Board. Mrs. Joy Grenair, Junior Education Officer, Ministry of Education. Miss Annabelle Phillipson, Principal, Marcus Garvey Primary School . . ." Miss Watkins had warned her that she had to read these names at the beginning; it was the proper, expected thing to do. What Miss Watkins hadn't told her — they hadn't rehearsed that part of it, Miss Watkins had just typed them in — was Miss Phillipson's first name: Annabelle. Pollyread didn't know anyone in Valley named Annabelle, but that wasn't it. Annabelle was a child's name. The picture of Miss Phillipson as a baby, fuzzy one second and very sharp the next, a few days old like Keneisha's baby, Abeo, but with half-glasses and large ivory-colored teeth, flooded Pollyread's mind. The markings in front of her, just when they had become words, went silly again. Disaster rushed toward her in a mighty wind that tore at the paper in her hand.

Except that the wind was not of disaster but, Pollyread recognized immediately and with rapturous thanksgiving, of salvation.

Enough! said Massa God with a roll of his thunderous shoulders, and shook all the rain in the world from his dark gray cloak of clouds.

"Man scatter," was how Poppa described the scene later, cackling like a schoolboy.

The rain fell like a plague of little stones flung into the crowd. People dodged and danced in a futile attempt to avoid the missiles. Pollyread, struck still by the sudden barrage and numb with relief, watched, fascinated, as the paper in her hand folded around her fingers like a bandage, dribbling streaks of red and black onto her wrist and the ground. It didn't occur to her to get off the open stage to shelter. In a few seconds her uniform became a slimy second skin and she could taste the sweat and pomade from her scalp running into her mouth. The rain on the zinc roof of the old school building drowned out her very thoughts. Her mouth tasted salty and her eyes were burning. She realized, saltiness rising behind the floodgates of her eyes, that she had started to cry. She swallowed her rainy tears, hoping nobody noticed. Just as she thought the barriers would give way she felt a hand on her shoulder, turning her around. "Come, pickney," Miss Watkins said, tender but urgent. "You favor wet chicken. Come."

With as much dignity as she could command, Pollyread allowed herself to be led off the stage by Miss Watkins, into the shelter of the staff room. As they walked past the sound system box, there was an explosion and a flash of blue and red lights and a sharp smell of burning that made both of them cough and laugh.

Miss Watkins, who was none too dry herself, got a towel from somewhere and shared it with Pollyread.

"We'll have to call you the rainmaker, Penelope," said Miss Phillipson from right beside her, making Pollyread jump. The principal's voice was as cool as the air. As if Pollyread was responsible for the deluge. But there was a little twinkle — it may have been rain but Pollyread decided it was a twinkle — in the corner of Miss Phillipson's eyes. And she remembered that calm, quiet voice that had saved her from doom. Pollyread gave up her straight face for a smile.

"Yes, Miss," said Pollyread, and found herself bobbing

in a curtsy, something she only did when she and her friends were practicing quadrille for the festival — the rain must have seeped into her brain.

Not quite the *vale* she had envisaged. Closer to a vale of tears. But she was still standing.

Leaving

Miss Phillipson was a magician. As soon as she dismissed the school for summer holidays — a distant matchstick figure on the stage waving frantically and shouting at people who mostly couldn't hear her — the rain stopped. Within five minutes, the sun was out, blades of light flashing off the puddles of water.

In a jumble of emotions as thick as the shifting clouds, Pollyread walked out of the school yard of Marcus Garvey for the final time with Mama. Poppa, Jackson, and other grade-six boys and some fathers had remained to help stack up the chairs. *Wherever life takes us,* her undelivered speech had proclaimed, *we will always carry a piece of Marcus Garvey Primary School in our hearts.* At the time of writing it, she'd joked to herself, *Which piece? The coolie plum tree?* Her favorite place at the school, especially in season — *that* she'd miss. Miss Watkins had asked her what she meant and the best she'd been able to say was, "Like a smell that you never smell again, but you always remember how it smell."

She'd said good-bye to all her teachers, solemnly promising those who asked that she would indeed come back and see them. She didn't know whether she would, or whether she even wanted to. She was already missing Miss Watkins, and already forming the determination to be a teacher too, and come back to Top Valley and teach, eventually becoming principal — though not a principal like Miss Phillipson. But Miss Watkins lived below Cuthbert Ridge so maybe, when Pollyread and Jackson came home for holidays . . .

The future suddenly yawned at her like a hungry dog . . . weeks and months away from (she swiveled her head) all this . . . down in that violent city full of wicked people who mocked country bumpkins while they were busy killing one another and smoking God knew what — cocaine! . . . There was one comforting thought: They would be with Aunt Shiels and Uncle Josie. They were family and had a large house — the twins would each have their own room for the first time. But most of the time they would be at school anyway, at the mercy of those crude Town children. . . . Maybe Jackson was right: Stay home where you belong and where you have your place and people.

But as she was walking between the cracked concrete gateposts of Marcus Garvey Primary, clinging like a baby to Mama's damp dress and inhaling her familiar smell,

Pollyread knew that the contraption of barbed wire and fence posts posing as a gate that Mr. Wadsworth the caretaker would drape across the opening when everyone was gone was already separating her from whatever her life had been up to that moment.

For a Monday afternoon, especially a rainy one, Shim's Grocery and Saloon was well patronized, both sides of it. There was an unusually large population of children, especially grade sixers, who had been aware from grade three or four of the tradition at Shim's that on the first day of summer holidays every grade sixer got a double scoop of ice cream — free. Mrs. Shim knew all the children anyway, so even overgrown grade fivers didn't have a chance of fooling her. In any case, all other children got their cones at half price.

Miss Clarice had three fires going that she had kept valiantly alive through the rain. On two of them kerosene pans were perched, one with her mainstay soup, the other with boiled corn. The heaped coals of the third fire bore, among the hot stones and ash-caked wood, chunks of yam with blackened skins, pieces of saltfish, and cobs of corn roasting to black-and-yellow perfection.

There was no need for anyone in Valley to cook supper tonight. *Pot turn down*, as Poppa would say.

Jackson was one of a fluid group of boys, between six and ten in number, who were challenging one another to one-hand catch with a rubber ball — the other hand bearing an ice-cream cone or a cob of corn, or in Trucky's case, both. Good-natured mockery and teasing fell sooner or later on everybody, because catching the ball was of less importance than keeping the food safe in hand.

Keeping his eye on the yellow rubber ball, which seemed to get smaller and darker as the evening came down, Jackson tried to focus on tomorrow. He would be able to lie in bed if he wished, or get up as early as he liked and go out into the backyard and inspect the plants. The damage there had not been entirely repaired — there was still work to be done, and he could start on that bright and early tomorrow morning if he wished. Or he could wander around Valley, looking for some of these same friends he was playing catch with. *Free as a bird,* he thought, catching sight of a flock of white wings whispering home in the purple light.

But he wasn't free yet. Tonight still had to be got through. There he'd be caught between his parents' eyes, with Pollyread skewering him for good measure. Tonight, Jackson thought as he flung the ball at Janja, was going to be the night of decision. Nothing had been said by anybody, but Jackson knew. This being the end of term, there would be talk of the summer holidays — and beyond. Plans would be made about uniforms and books and organizing with Aunt Shiels and Uncle Josie for them to stay there during the next term. Everybody talking around Jackson, as though, despite not getting first choice of St. Giles, he would still be going there. Mama, unusually for her and without telling the twins why, had dressed herself up one morning and gone as far as Stedman's Corner with them a couple weeks back, and caught the bus to Town. She was back home by the time they returned from school, still closemouthed. Talking it over, the twins had agreed on her mission: to organize for Jackson to go to St. Giles. Pollyread was delighted, as though the whole thing was her idea. Jackson had kept his own counsel.

He wished he knew what he wanted. He knew what he *really* wanted, that hadn't changed since he'd known himself: to grow things. To work the backyard, and the ground by Bamboo River and, now that Jammy had been evicted by Corpie and the judge in Town, the ground at Morgan's Mount. That was what he still wanted: to work with Poppa and grow things to sell, for people to eat, and flowers to make houses beautiful. The thought of being surrounded all the time by the big buildings of Town, walking on the dirty asphalt streets, heat and sweat and noise all the time . . .

But he probably wouldn't be allowed to do what he wanted. He was beginning to accept that. And he had had time to think about things, and was getting used to the idea of King's College. By himself. Without Pollyread. Just boys for a change. *Like now,* he thought, watching the ball fly between his friends. None of them would be at King's, indeed no one else from Marcus Garvey. He felt sad about that. But they had the whole summer ahead now. And perhaps there would be new friends to be made in Town. Maybe Town wouldn't be too bad after all. Miss Pollyread would just have to manage at St. Giles without him.

Still, maybe he needed to talk to Poppa before they got home. Man to man.

Leaning against the doorpost of the grocery side of Shim's, nibbling on her roast corn, Pollyread watched the boys playing and the smaller children running after one another outside the circle of the ball game. Light and shadow, sun and cloud, chased each other across the open ground also, playing. Distantly, thunder rumbled every few minutes. Behind her, Mama and her friends were enjoying soft drinks and beers inside the grocery. The men, including Poppa, were on the other side, in the rum bar. Women were not unwelcome in the bar, but when gathered in numbers like now, they tended to stay in the grocery, which had a longer counter. Today Mr. Shim had found extra stools from somewhere and everyone who wanted a seat had one, including Mama, who looked tired.

But Pollyread wasn't listening to what the group of women behind her was saying, nor was she paying much attention to the children scattered around Stedman's Corner. Pollyread felt distant from it all, unable to share in the jollification of her schoolmates. Her thoughts were coated with the cool moist evening that was coming down, darkening Stedman's Corner.

From she'd known herself, Pollyread had always had two ambitions in her life. The first one changed from time to time. One month it was to be a teacher like Miss Watkins. Though she didn't know whether she could deal with bad-behave children. Or a librarian, like Miss Brimley, because Pollyread couldn't imagine a greater joy than having books end to end in her life.

But her other ambition was as fixed as the time of AME's Sunday morning service, from ever since she was small until now. It was to sell produce in Redemption Ground market at the edge of Town. Like Mama.

Listening to the women inside with Mama, who had known Pollyread for as long as she'd known herself, Pollyread was remembering when Mama used to take her, or send her with Aunt Zilla, to Redemption Ground. Remembering the banana trash and the orange peel and the flies, and the smell of meat and fish from the butchers at the other end of the big shed that was the main market. Remembering the fruit that was always there to eat, and the other vendors' children to play with, jumping over the piles of produce and baskets, the vendors grabbing and shouting after them. Mid-morning, the fried dumplings and saltfish that would appear like manna in the white-and-blue enamel bowls. In the late afternoon before they started packing up, a little corn pork or oxtail and boiled green bananas, with hardo bread and, in season, poor people's butter, avocado pear.

But what Pollyread remembered most keenly from those times was the feeling of being at the center of the business of the world. The customer's fingers testing fruits and vegetables under the watchful eye of the vendor. The quiet haggling for the best price, the quarrels and making-ups, the loyalties between purchasers and vendors that extended over years and generations. Mama's deep apron pockets, where the crumpled paper money and the tinkling coins lived.

Every now and then someone would want to buy something and Mama's back would be turned, or she'd have gone to the toilet at the far end of the shed. "Watch these things for me, Miss Gladys," she would call to the tall, thin lady with the gold front tooth who had occupied the spot next to theirs from before Pollyread was born. "Two dollar fifty for cabbage," Pollyread would sing out right after Mama left, knowing that cabbage was the scarcest thing that week and everyone else had it for three dollars or more. And once the customer stopped, Miss Gladys could only look at her hard, because to say anything about the correct price would drive the customer away. Pollyread would sell several kilograms of cabbage before Mama came back to hear the tale from Miss Gladys. "I never know, Mama," she would say innocently, plum juice and syrup in her voice. "I think I did hear you say two dollar, I was trying to make some more money." And she would push the money down into Mama's big apron pocket and walk off, looking contrite and aggrieved at the same time, but filled with pride in herself. But for her having been there at that particular time, she would say to herself, the cabbage wouldn't sell at all. Miss Gladys still had a big pile of three-dollar cabbage in front of her!

She missed all that excitement, even the scoldings. Between studying for the Common Entrance exam and recovering from it, she had not been down to Redemption Ground as often as before. And now . . .

Phrases like *big opportunity for the pickney dem* and *better life for herself* were repeated over and over by the women and men inside Shim's until they floated in the air like banners.

Book is like bird, Mama was always telling the twins. *You can go anywhere in the world in them, and them will take you anywhere you want to go.* A book was a world for Pollyread, and she spent a lot of her time in the world of books, happy as the day was long — and the day was never long enough for a good book. Books, it seemed to her now, were taking her away to a new life — so people said over and over. Pollyread wasn't sure how she felt about that. She felt, inside herself, a closing of windows.

She jumped as she heard her name called, as if from far away. It was Poppa's voice calling her. She looked into the bar section, where he was sitting at the end of the counter, and met his eyes smiling at her. He beckoned her with a toss of his head — *like the goat,* Pollyread thought.

Once upon a time, up to not so long ago, Pollyread would have gone immediately to him. From she'd been a little girl she'd loved the rumbling sounds of the men's voices, and the smells of sweat and liquor mingled in the air around her. The men and Mr. Shim had known her from she was born. They'd tease her and pat her head and give her sweets. Tonight — which was probably why Poppa was calling her — they would make much of her accomplishments. But lately, she didn't know why, the men's voices seemed to pause when she came in, as though secrets were being passed around with the cigarettes the men offered one another. When she thought about it, as she did, she realized that this change had coincided with her starting to grow taller. Shooting up, as they said, like she was a plant. But it wasn't being compared to a plant that she minded either. She wasn't sure what it was. But now she felt uncomfortable inside the bar, as she had started to feel sometimes inside her body.

She shook her head at Poppa, slowly, to let him know that she really didn't want to go to him. Thankfully, he shrugged, still smiling, and turned back to Mr. Cowan beside him.

"Come, Pen," she heard Mama say beside her, easing off the stool. "Call your brother and let we go home. Night falling."

Jackson didn't mind being pulled out of his game, but he wasn't pleased that Poppa wasn't coming home with them. He ran back into Shim's and Pollyread, waiting with Mama at the start of the path home, watched him in earnest conversation with Poppa for several minutes.

Encounter

Accompanied by mist, they climbed into the night. Trees, boulders, bush floated around them. They seemed at times, the vapor curling around their legs, to be floating themselves. The widely spaced lampposts on the path wore skirts of gold and silver that faded completely after a few steps. Mama's flashlight, which she'd remembered this time, did what it could in between. The three Gilmores kept up a steady stream of conversation, less to say anything important than to make their presence known to anyone who might be themselves afloat in the silvery darkness. "Is you that Maisie?" "Yes, Gertie-chile." "Stand steady where you is, we coming through." "All right, come." Familiar shapes and smells would glide by like phantoms and disappear.

By the time the twins and Mama reached up to the house, they were exhausted. Even Cho-cho's greeting was restrained, as if muted by the mist. He whined happily but didn't bark. The nose he nuzzled everyone with was cold. The house seemed far away, looming around the single light that had been left on in the shed, which wore a yellow halo. Mama rested on the big stone by the gate, ignoring the wetness of it — something, Jackson noted, that she would not have allowed either of her children to do in their nice school uniforms.

"Lord, me tired," Mama sighed. Her face shone with perspiration, her voice with relief at reaching home. Pollyread sidled over to her mother and leaned against her, like a fading plant seeking support, Jackson thought. He just wanted to get inside, and turned to look at the house in order to make his point.

And as Jackson stared at the house itself, cradled by the whiteness that edged its familiar outline, the light in the shed seemed to split it into two shapes: the house itself, solid and immovable, and — something that moved. A person. A man. A man with something in his hand that danced in the light. Jackson knew it right away. A cutlass. And after the bubble of fear had subsided and he looked closely, he identified the man: Jammy. Back again. He recognized him from the shape of his bare shoulders and the way he walked, because there was something different about Jammy's head — ah, no dreadlocks. In fact, a cleanly shaven head. It glowed like another light.

Cho-cho exploded toward the figure, yapping furiously. Jackson felt Mama freeze beside him, Pollyread stand up straight and still. Jammy was strolling toward them, casual as if he were in his own yard, and for a moment Jackson felt as if *they* were intruders. Anger rose in him, absorbing fear.

"Modda," Jammy called out. His voice was hoarse, fractured. People of all ages would sometimes address older women, out of respect or affection, as "Mother." But resentment flared in Jackson at the unwarranted familiarity from this near-stranger who was suddenly trying to destroy their lives and had now — for at least the second time! — invaded their home. He heard a faint growl that he thought was Cho-cho but in fact was coming from his own throat. Mama grabbed his arm just as he was about to rush at Jammy.

Her voice was dry and flat, unafraid. "What you begging, James?"

Her scathing tone stopped Jammy in his tracks. Jackson, still unable to see any but the outline of his face, saw the muscles of Jammy's shoulders tighten as he shuffled forward a few more steps and stopped.

"Cho man, Miss Maisie. You don't have to go on so."

"Go on how?" Mama asked, her voice rising. She rose from the stone. "When *you* feel free to come into *my* yard" — she let go of Jackson and slapped her own chest, stepping toward Jammy — "and mash down *my* things" — another slap, another step — "and threaten *my* children" — slap, step — "then, boasie as you please, come *back* into me yard" — step — "to tell me that *me* don't have to go on so? Bwoy?" Mama stopped, her children a step behind. "Weed must be boil you brain."

"I-man coming here in peace, Modda." Jammy was five or so meters from Mama. His voice was soft, pleading with Mama. Jackson could see now his eyes glowing at them, and a dull shine on his lips.

"Peace?" Mama's anger was still on the boil. "You come here in 'peace' with a cutlass in you hand? What you know 'bout peace, James? Everywhere you go is war. And now you bringing war to my house."

He slid the cutlass quickly into his belt. "Not true, Miss Maisie."

"Not true?" Mama stepped closer to Jammy, Jackson and Pollyread, on either side, following. Jammy took a step back. "Is not you come in here one night in thunder and storm to chop down everything decent people plant and have growing by the sweat of honest labor?" Mama's words were tumbling out in panting breaths.

Jammy turned his head slightly away, as if to avoid the torrent. He found himself looking directly at Cho-cho, who, poised on coiled legs, was directing a steady snarl in his direction.

"Is not you grab after the girl pickney here?" Mama continued. "Minding her own business just going to school."

"I wasn't going to hurt her, Miss Maisie. I wanted to talk."

Mama brushed aside his words with her hand. "And is not you planting poison to kill people up yonder?" She pointed beyond Jammy in the direction of Morgan's Mount.

"Is not poison, Miss Maisie," Jammy said.

Each time he spoke, it seemed to Jackson, Jammy drew more into himself and became more compact. Or perhaps it was the air, now churning around them as though stirred by Mama's wrath, which made him seem less substantial.

"So tell me what you growing up there if is not poison?" Mama's hands went to her hips, a challenging stance familiar to the twins.

"Cocoa. Is a new kind of cocoa. Sell for plenty money." Jammy's chest opened up with pride and Jackson saw the old insolence back in his eyes.

"Plenty money, yes," Mama mocked. "Blood money."

"What you mean, blood money? Cocoa can be blood money?" His eyes and lips spread wide with scorn.

Mama looked at him with openmouthed wonder.

Jackson and Pollyread looked at each other. Was Jammy playing a game?

And then Mama laughed. She threw back her head and it was as if laughter was being pulled out of her throat on a string up into the night air. The twins watched her in astonishment, glancing nervously at each other. Jammy's eyes glowed bright as he watched Mama, and then darkened, clouding over with anger. In the uncertain light the mist seemed to divide into ribbons around his shining head. His mouth opened and an animal roared from inside him, matching its sudden rage to Mama's laughter. Jackson felt a chill in the air — *somebody walking over my grave.* Growing enormous in the flickering light, Jammy rose up on his tiptoe and his hand went to his belt.

Jackson lunged forward, propelled by fury and fear. Pollyread was even quicker and smashed her book prize into Jammy's face, spinning him off balance. Jackson jumped on his shoulder and locked his arms around Jammy's thick neck but realized immediately that he was losing his grip from the sweat on Jammy's skin. Cho-cho was hysterical, though he didn't attack Jammy. In fact the little dog was pointing in the opposite direction. Pollyread meantime had both hands fastened onto Jammy's hand that held the cutlass as he struggled to free it from his waist. He twisted and bucked to throw them both off. Mama's laughter turned to screams. And then everything — the twins, Jammy, Cho-cho, Mama — was swallowed up in a silent explosion of whiteness that blinded Jackson and threw Jammy and the twins hard onto the ground, knocking everyone's breath from their bodies. Everything *became* light.

And then became — silence. Dancing lights and silence. As of the grave.

Pollyread's head felt like greasy dishwater was swishing around in it. Her mouth tasted dirty, and her stomach was about to display its contents right there in front of her. Which would cover Jammy's chest and head, so it might be worth it. She was lying half on top of Jammy, her head on his belly, she realized, her right hand pinned between her own head and the hard wooden handle of Jammy's cutlass. Everything hurt. *Better before you married,* she heard Poppa's voice in her head, teasing as he always did when she hurt herself. She was glad she could think or remember at all; she wasn't sure she could move.

Then something did. Jackson, sprawled on the ground next to Jammy's head with one arm tight around his neck. He lifted his head and found her eyes. The air between them seemed to be in motion. As she struggled to get off Jammy and stand up, her eyes and stomach swimming, Pollyread felt as though they were in a spotlight. And the little piece of her brain that still worked knew the reason.

Towering over them all in the swirl of haze, Pollyread saw the goat's head, unmistakable, looking down at her and at Jackson. He seemed to be grinning at them, lips pulled back over those large yellow teeth.

Pollyread was also aware of something flickering like a candle close by: Jammy's eyes, wide as windows, blinking in the direction of the goat as he tried to raise himself off the ground, mouth hanging open. Through her own pain and astonishment, she found laughter bubbling up toward her lips.

The goat's eyes sparkled with amusement, stars in a pillow of mist. It was nodding at her. *Well done*, it seemed to be saying. Then it looked away — to Mama.

But Mama was staring at the twins and holding her belly. Her maniacal laughter was a distant memory. Wide-eyed and openmouthed, she came toward Pollyread on stiff legs.

"You all right, pickney?" Her voice croaked with concern and confusion. "Jackso?"

Jackson raised himself on his elbows and grunted.

"Yes, Mama," Pollyread answered.

"What just happen?"

Pollyread looked in the goat's direction — *there you go again,* she thought, *expecting it to talk.* It had moved farther away from them, nearer to the side of the house from which Jammy had emerged. Its eyes, fixed on Mama, still smiled, but there seemed a touch of sadness there too. Was it leaving them? Was it telling them something bad about Mama? And Cho-cho! The dog seemed to be stalking the cloud shape, raised hairs marching down his spine to his rigid little tail. The goat's eyes flicked down and noticed the canine. Its teeth gleamed for a moment, in a smile or a grimace, and a breath of vapor flew at Cho-cho. Who yelped and scurried behind Jackson's legs. Pollyread giggled, all fear dissolving.

As did Pollyread looked up from Cho-cho to see a white stream flowing toward one side of the house as if it was being poured through a funnel there. The yard became a clear pool of silence. The surrounding mist had disappeared too. The lightbulb under the shed glared at them, naked and plain.

"What happen?" Mama asked again.

"Jammy —" Jackson began, and then stopped.

Jammy himself was getting to his feet, one hand pressing the place where Pollyread had fallen on top of the cutlass handle, the other rubbing his neck. He looked around him, his eyes focusing.

"What you all doing out here on the ground?"

Poppa's voice came from the gate. Startled, they all turned.

"You lock yourself out of the house?" Poppa's tone was light, teasing them. Then, coming closer, he saw Jammy. "What *him* doing here?"

"Gilbert." Mama's voice cautioned her husband, but about what, Pollyread wasn't sure.

Jammy, still groggy, didn't seem to even see Poppa.

"What smell like that?" Poppa asked, sniffing, his head turning from side to side.

Everybody sniffed. Pollyread's nostrils prickled, as though orange rind had been squirted into them.

"Like something dead," said Mama.

"It not dead."

"What you doing up here?" Poppa's eyes were fixed on Jammy.

"I come . . . to talk to you . . . Mass Gillie." Jammy's voice was hoarse; he sounded drugged. He was looking around for something.

Poppa's short laugh was bitter. "Pity you never think

to come talk before you start all this." He stepped briskly past the small group and toward the house, not looking at any of them.

"Mass Gillie." Jammy's arm lifted as if to stop Poppa as he passed. "I didn't know."

Jackson's eyes had become accustomed to the semi-darkness again. Now he was seeing Jammy clearly. And what he saw amazed him. Jammy's face had collapsed in on itself, his mouth turned down and trembling. His eyes shone, but not with anger anymore. Jackson saw what looked like a tear on his cheek.

Poppa brushed past Jammy. "Didn't know what?"

Jammy struggled to speak but only heavy breaths came out.

"What you didn't know, James?" There was that name again from Mama. Jackson had noticed when Mama had used it the first time tonight, just before the goat came, challenging Jammy's presence in their yard. Now Mama's voice was surprisingly gentle, as though speaking to one of the twins. Pollyread's eyes were full of questions also, but both of them knew not to speak if they wanted answers.

"Me father," Jammy croaked.

Revelations

Jackson and Pollyread exchanged quick glances again, minds racing. Miss Mildred's four children, they knew, didn't all have the same father, but that wasn't remarkable. The same was true for many of their friends. The web of paternal relationships stretched across Valley and the district to Town and foreign. Not every child knew his or her father; a few didn't know their mothers either.

It had never before occurred to Jackson to wonder about Jammy's father, whoever he was. He had heard people call Jammy "the devil's own spawn," but that was just bad-mind because of some of the things he'd done.

And then something caught his eye. Eyes. Poppa's eyes. And Jammy's. A few feet apart, looking at each other, and he could see both faces. One eye, the left, slightly smaller than the other. In both faces. In his own too: *You favor you father* had been a point of pride with Jackson all his life. Now?

"What about you father?" Poppa asked, his voice like Mama's, suddenly milder. "You hear from him?"

Jackson felt himself and Pollyread suddenly excluded, eavesdroppers on a private conversation. He stood rock-still, aware of the dark cool night surrounding them. His own thoughts were swirling, his eyes bouncing between the two men's faces.

Jammy, as if not trusting himself to speak, shook his head.

"So what, then?"

"I find him."

"Where?" asked Mama.

"In church," Jammy said.

Things were getting *really* strange, Jackson thought. Jammy saved! Was that why he'd shaved his head?

Mama laughed, but not unkindly. "If you live long, you see everything."

"Not that, Miss Maisie." Jammy sounded like a confused little boy. "In Tower Street."

"Prison?" Pollyread yelped like someone had stuck her in the side.

"You father in prison?" Mama asked.

Jammy shook his head and shrugged his shoulders at the same time, not looking at either of them.

"So what?" Poppa was impatient. "How you find — you father?" It seemed to Jackson that Poppa had been about to say something else.

"Reverend Spence," Jammy said, a flash of his old defiance in his voice.

"Who is Reverend Spence?" Pollyread snapped, as impatient as Poppa at Jammy's apparent stumbling.

"Pen." Mama's caution zipped Pollyread's lips together.

Jammy turned slightly to acknowledge Pollyread, and then turned back to Poppa. "Him is the prison chaplain. Visit every week."

"Reverend Spence is you father?" Pollyread again.

"Pen." Poppa this time. "Give the man chance to speak."

"He say he recognize me," Jammy pressed on. "Say I favor somebody. Somebody he know. He say this about three time. Each time he say the same thing and then go away, and come back the next week and say the same thing again. Then one week he go away, and next week he bring a paper, show me that is he baptize me. In his church. When me was little baby." Jammy smiled at the thought of himself as a baby. "Say he remember me. I was sick onto dying, he say. That is why my mother bring me there. She come wake him up in the middle night. She never even belong to his church, he say, he never see her before that. But he baptize me to save my soul." He beamed at them. Jackson hoped his sister would be silent on the question of Jammy's soul, saved or otherwise. "My mother name me James. And Reverend name me Bartholomew. 'Cause the day my mother bring me to him to baptize was his day, Reverend say. James Bartholomew. That is what he call me too. In Castle Street, once he find out who I-man is. Bartholomew." Jammy's tongue pushed the name out in syllables, with pride. No one else in Valley, or anywhere else that Jackson knew of, was named Bartholomew. He couldn't remember hearing the name before. And Jammy would be the least likely candidate for such a grand name.

"So, James," Mama said. "The parson man remember you from when you was a little baby?"

Jammy laughed. "No, Miss Maisie. He remember my modda. He tell me that after he baptize me, she join his church and come every Sunday. Even though she is born and bring up Adventist. And few time she bring a man with her that parson believe is me father. And then they disappear, he say, and he never see either of them again. Every time he come to the Castle, he just looking at me and looking at me and say that he know me. Every time. And one day he come back with that paper from his church, the cerfiticate. He say he remember me mother through I look so much like her, and that lead him back to the cerfiticate."

Poppa's voice was quiet. "James Bartholomew what?"

"What you say, Mass Gillie?" In the telling of his story, Jammy had become more and more relaxed and now, as he seemed not to hear Poppa clearly, he sounded almost offhand.

"Is not only James Bartholomew that is on the baptism certificate," Poppa said. "It must have another name. The name of the father."

Jammy looked Poppa straight in the eye. "You know that name, Mass Gillie." The sly, arrogant tone that Jackson had first heard that morning up at Morgan's Mount was back.

And Poppa, just like then, bristled. "*I* know?"

"Yes, Mass Gillie," Jammy said softly, teeth gleaming in a slow smile. "'Cause is your name," Jammy said quietly, and as if he was offering Poppa a present. "Gilmore."

The four of them stood like trees. Pollyread's head felt as it did after a long bout of studying, ready to burst. The pain from the fall with Jammy and the confusion of the goat was all gone, but her brain felt stuffed with cotton wool.

Was this what the "story" had come to? All the hints and sly looks between Bollo and Trucky. The sudden, curious changes in tone of their parents when talking about Jammy. Is that what Jammy's story *meant*? That his name was really Gilmore, same as everybody else in this yard? That he was *family*?

Worse — Poppa's outside pickney!

Pollyread's mind bounced off that idea like a rubber ball, seeking other explanations for comfort. There was none to be had from the many that shuffled through her head like a pack of cards. As people said, *Friends you choose, your family choose you.* And *that* was no comfort at all.

But Pollyread had no choice but to come back to a sinking feeling, like undigested food at the bottom of her stomach, that Jammy wasn't lying. Mama wouldn't be so calm. Maybe she knew all along. It wasn't unusual for families, especially the women, to harbor the offspring of other liaisons (a Common Entrance word that caused a lot of giggles) and raise them. If Jammy was Poppa's outside pickney . . . The ball started bouncing again. . . . Coming back to Poppa, who looked so — what? Defeated. Why was he looking like that? Defeated by Jammy! *Lordy.* What was Poppa seeing on the bare hard ground he was staring at? Shame that his children should find out? *Truth is the lightest basket to carry.* Now the truth, Jammy, rested as heavy on his shoulders as if the real person was sitting there.

"Gilmore?" Pollyread heard her own voice breaking the silence, squeaking like a rusty hinge.

"Say what?" Jackson asked in a croak.

The parents said nothing.

"Trueblood name Parchment," Jackson insisted, speaking of Jammy's brother Vincent, in grade four.

"And don't *your* name is Parchment?" Pollyread heard her own voice coming from far away.

"That is what I am *called*," said Jammy, crossing arms on his chest.

You mean, that is what is written in the book at the police station, Pollyread thought. *Thank God is not Gilmore.* She turned to her mother, who was closest to her, for some kind of understanding. Mama was looking at Poppa, waiting for him to speak. Poppa walked off toward the house.

Jammy looked pleased with himself. Pollyread felt anger puddling in her stomach. But she also felt helpless. Off-balance. Usually, words were how she helped herself to understand her world, and her thoughts, her feelings. She would say something, or ask a question — sometimes without actually thinking about what to say. And clarity would present itself like a light, or like a wise person, smiling and showing the way through the macca bush to understanding. Tonight, though, she didn't trust herself to say anything more. The words that had spurted out of her had only brought confusion and rebukes from her parents.

Poppa sat down heavily on the steps to the house, its dark shape looming over him. In the stark light from the overhead bulb he looked tired. Older. His stillness seemed to draw everyone else toward him, including Jammy. Mama, still cradling her belly, sat beside Poppa and rested a hand on his knee. Another silence settled in like the mist, which had returned.

Poppa looked up finally, at Jammy. "It was for your mother to tell you," he said. Pollyread took comfort from the tone. Like he used to explain a homework problem.

Jammy's laugh was coarse and bitter. "If I didn't go to prison I would die without knowing who my father is."

"It wasn't in my place," Poppa repeated.

"What did your mother say?" Mama spoke softly. Everything was hushed, Pollyread noticed.

Jammy snorted. "Might as well I tell her I find some money on the road. She don't care. Is like she blame me for her fall. She's a hard woman, Miss Maisie."

"She wasn't always so," said Poppa. He looked out toward the gate, staring into the mist at what only he could see. "She have a hard life. She is a good woman. She never expect you but she never dash you away, and there was plenty people telling her to do that."

"My father too?" His face was expectant.

Poppa thought for a moment and then nodded. The answer turned off a light in Jammy's eyes.

Pollyread realized that she had been taking very shallow breaths. Remembering Miss Phillipson's timely advice earlier, she drew in deeply and exhaled. Her fingers, which uncurled themselves from a fist, ached. She took another deep breath and let out more of her fear with it. Her whole body felt weak. She looked over at Jackson, whose eyes screwed up with questions.

"But it wasn't as simple as that," Poppa said, his voice as dark as old wood. "By the time you mother confirm with you, Royston did get a paper from the Ministry for farmwork in Canada."

"So?" Jackson couldn't see into his eyes but Jammy's angry tone was a challenge.

"He felt he had to go."

"Had to?"

Poppa waved his arm at the night. "This was going to be his, not mine. Paps was leaving it for him, we all

315

know that from we born." Poppa looked past them again. "But if he gave up that farmwork paper, another one wouldn't come again for a long time. If at all."

Jammy, eyes fixed on Poppa, was silent.

Farmwork was something that all Valley children knew about. Next to your birth certificate, and if you were lucky a land title, a paper from the Ministry in Town, entitling you to go to the United States or Canada to work on a farm chopping sugarcane or picking apples or tobacco, was the most valuable piece of paper you could hold in your hand. Many were called — when the Ministry appointed a day for interviews, thousands of men from all over the island found themselves at the Ministry gate from the day before — and a comparative few were chosen. The chosen didn't always return. The unchosen kept trying, again and again and again. Jammy's father had been blessed.

"I was in Town," Poppa said, "setting up my life." He squeezed Mama's hand on his knee. "Going on fine." He gave a little chuckle and Mama smiled. Then he looked up at Jammy. "Is through you that my life change."

"Me? How?" Jammy's natural belligerence coarsened his voice.

"Is a long story," Poppa sighed. Jackson groaned inwardly, but was dying to hear it.

"When your mother come to Town, I didn't know her," Poppa said. "Your father bring her to introduce to me, and ask me to look out for her. Being as she was new to Town and I'd been there over a year."

Pollyread knew some of this story: how Gilbert, the second son, had been sent to family in Town to learn a trade because the land was going to Royston, the eldest.

"What she was doing in Town?" Jammy's resentment had subsided again. Like the twins, he wanted to hear the story.

"Her family send her." Poppa's voice had a harder edge. "Because of you."

"How you mean, Mass Gillie?"

"Is Town you born. But you make up here."

Pollyread understood. Miss Mildred, like many a girl before and since, had been sent away to some other family member for being pregnant. To wipe shame out the eye of the family. Jammy was the shame, Mildred's the punishment.

"Things was going fine for me," Poppa resumed, winking at Mama. "I was learning carpenter trade, and mason. I was going to night school, studying accounts and commerce. I was going to be a contractor, like Mass Jonas, Pops's cousin."

317

"And I was training for nurse," Mama said. Which the twins knew.

"The family in Town was taking advantage of Mildred, working her like a slave. She eat what leave from their table. I used to have to carry extra milk and other little things for her," he said, "like how she was eating for the baby as well."

Mama laughed. "He was so attentive to Mildred, I thought your father was the babyfather." Pollyread didn't find this funny at all.

"You mother and me was just getting to know each other then," Poppa explained, looking a little embarrassed.

Big brother Royston came to Town from time to time, to see Mildred and to leave what money he could to buy things for the baby. "And then one time he come and show us the paper he get from the Ministry, for farmwork."

There was no question of his not going.

"But what about Miss Mildred and the baby?" Pollyread interjected, angry with her unknown uncle.

"It was too good an opportunity to pass up," Poppa said.

"Too much money, you mean," Pollyread argued, as if money was not a good reason for anything when weighed against the needs of a mother and baby.

"When you poor, child," Poppa sighed, "money can seem like everything. Farmwork is also an opportunity. Like scholarship." He looked at his children, quieting them with his eyes.

Royston promised everybody — his father, his brother, his babymother — that he was coming back. A cousin of Mildred's from the district also went to do farmwork. He didn't return either.

So, after more than a year with no word from Royston, Gilbert was summoned home.

"I didn't want to come," Poppa said, glancing down at the ground. "But if I said no, Pa would have had to go on working the ground until he drop dead. And it wouldn't have taken very long for that to happen. Only two years as it was. But at least I was able to give him that."

They were talking around Jammy, who stood there like a statue, only his head moving as his eyes followed the speakers. Pollyread guessed that a lot of this was news to him too.

"So what happen to Miss Mildred?" Pollyread asked.

"She try to make it in Town, but it was too much for her. And as big and strapping as you see Jammy there, as a baby him was sicky-sicky, always taking to doctor. She just couldn't manage on her own."

Pollyread and Jackson, looking at each other, struggled to imagine Jammy as a sickly child.

But Mildred was lucky, Poppa said. There were only girls in her family, so when time came it was she, the eldest, to take over the family ground near Cross Point or leave it to be captured by somebody else. "She work like a black on that ground." Pollyread had heard the expression before and never quite understood it, since the people saying it and about whom it was said were all black.

"So how he come to be up here with you?" Jackson asked, as if Jammy wasn't right beside him.

"Very helpful too," Mama said with a smile. "Help me round the house and help your father at ground. A nice little boy."

"Them days," said Poppa.

Jammy showed emotion for the first time, a soft smile warming his face. As if he too was remembering a nice little boy.

"Why?" Jackson insisted.

"Family business," Poppa said. "Miss Mildred was trying to raise another boy pickney, I don't even remember his name now, he leave up here long time with his father."

"Melrose," Mama supplied.

"And Melrose father treat Jammy rough. Jammy own way from he small, and not accustomed to having man telling him what to do. Plenty quarreling in the yard." Poppa turned to Jammy. "You remember?"

"Wicked and dreadful," Jammy growled. "Him was wicked to I-man."

"So Mildred ask you father to take him over for a while," Mama said. "To teach him things and make himself useful."

"And he was useful," Poppa said. "Very useful."

"So what change him?" Pollyread wanted to know.

"Ask him." Mama challenged Jammy: "Why you just disappear so?"

Jammy snorted. "The little pickney start taking up all you time," he said, looking from Mama to Poppa and back. "It get so you never even notice if I was here or not."

"They were little babies," said Mama in simple explanation. "They needed us more."

Jammy didn't respond, but his memory of that childhood time was clear on his face. Pleasure and pain were like one of Mama's marbled cakes.

"And that was when I needed *you* most," Poppa said, "'cause Maisie couldn't help me at ground after they born. And you just disappear so, braps."

"Disappear with my brooch," Mama said. Her face and voice had hardened.

"No, Miss Maisie," Jammy exclaimed, trying to object to the accusation. But Jackson, who had no idea what Mama was talking about, knew from looking at him that Jammy had taken the brooch.

"You and the brooch disappear same time." She slapped one hand against the other to emphasize her point. "What we was to think?"

"The brooch disappear long before me," said Jammy with a last effort at argument.

"If you never take the brooch," Mama said, "how you know when the brooch disappear?" Her tone, which Jackson knew well, was like a searchlight into the darkness of attempted untruths.

Jammy looked down at his feet again, silent for a moment. Then he looked up with a little smile. "I will get it back for you," he said.

"Get it back?" Mama's eyes crinkled.

"From where?" Poppa asked.

Jammy grinned like a mischievous little boy. "Jackso. Go get a flashlight."

"What you want flashlight for?" Poppa asked.

Mama handed Jammy one from her handbag. "See one here."

They all watched and listened, entranced, as Jammy directed Jackson on his belly under the house, Cho-cho tagging along and getting in the way. Jackson returned, choking and spluttering, with a puzzled look on his now gray face and a matchbox in his hand. He held it out to Jammy.

"Give it to your mam," he said. Which Jackson did.

Trembling with nervousness, Mama inched the little yellow-and-black box open. And sneezed.

Everything flew, landing in different places on the ground. Pollyread, quicker than Jackson or Mama, who cried out like a little bird, saw the brooch glinting in the half-light and pounced on it. A small golden bow nestled in the palm of her hand, dusty and in need of cleaning. A red jewel tied the knot. Beneath the grime, it was the most beautiful thing Pollyread had seen.

"My mother give me that," Mama said with pride in her childlike voice. "I did plan to leave it for you, Pen."

No one, it seemed to an irritated Pollyread, smiled more broadly than Jammy.

"But we don't finish our business here, Mister Jammy," Poppa said, solemn like in church.

"What you mean, Mass Gillie?" Jammy's back straightened and his chest lifted. For the first time, and to her dismay, Pollyread noticed. Poppa said Jammy stood like his father, Poppa's brother. He stood like Poppa too.

There was another presence here. A presence that was an absence. Pollyread felt it. A presence. An absence. Uncle Royston — Jammy's father. (*Whew!*) Absent from Jammy's life. But present in it by his absence. Jammy's badness had grown out of his father's absence. Badness that had brought them now into this circle of light in which the four Gilmores — the *five* Gilmores — were present. And present still in Poppa's life, in his tenderest thoughts. Someone Pollyread had never seen. Not real. Like Goat. But very real. Like Goat.

And Pollyread realized that Uncle Royston's absence was a presence in her life also, and Jackson's. If he had not got his paper to Canada, *he* would have been the proprietor of the Gilmore land in Top Valley. Jammy would have had ground to plant, maybe even the ground at Morgan's Mount, and would be growing food there instead of a devil weed. And Poppa and Mama would have remained in Town. And the twins would have been born there. Valley would be somewhere they visited, to see their country cousins . . .

Mama and Poppa's anger swept Pollyread's thoughts away like cobwebs as they laid into Jammy, verbally, about all his transgressions. *Kicking a man when he's down*, Poppa would have called it under other circumstances, but gave no mercy on this occasion. Which seemed fair to Pollyread: Jammy had shown no mercy to them.

He'd felt an entitlement to the ground at Morgan's Mount "as 'cording to how we is family and all, Mass Gillie," he'd said with a nervous smile.

Poppa laughed harshly. "So you come to threaten me on *my* land because you think is your *father* land, and him would want *you* to have it."

"Seen," Jammy said, thinking he had finally made himself understood.

"Well, for your information," Poppa said, "that is not the ground Royston was to have. That land that you is planting your funny bush on —"

"Poison bush," said Mama sternly.

"Poison bush," echoed Poppa, "is paid for by *my* money, for *my* son." He pointed over to Jackson, who looked slightly embarrassed to be identified as a landowner. "You is trespassing on *his* land."

Pollyread saw defiance and talk-back flare in Jammy's face, hover there for a moment, and then fade.

"And then," said Mama, "you add insult to injury. Come into people yard in the middle of the night and chop down everything like a rampaging beast. Why, James?" She seemed more puzzled than angry.

Everyone looked at him. Eyes falling to the ground, he wilted in their collective glare like a flower. They waited.

"Why?"

Jammy shrugged. "Weed twist up me head that night, Miss Maisie," he muttered. "I sorry."

She stepped closer to him and pointed a finger at him, something she discouraged in her children. "And after you see how weed can make people mad, you still persist in planting that pernicious bush up so? To make other people pickney even madder?"

"I never know what it was, Miss Maisie." Jammy's face looked about ten years old. "A man come and say that if I plant it for him, he will give me a big money. Him never directly tell me what it was."

"What kind of man?" Poppa asked.

"A white man. He never talk English too good. I hear say he come from foreign. And he have other man planting the bush for him all about."

The Gilmores looked questions at one another. "Up here?" Pollyread asked.

326

"No. But other mountainside here and there. The land have to be high up, he say. He send another white man to check us out, and bring money to pay for labor." Jammy, for a moment, began to look like his old self, prideful and arrogant.

"And you take it buy weed," Mama said scathingly. Jammy looked down at his feet, the little boy again.

"When I go to Town this last time . . ." He paused, looked embarrassed. "On the weekend. I hear say Babylon scrape up the white men, and some of the man that was planting for them."

"Babylon looking for you too, James." Poppa's tone was solemn.

"What you mean, Mass Gillie?" Jackson was relieved that Jammy didn't call Poppa "uncle." He was still recovering from the moment of terror that had seemed to be an hour long, when he'd thought that Jammy was Poppa's son, his and Pollyread's brother. Even cousin would take getting used to.

"I mean, James," Poppa said patiently, "that you assault a police officer. That's one." He held up a hand and ticked its fingers off with the other. "Two, malicious destruction of property, namely *this* property. Three, you are in illegal occupancy of property not yours. Sake of my brother, I will talk to Corpie and won't press charges on those two. But four, you are growing an illegal substance, and is worse than ganja so the sentence will be longer. Five, you disarm a police officer in the lawful exercise of his duty." Mama had a way to tease Poppa, when they were arguing, that he should have been a lawyer. Jackson, impressed by his father's calmness, felt like saying that now. "Six, you resist arrest."

"Him never arrest me," Jammy said, voicing his own feeble defense.

" 'Cause him never hold on to you," Poppa said, serious and calm as a judge on television. "And is only because I talk to him why he don't make a full report about you and set every police in the island looking for you." Poppa paused. "Yet. But next time he see you, he might shoot you."

Pollyread's breath whistled.

"You are a wanted man, James. A fugitive." The word hung in the air like an unpleasant odor. Jackson saw its meaning seep into Jammy's eyes. It wasn't the first time, of course, but nothing before had been as serious as this. Jammy's eyes searched the darkness for escape.

"If you run this time, James," Poppa said quietly,

exposing Jammy's thoughts, "nobody can't help you again."

Jammy's eyes wandered the darkness a while longer, then came to rest on his uncle's. "I need help, Mass Gillie." His voice was broken, his bowed, newly shaved head a small moon under the shed.

Signs and Wonders

Jammy — *James* still sounded funny in Pollyread's ear — had been sent to make peace with his mother, after a solemn promise to meet Poppa at Stedman's Corner tomorrow morning for them to go and see Corporal Letchworth and "face you music," as Mama put it. And it was as she cleared the table after supper — warm cocoa and hardo bread, not really supper, they'd all eaten something at Stedman's Corner — that Pollyread remembered the book Miss Brimley had sent home with her. In all the excitement of the last few days, she'd completely forgotten.

It was an old book, and as she put it on the table Pollyread got a whiff of mildew and dust. The smell of Cuthbert Bank Library. *This*, she always thought, *if it had a smell, is what time would smell like.*

The pages were brownish and speckled, somewhat like Miss Brimley's skin. Some of the pages were eaten away at the edges; they looked like old plates that had been chipped. *An Encyclopedia of Myth and Legend,* it said on the cover and title page. In pale blue ink on the inside cover was written *Evangeline Brimley, Edinburgh, 1938.* As Pollyread turned the pages carefully, there were illustrations of weird animals, half this and half that, and of men with beards wearing miniskirts and women in clothes, when they had anything on at all, that would have had them run out of AME Church any day of the week! She hurried through to the G section.

And as she found the correct page and opened it flat on the dining table, Pollyread's breath caught in her throat and she spluttered.

"See him there!"

Mama called out from her rocking chair, her sewing chair as she called it, where she was settling down to mend something: "See who, Pen?"

"Goat!"

"Who?"

"Goat!"

"Who goat?"

Pollyread caught herself. Said nothing further. But Mama was already easing out of her chair and coming over to the table. Pollyread held her breath.

Her finger was also stuck. On a drawing of Goat. One of a dozen or so displayed across two pages of the

encyclopedia. Just the heads, no bodies. Exactly like . . .
Goat — the old man's beard, the all-seeing yellow eyes,
the towering Joshua horns arching back like question
marks . . . their Goat!

"That is a pretty goat," Mama said, standing over
Pollyread. Smiling. "The prettiest one on the page. I
wonder if Mass Cleveland have any goat look like that?
I never see one look like that before."

Yes, you have, Pollyread thought.

Her eye caught the sudden movement of Mama's
hand, dark against a pale yellow dress, which had been
resting on her stomach as she looked at the book. Her
fingers clutched at the cloth, involuntarily it seemed to
Pollyread, with a life of their own. And then relaxed.
Clutched. Pollyread looked in Mama's face. Something
like the shadow of a bird fluttered across her eyes,
pinched her lips. And was gone.

"What happen, Mama?"

And as she heard her own voice, seeming to come
from far away, Pollyread understood. About Goat. And
Abeo. Even about Jammy. Most of all, about Mama.
Finally.

She heard herself answer her own question. "You
making baby."

Mama's eyes, calm again, swallowed hers like a cat
swallowing milk.

*   *   *

Jackson, outside under the shed with Poppa, cleaning and tidying away tools, heard his sister's shriek:
"Is true?"

"What happen with you sister now?" Poppa asked as
Jackson headed up the steps.

Pollyread heard her brother in the doorway and spun
toward him, face ablaze. "Mama pregnant!" she
announced. As though the information was her exclu-
sive possession.

Jackson felt himself held and released, as if by a sudden hug. And he felt the relief of finally knowing
something he'd wondered about. But he didn't know
what to say. And Pollyread's eyes clearly expected him
to make some response to her declaration.

Poppa saved him by coming into the house. "What is
all this commotion in here?" A little light in his eye told
Jackson right away he was teasing.

"Mama pregnant," Pollyread said before anyone else
could draw breath.

"You don't think I know?" Poppa smiled to soften the
retort, but Jackson saw his sister shrink a little.

Jackson found his voice. "You sure?" he asked
Mama.

"So them say." Mama shrugged, and then giggled like

a girl. "Shiels send a note from the doctor about the tests."

The twins looked at each other. Doctor? Tests? Aunt Shiels was Mama's big sister, a nurse at the university hospital in Town. When had Mama gone for tests? That time they thought she'd gone to see about Jackson and St. Giles? Parents could be sneaky.

"Everything all right?" Pollyread asked.

Mama nodded. Her eyes shone, her face seeming a shade lighter from a low flame just below the surface of her skin.

Jackson felt the shadows around him, the night enclosing the house, softening the lines of doorway and window. Shadows within too, like soft dark fingers tightening his stomach. The last time. The darkness of it, coming back at him from a long way, two years, shot through with pain like lightning. The excitement of the first news, like being plugged into electricity. Then slowly being unplugged. The long months of Mama in bed by doctor's orders. Her body changing. Everyone on eggshells, for reasons the twins only hazily understood. But understanding one thing very clear: that something terrible could happen. And it did.

They were in grade four, learning new words all the time. That word, however, they didn't learn at Marcus

Garvey, and never discussed even between themselves. Miscarriage.

It seemed to Jackson, held for a moment in the hand of those memories, that a long silence had followed, like the coolest, darkest period of the night before first light.

And now, suddenly, there was an unknown presence in their midst. Again. Almost as if his eyes were pulled there, Jackson looked at his mother's stomach. He wasn't even sure that it looked any different, but now that he knew . . . maybe just a little fatter.

Abashed at his own thoughts, he looked away, down at the dining table. And saw Goat in the book lying open there. Exactly Goat. His head floating on the page . . . Like it had done . . . There was writing under the drawings that he bent slightly to read. *Throughout history, goats have been symbols of fertility and life in many cultures,* it began. Jackson knew about fertility. Poppa talked about the fertility of Valley soil, which made things grow well with a minimum of chemical help. Mama sometimes joked that "if you leave you finger in the ground too long, a finger tree would grow." Now something was growing in Mama's soil.

As Mama herself might say, *Signs and wonders.*

Jackson smiled.

Beginnings

You want a little brother?"

"Don't matter. You want a little sister?"

"Most definitely not."

"Why? Don't you was going on so about Abeo?"

"Abeo isn't my sister."

"So, suppose mama have a little girl?"

"They have machine at University hospital that can tell you if is a boy or a girl."

"And suppose is a girl?"

"Machine can be wrong."

"Machine or no machine, boy or girl, baby coming."

"I thought she went to Town to see about you and Saint Giles."

"Me too. She fool us."

"Well, Poppa going have to deal with it."

"Deal with what?"

"Saint Giles."

"What you mean?"

"Don't play idiot with me. You know what I mean."

"I talk to Poppa already."

"And?"

"And nothing. He say to leave it with him."

"Leave what with him?"

"   ."

"We lucky, you know."

"We? How?"

"We never drop out of Mama's belly."

"Where you think they go?"

"Who?"

"The babies."

"Which babies?"

"Mama's."

"Mama don't have . . . Oh."

"Where?"

"I don't know."

"What you think? They must go somewhere."

"But they not alive to go anywhere."

"How we know?"

"If they was alive, they would be here. Like us."

"But maybe they here."

"Where?"

"With us."

"You see them?"

"Don't be stupid."

"I stupid. You smart. You tell me where they are, then."

"I don't know."

"Well then, Miss Scholarship."

"But they must be somewhere."

"Why?"

"Everything is somewhere. Miss Brimley show me in a book. It say things cannot be created or destroyed."

"What that mean?"

"I don't know."

"You ask Miss Brimley?"

"She say is science."

"Obeah."

"Not obeah. Science. It name science."

"Sound like obeah to me."

"Old people say if spirit don't have the proper burial, it wander. All over the place."

"That is obeah. Don't make Mama hear you."

"They must go somewhere."

"Who?"

"The babies. They can't just wander around in space."

"Astronaut."

"That is not funny."

"Maybe they in the same place with the goat."

"How you mean?"

"The goat that —"

"I know which goat you mean."

"We don't know where the goat come from, right?"

"Okay."

"And we don't know where Mama's baby go to."

"Right."

"Maybe is the same place."

"Jackso."

"What?"

"When we in Town, where the goat going to be?"

"How you mean?"

"Is it going to be here with Mama?"

"Or in Town with us, you mean?"

"Yes. Plenty wickedness in Town for it to deal with."

"True word. We might need it more than Mama."

"And we not going to be even here."

"Here where?"

"You sleeping?"

"How I must sleep with your chatta-chatta right next door."

"Well, excuse me for breathing."

"We not going to be here when?"

"When the baby come."

"When it coming?"

"February."

"So long?"

"Ha-ha-ha."

"What so funny?"

"You think baby is puss or dawg?"

"No. But it still seem long."

"Well, is February."

"If nothing don't happen."

"Don't say that!"

"But suppose something happen to her?"

"Hush up."

"But suppose —"

"Poppa!"

"What?"

"Jackso in here telling duppy story."

"Jackso. Stop frighten your sister in there.

"The two of you say you prayers and go to sleep."

*   *   *

"Why you do that?"

"You *was* trying to frighten me."

"I just ask a question."

"Is what you ask about. Mind you put goat mouth on Mama."

"The goat is Mama friend."

"Not that goat. Old people say if you talk about something bad, it might happen. That is goat mouth."

"I know that."

"Nothing bad going to happen to Mama."

"Okay."

"The goat will see to that."

"But suppose it follow us to Town instead?"

"Our Father."

"Who art in heaven . . ."

"Hallowed be . . ."

Acknowledgments

I'm very grateful to the taxpayers of Canada, whom, unbeknownst to most of them, contributed greatly to the writing of this book through timely grants from the Canada Council for the Arts, the Ontario Arts Council, and the Toronto Arts Council.

Several people contributed critical support of different kinds at different times in the long gestation of this project. Some of them, alphabetically: Lori Bollinger, Marlene Bourdon-King, David Findlay, J. Fitzgerald Ford, Nalo Hopkinson, Hiromi Goto, Larissa Lai, Amanda Preston, Olive Senior, Jennifer Stevenson. Many others also provided insight and sustenance; they know who they are.

A special thanks to Jean Pollard, my sister, who paid for writing lessons when I was just a little older than the Gilmore twins; trees from acorns.

Thanks to Margaret Hart, my agent, who knew what she wanted from the start. Arthur Levine and Rachel Griffiths believed in the book when I wasn't sure myself.

More than anyone, Rachel has made it what it is, though I take all responsibility for what it is not.

I have derived much inspiration and encouragement from David, Rachel, and Daniel Mordecai, who, not generally patient otherwise, have waited most of their lives to see this book, cheering it along the way with opinions (generally correct) and suggestions (not always taken).

Pam Mordecai has been the most patient, most supportive, and least opinioned of all. What more can one ask in a life partner? One who writes so wonderfully to boot.

Give thanks and praises.

This book was art directed by Lillie Mear.
It was edited by Rachel Griffiths.

The text was set in Minister Light, designed by Carl
Albert Fahrenwaldt for the Schriftguss type foundry in 1929.
The display font is Sodom, which was based on a letterpress
type design released by the Hamilton Type Foundry in the 1930s.
Designer Bill Moran printed the letterforms off of the original
wooden blocks, and the alphabet was then converted
to font format by Darrel Austen and Chank Diesel.

The book was printed and bound at
R. R. Donnelley in Crawfordsville, Indiana.
The book production was supervised by Susan Jeffers Casel.
Manufacturing was supervised by Jess White.